James Moloney is one of Australia's most loved writers. He grew up in Brisbane, coming of age in the 1970s when Sir Joh Bjelke-Petersen's Country Party dominated Queensland politics. It was a time of unrest and frustration for young people, who could see the dawning of social and political freedom elsewhere. This experience inspired the writing of *The Tower Mill*, his first novel for adult readers.

www.jamesmoloney.com.au

The Tower Mill

JAMES MOLONEY

UQP

First published 2012 by University of Queensland Press
PO Box 6042, St Lucia, Queensland 4067 Australia

www.uqp.com.au

Cover design by Christabella Designs
Cover photographs © Millennium Images; Queensland riot police
    beside the Tower Mill, Brisbane, 1971 © Newspix
Author photograph by Jen Willis
Typeset in Bembo 12/15.5 pt by Post Pre-press group, Brisbane
Printed in Australia by McPherson's Printing Group

National Library of Australia cataloguing-in-publication data
is available at http://catalogue.nla.gov.au/

The Tower Mill / James Moloney

ISBN: 978 0 7022 4932 7 (pbk)
         978 0 7022 4862 7 (pdf)
         978 0 7022 4863 4 (epub)
         978 0 7022 4864 1 (kindle)

University of Queensland Press uses papers that are natural, renewable and recyclable
products made from wood grown in sustainable forests. The logging and manufacturing
processes conform to the environmental regulations of the country of origin.

For Betty Moloney,
who might have written novels,
but chose other ways to let us know she was here.

HE TURNED with an animal's impulse to save himself, instantly throwing his light frame backwards into the melee. Everyone was doing the same, hundreds of bodies in panic, a wave moving into the false refuge of the park below. Girls screamed, legs tripped over one another and then they were all running downhill into the darkness.

He fled to the right and, since he was light on his feet, quickly outpaced the danger. Then he stopped. The charge had come so quickly; there'd been no time to think. Now, while he snatched breaths and heard the wails of terror all around him, he called her name tentatively.

He tried again, this time with the urgency he no longer felt for himself, but for another. 'Sue!'

But how could she hear him in the mayhem? There was no light in the park, but from the shouting he could tell the demonstrators were being chased towards Albert Street. Sue would be with them and, Jesus, the pigs were still after them.

ONE

TOM

After an anxious hour at the Qantas desk, I fell heavily into my seat, a reckless move given the belt buckle then had to be fished out from beneath me. Contortions completed, I stared absently through the porthole and there they were, four digits picked out by the glow from the terminal. Even if I'd missed them in that first brief glimpse, the little beggars would have been there for me to see in the dawn over Turkey, taunting me to give them meaning, when others would have seen only numbers stencilled on an aircraft's wing.

Why were they there? A serial number for the maintenance crew, perhaps, but why in that particular order when, lined up as they were, they made such a blatant connection to my presence on board that plane? Why not 7-1-9-1 or, if they were so keen to reference the twentieth century, why not 1-9-1-7? I turned away.

Did anything truly important happen in 1-9-7-1? Nothing came to mind while I fastened my seatbelt. There must be almanacs with the tides and temperatures and obituaries for the good and the great who'll forever have that date bracketed after their names, but I wasn't interested in any of that.

A year of minor events, then. A year of things that influenced only the lives they touched intimately. I wondered whether an almanac on some duty shelf somewhere recorded that, in 1971, the South African Rugby team toured Australia and my fathers fell in love with a girl who married one of them, when it was the other she loved? Not the second part, surely, and even if there was such a record, there'd be no mention that the marriage didn't last, since a marriage needs time to disintegrate and almanacs end abruptly on New Year's Eve. No mention, either, that it would be another ten years before the woman settled down with a French banker who, somewhat irrelevantly, was mad about Rugby.

Football and blighted romance; to most eyes, they must seem disparate entities, yet they came together in me, since that tour by South Africa's Springboks removed a significant obstacle to my birth, while my mother's romances have shaped my life in ways that took me a long time to work out. I was still working out what to do with my accidental life on the night that plane rose into the sky over London.

My mother is Susan Kinnane. To many people, that name means nothing, I'm sure, but at the height of her career it appeared in the newspapers almost daily; not articles about her – she's not an actor or a model or a politician – but those who read front page leaders or the occasional opinion piece will know who she is.

She wasn't a columnist, though, in 1971. Thanks to the Springboks' tour, journalists of the day quickly learned the politics of Rugby at a time when that ugliest of words, apartheid, set South Africa apart. Some dusted off grim obfuscations such as *defenestration* to describe the fate of activists who died during police interrogation in Johannesburg, raising a chuckle among the besieged Afrikaners, no doubt. But if there was a rigid middle finger the regime most liked to shove in the face of noisy scolds, it was their triumphant Rugby team.

And in the winter of 1971, the Springboks came to Brisbane where I'd recently been conceived, where I grew up and where, as my plane backed away from the terminal at Heathrow that evening in 2003, I hadn't set foot for many years.

I listened half-heartedly to the safety briefing, with the window teasing me on the left and one of Susan's unwanted lovers on my right. There wasn't much room, since we were both over six feet tall, but it was all the space we'd have until we stretched our legs more freely on the other side of the globe.

'We made it,' said Dad. 'I was afraid they'd send us back to your flat.'

He leaned across me for a glance through the porthole, but if he saw the numbers on the wing they didn't speak to him as they had to me, and with little to see he sat back, slipping a well-thumbed collection of verse into the seat pocket. He noticed me eyeing the poems. 'Suzy Wilson wants me to do a reading at Riverbend Books next week.'

'Must feel good to be feted, at last,' I said.

'Feted? Being read is enough.'

'If I was staying in Brisbane longer I'd be there.'

My return flight was already confirmed, which was a relief. Our seats *to* Australia had needed hours of pleading calls just to get into the stand-by queue and in the end Dad had been forced to play the bereavement card. By rights, it should have been me on the phone. I was the grieving son. Sometimes I felt that was my only identity.

I was ten years old before the laws of biology caught up with me and I discovered that a boy can have only one father and one mother. Until then I'd had two of each and wondered why life was so parsimonious towards my friends. Nothing had been kept from me, or none of the basic facts, at least, and I didn't suddenly lose my surplus parents to this disconcerting news, either. All four had names, and if one lacked a face, I didn't question why it remained hidden in those shadows that children know, on trust alone, are not to be looked into. Until trust erodes, of course, and once it's gone you're not a child any more. That was a fair definition of growing up, I discovered – the slow weathering of God-like beings who once rose above you as immutable as a mountain range.

The aircraft's slow taxiing became a surge until we were suddenly in the clouds and banking towards the English Channel.

'It's a long way,' said Dad.

'Long-haul flights are a birth-right for Australians,' I said, to tease him. This had been his first trip to England; my sisters and I, and certainly Susan, had all beaten him there.

He responded with a shrug, as though he was in no mood for such banter. I did my best to accommodate him, only for him to pipe up soon after.

7

'You've gone quiet.'

'I'm thinking about the funeral,' I said. 'There won't be anyone there named Stoddard, not even me.'

'You don't have to share a man's name to carry his blood in your veins, Tom.'

'Doesn't seem right, though. I should bear his name for one day, at least, even if it's his last.'

'We certainly managed to confuse things for you,' he conceded, although no one did more to see I lived a carefree life than Dad.

We did fall silent after that, while the rest of the passengers fidgeted, swapped items from seat pocket to overhead locker, then settled finally, until most seemed lost in their own little world and content to stare at the seat-back in front of them. Twenty-four hours in an airline seat leaves a lot of time for thinking. Was that part of an Australian's birth right, as well? After those numbers on the wing, and then the exchange with Dad, there was only one thing I would contemplate, all the way to Brisbane.

Whenever my thoughts drifted onto my unusual provenance, it was the Kinnanes who took priority. Susan's parents, Len, and especially Joyce, were the ground I grew out of, it was their DNA I could feel in mine, even though theirs was another name I had never carried. Years ago, I was shown an anniversary portrait of them surrounded by their children, the youngest of my uncles lying in his mother's arms at the centre of the photo, his legs like pudgy sausages and his feet in snow white booties. Seated beside Joyce, Len balanced another of my uncles on his knee and there at his elbow, solid on her six-year-old legs and with a face that would frighten lions, was my mother.

'Why does she look ready to eat someone?' I'd asked when shown the photo as a teenager.

The picture was thirty years old, but my aunty Diane had a ready answer: 'Because Mum had just told her off for making faces. We were all in a silly mood, specially Ritchie.' She pointed to a boy some inches taller than my mother. 'But it was Susan who copped Mum's wrath.'

Even then, I thought. I must have been fifteen at the time – old enough to sniff something toxic between them. Grandma Joyce was kryptonite to my mother's Supersusan, or perhaps I had it the wrong way around. I'd had to piece so much of my mother together over the years, little by little, whenever she gave me the chance. I learned to love her in the same way.

It was Diane who pushed the photo into my hands that day. She told me, too, that Susan hadn't been quite old enough for her to play with as an equal, yet she wasn't so much younger that Diane could mother her, as she did the two younger boys. A born mother was Aunty Diane; at least one of Joyce's daughters took to the role.

The Kinnanes were good Catholics, of course. Their boys went to high school at St Laurence's, and, for the girls, Avila College was across the road from St Teresa's, their parish church. Apparently, when the sisters seemed sure Susan would win a scholarship to university Joyce began to get ideas: what a wonderful thing it would be if her daughter ended up teaching at Avila, now that the ranks of Irish nuns were thinning out.

My mother quickly scuttled that plan, but she did take me to Avila College, once – on the same day I was shown the family photograph, in fact; she just veered off Logan Road on an apparent whim and pulled up outside.

She was delaying the moment with her mother, I realised later; Joyce had only recently been diagnosed with cancer. Must have been Christmas, 1987, then, because Susan had been back in the country only a few weeks and it wasn't until after my birthday in March she began coming to Brisbane for the Fitzgerald hearings. Whatever the dates, I was in my mid-teens so no wonder I cringed with the self-consciousness of a schoolboy made to traipse around the silent buildings of a girls' school.

'It hasn't changed much,' she decided, as we, or rather *she* explored the playground. 'Bit more money to spread around for walkways and gardens.'

I remember she pushed aside an agapanthus that drooped from a raised flower bed beside the path and kept on, with me slouching, hands in pockets, behind her until we reached a stairwell. There were no gates, no security patrols, nothing to stop us climbing higher to wander along the balconies and peer into the classrooms.

'Come on, you can see the city from up there.'

What could I do but follow?

'They added this top floor while I was in Senior,' she told me, with her back pressed against the railing. 'Finished halfway through the year. In fact, Mrs Fenster taught the first lesson in that room.' She pointed to the middle of three. 'I remember because it was my history class and we talked about Vietnam and how the war was turning against the Americans.'

She was suddenly overwhelmed by an enthusiasm to tell me things, even though our relationship at the time was so fractured we struggled to find anything to say at all.

'It was 1968, you see. What a year that was. Student riots in Paris, Russian tanks in Dubcek's Prague . . .'

She stopped, her eyes seeing into a past that I had no way into, then she corrected herself, 'Except it was in religion class that we discussed that. Sister Bernadette railed at the Godless communists and what they would do to the poor Catholics, as though religion was the reason for the invasion. I remember being as stirred up as she was, though, because it was oppression, pure and simple.'

Swept up in school girl reminiscence she turned around to look out towards the distant skyscrapers. 'It's odd how some years slip by without a whimper and others stick in your mind. Sixty-eight was a year that just wouldn't quit.'

Pointing to the flagpole at one end of the playground, she said, 'I remember the flag at half-mast because the premier had died suddenly. Did he ever have a name, whoever he was? We didn't give a damn who replaced him, although we should have. Oh Christ, we should have.'

She turned to me. 'Do you know who I'm talking about, Tom?'

I shook my head and saw in her face a smug vindication, made all the more bewildering by her obvious disappointment. She offered no name to enlighten me.

'Even the Pope got in on the act that year,' she went on, as though determined to befuddle me entirely. She was staring at St Teresa's across the road, giving some context, at least.

'Diane was married in that church. 1968 again, you see. Christ, the planets must have aligned, something like that,' she said, with a bitter laugh. 'And there was a confirmation, too. One of my brothers. Can't remember which one . . .'

By this time she wasn't talking to me at all. Just as well, because I didn't have a clue what she was on about.

SUSAN
1968

I swapped the straps of my school bag from one red palm to the other, wishing, as I often did by the time we reached this corner, that I'd caught the bus instead. Karen strolled shoulder to shoulder with me on one side and Cathy Betts on the other. It was always this way, with me in the middle. I had further to go so maybe they let me have the narrow footpath to make the walking easier. We'd never talked about it.

Cathy always had fags in among her school books and we had just shared one among the overgrown trees on a vacant block set back from Logan Road. Whether we were smoking or walking or simply standing together on a street corner, we talked, not about anything much, but friends didn't talk about important things; that *was* their importance. It made a nice change from school, because in the classroom, where the topics were more serious, I talked myself hoarse.

Susan always has something to say in class and expresses herself resolutely, Sister Bernadette wrote on last year's report card. The bitch was having a dig, of course.

Mum chuckled to herself when she read the words but there was real pride in her face, I think, and later, too, when she'd shown the comment to Dad.

'Good to see you give your teachers the run-around and not just me,' she said, slipping her arm behind me while she stirred the gravy. Joyce was always quick with a loving hug when it was something she approved of.

As we crossed a side street, Karen tugged at her waist to adjust the folds of her uniform already bunched over her belt. We all used the same trick to look more like the models in *Seventeen*. Whenever the nuns sprang a uniform check, we just let the material fall naturally and sure enough, our hems finished perfectly in line with our knees.

'Any higher and some dirty old man will drive his car into a telephone pole,' I said to Karen, and all three of us sniggered at the mayhem we were capable of.

Actually, my legs were better than Karen's, which were too long and shapeless, like a giraffe's. Men liked my legs; I'd seen them looking on the way back from communion each Sunday, when I wore my skirts as short as Mum would let me.

We continued our weary way home, peering into brown backyards much like our own. First Cathy turned into her street, then Karen, who lived higher on the slope overlooking Holland Park, leaving me to lug my heavy bag another half-mile. Our place was a weatherboard Queenslander, like every other house in the street, although Dad had built a fibro extension at the side for my little brothers. It stuck out like an angry pimple, if you asked me. Even with the extension, I was the only one with a room to myself, and that was a recent privilege thanks to my sister getting married.

When I arrived home that day, the Torana parked out front told me Diane had come to visit. Great, there'll be cake, I thought, and my mouth began to water.

But there wasn't any cake. Mounting the front stairs I found Di in tears on the settee and Mum red-faced in the kitchen. I went back to the lounge room and slipped onto the cool vinyl beside my sister.

'What's happened?'

'You'll find out soon enough,' she answered, with a bitterness that just wasn't her.

'What does that mean? Has something happened to Jim?'

But I knew that if anything had happened to Diane's brand new husband, Joyce would be all sympathy and consoling arms around the shoulders.

Di stood suddenly and left the house without saying goodbye, and still none the wiser, I took my questions back to the kitchen.

'You're too young . . .' Mum started to say, then stopped herself, afraid of tears. My mother wasn't one for crying.

At school the next day, I told Karen.

'I haven't seen them like this before. They never fight. I can't work it out.' Karen was the youngest of four sisters, but with so little to go on, not even she could come up with a cause.

Diane rang the next evening and spoke to Mum for a long time, and this seemed to clear the air; enough, at least, for me to stop talking about it with my friends. It wasn't over, though. I saw the suspicion in Mum's eyes every time Diane came round, until I couldn't stand it any longer and demanded answers.

'She thinks I'm still on the Pill.'

I knew she was on it. Before the wedding, while we'd waited at the dressmakers for the final fitting, she'd opened her handbag and taken out a long silver card with a colour-coded arrow printed over the back. The tiny pills rattled like a baby's toy when I took them from her hand. They seemed so grown up, so forbidden to someone like me. My finger flicked at the broken foil.

'I've started taking them already. You have to, so it will be safe on the honeymoon.'

Oh God, hadn't we blushed then. She was still a virgin that afternoon, I'd have bet my life on it, but the open packet announced what she'd soon be up to in a way that white gowns and wedding cakes did not.

Now, in the bedroom we'd shared until a few months ago, I asked innocently, 'And are you still on it?'

'No, I can't be, can I, not after the stupid Pope had his say. Bloody Mum, though. There's only one way I can convince her, isn't there? Only one way to show I've stopped.'

The stand-off festered, unnoticed by the rest of the family, all conveniently male, of course, but not by me. How could poor Diane prove she *wasn't* doing something so invisible. It was like a test for witchcraft; throw a girl into the pond and if she drowned, then her innocence was proven, but if she stayed afloat, haul her off to the stake.

I was the one who burned. The flames might have died down a little between Mum and Diane, but I still felt them like a blow torch. It was so unfair!

Then the archbishop came to St Teresa's for confirmation and among the twelve-year-olds rounded up for a ceremonial slap on the cheek by his Grace was my youngest brother. It occurred to me, as we were filing in to a pew, that Diane couldn't take communion if she was guilty of a mortal sin and, if she was still taking one of the tiny pills each morning, then in the eyes of God and Joyce Kinnane, she certainly was.

With eight of us, plus Jim Wells, we took up a whole row, and, when it was our turn to head down to the communion rail, first my newly confirmed brother stepped into the aisle, followed by our parents until, with Mum turned round to watch, Diane stood also, resigned but strangely triumphant. She had knuckled under for the sake of peace in her soul, or was it simply for peace with Mum.

I watched as the rest of my brothers trailed listlessly behind Diane. It wasn't right. There should be a Kinnane left sitting here in defiance and if it wasn't one sister, then it would be the other.

Mum had thunder in her face when she saw me still sitting there, but held her tongue until she had me alone in the house.

'What do you mean by that, back there in the church?'

'I couldn't go. I wasn't in a state of grace,' I said boldly.

Sin wasn't something you talked about. If you'd scored a big one – my Johnny Farnham poster caused occasional lapses of purity – you went to confession without a fuss. No, Mum knew me too well. I was up to something and she wouldn't have it.

'Did you think of your brother before you embarrassed us all in front of the archbishop?'

I wasn't having any of this, either. 'I know about Diane and the Pill,' I shouted. 'I know you made her go off it.'

Mum seemed flummoxed for once and, at first, simply blustered clichés. 'That's none of your business. How dare you talk about that. You shouldn't even know about Diane. I'm disgusted. It's over now, anyway; she knew what she had to do and I'm proud of her.'

'I'm going to take it,' I said, although the idea hadn't occurred to me until the words were out of my mouth.

'That's enough—'

'I don't care what the church says about it.'

'You can't just pick and choose to suit yourself.'

'I'll take it before I get married if I want to.'

Mum slapped my face, then stood looking at her hand as though it belonged to someone else. The shock made me burst into tears more than the pain.

Later, Diane sat on the edge of my bed and asked in her gentle, always reasonable tone, 'What are you trying to do, Suze? This is between Mum and me. You're only seventeen, for God's sake. It's not up to you.'

'You'll get pregnant.'

'No I won't. We're being careful and it's not like I don't want to be. It's the money really. We're trying to get a deposit together.' After a pause she spoke again, more firmly. 'You're not helping, you know. It's been hard the last few weeks, between Mum and me, but it's over now and I'm happy about it. Leave it alone. Please.'

I sat up on the bed and let Diane put her arm around my shoulder, coddling me, tracing a finger along the side of my face to sweep loose strands of hair behind my ear.

'That's better. Come on. You have to sort things out with Mum. You can't live in this family without that.'

She helped me up and together we went into the hall. There, where the hall opened into the kitchen, Mum waited like the archbishop watching candidates approach for confirmation, except on this occasion the slap had already been administered.

'I'm sorry, Mum,' I muttered.

But I wasn't. I'd come out of my room to save the peace Diane had bought by giving in. I played the penitent daughter and let myself be hugged, hating myself for it and hating Joyce even more for her motherly good grace that showed she'd beaten us both.

Bugger it! I didn't like losing and if opportunities for retaliation were limited at home, I had an alternative.

I began to bait Sister Bernadette in religion class until I could see the dread in the old bat's eyes before every lesson. I was good, too. The other girls watched me go at it, all of them fed up with school, but at the same time spooked by what lay beyond. I was a distraction for them, a spectacle.

In the final week, Karen, Cathy and I slipped away from the grounds at lunchtime, to a park at the base of the hill. There, we climbed onto the low branches of a fig tree and stretched out like leopards.

'It's so radical,' said Karen, breathing smoke slowly into the air above her face.

It was the third time she'd used the word in as many minutes. Cathy was almost as bad. *Radical* was their new word for everything, borrowed from the spaced-out Americans on television.

I was suddenly tired of it all. 'What's radical?'

The prickliness in my tone made their heads turn. They liked me getting feisty with Bernadette; not with them.

'Smoking, you mean? Pulling your skirt up so high we can see your undies? It's all bullshit,' I snapped.

Self-conscious now, Karen covered her thighs. 'I meant you, Suze. In religion, the way you face off with Sister about the Pill and every-thing. Half the girls think you're already on it, you know.'

I didn't miss the deliberate pause here to show that speculation extended to those present. I tried a non-committal smirk which didn't quite come off. Anyway, how did they think a schoolgirl could get hold of the Pill, especially with a mother like mine?

'You've got poor old Bernie guessing anyway,' said Karen. 'You can see her getting madder and madder when you argue with her. It's just so . . .' She caught herself in time. 'I don't know. At least it's not boring.'

And there it was, at last. That was all I was to these two, an antidote to their lethargy. No one else would take up the fight, either. Many had been my friends since primary school, but the truth was I was tired of them, their obsession with boys and clothes and being a rebel in just the right way to impress other girls, but never so much they crossed the line. I was tired of being watched and mimicked. I wanted something to give my whole life a damned good shake.

'The old duck'll be glad when we're gone and she doesn't have you in her face all the time,' Karen went on, still talking about Bernadette, school, the same old things.

Cathy was more thoughtful. 'Do you think you'll still go to church after you leave school?' she said. It was a question to Karen as well, but really it was my answer she wanted.

I thought about it: Mum standing in the doorway of my bedroom on a Sunday morning, calling me to hurry, the others all ready to leave.

'I'm not going to church. I'm going to uni.'

TOM

Susan took me out to the University of Queensland one afternoon. She'd arranged to collect me after school, on a day when the
Inquiry was in recess, I suppose, but since the name Fitzgerald was
just part of the background hum on telly, I had no idea of what was
going on. It must have been before she took me to see Terry at the
nursing home. While Dad didn't put any obstacles in the way of
us meeting after that, he didn't exactly encourage us, either, until I
started ringing her myself from the phone in the lounge room and
told him outright that I wanted more contact with her. He had to
back off, then.

We went to a park at first. Where was it? Certainly not Wickham
Park, not that day. There were some boys training for Rugby on a
field nearby and she caught me watching them. That set me going
and I told her I'd played pretty well in the trial games at school and
might win a spot in the First XV, even though I was still in Year
Eleven. I thought that was why she had asked to spend time with me,
to find out what I did with myself.

'Rugby,' she sneered. 'Greater Public School. Terrace is the last
place I'd have chosen.'

That was when she thought of going out to UQ. 'Come on,' she
called, already on her way to the car.

Students were leaving after the day's lectures by the time we
arrived and she had little trouble finding a parking space close to the
undergraduate library.

'This road used to go right through,' she said, as we followed the ring road to where the barriers had been built. I thought this trip was to be more reminiscence, like our visit to her old school the Christmas before, but I was wrong.

She took me to the canteen, the 'refec', she called it, and there we sat with a coffee for her and a Coke for me. She was more relaxed here, as though finally she had found a place from her youth that she remembered fondly. A raucous bunch of students roamed through the scattered chairs, three voices talking at once and everyone laughing. She watched them with obvious approval, recognising her former self among them, perhaps. It didn't last. She saw others hurrying by, alone and serious and these figures earned even more contempt than she had shown for my football.

'Look at them, scuttling off to their commerce lectures. Full steam ahead to an MBA, then into to the market place. All they can think about is that first BMW. It makes me sick in my bones.'

What could I say to that? I knew what a BMW was, but what was an MBA? I'd already tried to tell her what was important in my life and found it ignored, so I clammed up, miserable and hoping she would drop me home soon. It was then she leaned across the table, confiding in me in a way that suddenly made me realise this was my mother and she felt there was something vital I should know.

'I learned more in this refec than I ever did at lectures,' she said, happy at last. 'It's still the same. When you get out here yourself, remember that. And don't do a bloody business degree, either. You *do* want to come here, don't you, Tom?'

Hearing my name on her lips was a shock, especially as it was said with tenderness this time. She wanted something for me and I felt ludicrously grateful. 'I haven't thought about it,' I answered truthfully, wanting to be convinced.

'Well think about it now. This is the place. Even with yuppies fouling up the footpaths, I can still feel it. Can you feel it, Tom?'

Again she'd left me floundering. 'Feel what?'

'The atmosphere,' she insisted, lifting her open hands level with her shoulders for a second. 'This place was hopping when I came here for my degree. No teachers, certainly no nuns, just lecturers more radical than the students. We were all aping the Americans, of course, but Christ, it was the end of the '60s and we were changing the world!'

This meant nothing to me, praise for a time before I was born, though it somehow brought her closer to Dad in my mind because he raved about the '60s, too, dragging out old photos of him in shirts that looked vaguely Indian and with some friend of his flashing the peace sign in the background. It was a joke, and an embarrassment, but it was Dad all over and now my mother was waving at me from the same frame.

I think she felt the distance between us then, because she backed off, watching me. I wondered suddenly what she was thinking and decided she was trying to love me, this son of hers in a school uniform she seemed to despise. It was as though she knew she had to love me, but didn't have the first clue how to go about it.

She was on her feet quickly and I moved to join her but she waved me down again. 'No, stay there. I'll be back in a minute. You want anything?' she said, as an afterthought.

'Yeah, another Coke, please.'

She was back quickly, my Coke and another coffee on a tray, and there was something else besides – a packet of cigarettes. I hadn't managed the first mouthful from the Coke before she had the packet open and offered me one.

'I'm only fifteen, Mu—' Just caught myself. We had agreed I would call her Susan. It worried me that I could slip up so easily.

'Come on, Tom, all schoolboys smoke. It's like wanking.'

I didn't want to go there, so I took a cigarette from the packet and sat with it between my fingers, waiting for a light. But this frank embarrassment struck me as deliberate and I began to suspect the Benson & Hedges served the same purpose. She wedged a cigarette between her own lips then struck a match, leaning across with hands cupped to light first mine, then hers. I took a shallow puff and let the smoke out quickly, looking timidly around the refec.

'What are you looking for?' she said, challenging. She knew, but I told her anyway.

'I'm in my school uniform. I could get expelled.'

She laughed; it was hardly the considerate act of a loving mother. I still didn't realise what she was trying to do. With my free hand, I started to work at the knot of my tie.

'No, leave it,' she said, and laughed again, with an elbow propped on the arm of her chair and hand cocked to let the smoke trail away over her shoulder in a mockery of pretentious elegance. 'Take a risk, Tom,' she said. 'You spend all your time living by the rules, don't you? I'll bet you try every day to make your teachers happy and your football coach and most of all Mike Riley. You don't have to, you know. Has that ever occurred to you?'

What was she on about? I wanted to go home, but the way she looked at me, waiting silently across the table stirred me as much as it unsettled. Leaning back, she used her feet to position one of the empty chairs, then lifted her legs into it, folding one over the other. Took a long drag and let it stream blue-grey into the air. Smiled.

Suddenly, she broke her pose and positioned a chair for me to do the same and at last I understood the act she was putting on, an act for me, her son, a boy she hadn't seen for years. She didn't know how to act, so she was putting on a show.

I lifted my legs and let the heavy black shoes fall into the chair.

'That's better,' she said, and drawing back she worked her mouth obscenely until out floated a smoke ring. 'Can you do that?'

I had been practising since a mate had shown me how, weeks before. I tried, but managed only a wobbly square that broke disappointingly a few centimetres from my lips.

My mother, meanwhile, pushed ring after perfect ring into the air at a forty-five-degree angle.

To hell with smoke rings. I took a deep lungful and produced a satisfying smack with my lips as they parted company with the butt. She nodded her approval and watched as I dispensed the smoke through mouth and nose at the same time.

'Do your parents know of this expertise?'

'I've been caught once, so far.'

'Do you use mints for your breath?'

'Yeah, but they're a dead giveaway. Clothes are the real problem. The smell gets into the material.'

'Easy, you just say there were others smoking all around you. They can suspect, but they can't prove anything. Did it with my parents all the time.'

This exchange was the freest we had managed since she'd landed back in my life at Christmas, but I couldn't ignore the way she had talked about my parents, as though she wasn't one of them.

'I didn't know you smoked,' I said.

'I don't.'

'What about those smoke rings, then?'

'A misspent youth,' she said, laughing as she tapped ash onto the floorboards. 'I gave it up when I was pregnant with you. There were no warnings about smoking and pregnancy back then, but something made me stop.'

'Instinctive,' I said.

'Shit no. Motherhood's not instinctive, Tom, no matter what they tell you.' Then, out of the blue she nearly floored me. 'What would you think if I had another baby?'

'You're not pregnant, are you?' I asked. She squawked at the panic in my response, while the heads that turned our way made me self-conscious again.

'No, of course not, but I'm thirty-six and time is running out if I do want another one.'

'I thought you needed a husband.'

'Shows what lies those Brothers teach you. No, all you need is a man, Tom, and only for a few minutes.'

I was to discover years later that her little joke meant more to her than I was allowed to see. She had moved in with a new partner and a baby wasn't out of the question that day in 1988. Strangely, the idea appealed to me. I had two sisters, but much as I loved Gabby and Em, they weren't really my sisters. If Susan went ahead, then I'd have a half-brother or sister, at least. Was she asking my permission?

Across the table from me, she seemed to think for a long time about what she had said, avoiding my eye until, with a final drag on

23

the cigarette, she stubbed it out savagely. The action seemed to turn *her* savage, like the dog that snaps suddenly at a leash it has happily ignored for hours.

'Seems a bit ridiculous to have just one child,' she said. 'You either have a family or you don't. One's not a family, is it, Tom, but when a woman has that first baby, well, she's lost her chance for the purity of a childless life. No proud feminist choice to skip the oppression of motherhood.' This was said loudly, a parody for the benefit of the few faces that turned our way once more. Then softly, so that only I could hear, she said, 'I wanted to have an abortion back in '71, you know. I sat in this very place thinking about it. I even asked Mike to help with the money.'

Not then but later, after she had dropped me at home, I tried to work out why she had hurt me that way, my own mother, just when I'd felt something for her. No one had ever cut me so deeply, nor so deliberately, although I had been living a charmed life until then, under the roof of Dad and his wife, the woman I did call Mum.

TWO

TOM

'It was you who introduced Susan to Terry, wasn't it?'

My question wasn't entirely out of the blue, when Terry Stoddard was the reason Dad and I were both on this plane. Perhaps he had been thinking about Terry, too, because he answered immediately.

'At a rally in Roma Street Forum. The cops had beaten up some Aboriginals in Spring Hill, and the newspapers didn't give a damn. That upset Terry more than the bashing.'

It didn't surprise me that Dad remembered the cause even though that hour of placard-waving must have been one among many.

'But you've always said you hardly knew him,' I said.

'It's true. We ran with the same bunch, but Terry was in a different league. You could tell he would always be out in front, that he had big things ahead of him. We were in a tute together and I'd pretty much done an assignment for him when he was too caught up in one of his causes. When he spoke so passionately at the rally, Susan wanted to know who he was. I saw an opportunity to be useful to her, to impress her with the people I knew.'

'Not such a wise move then, introducing her to Terry. Were you already in love with her?'

'Intoxicated,' he said, then laughed at his choice of word.

'This was after you two hooked up on Gold Coast, wasn't it?'

'She's told you about that, has she?'

He looked a bit surprised and I wondered if it was fair to go on. I knew more than he'd be comfortable with about the holiday when Susan had been stuck with her family at Tugun, playing endless games

27

of Five Hundred and bored out of her skull. Then, on the beach one morning, there was a familiar face from the refec, and better still he had a car. Mike Riley had been just the distraction my mother needed, someone to have a bit of fun with in return for a kiss or two while they fed the seagulls.

'Susan says you fell in love way too fast.'

Dad shot a breath sharply from his nose, a mannerism I'd long linked to the way he weighed up what to say and what to keep from me.

'We drove up to Tambourine. Stopped for a swim at Cedar Creek with the water so clear we could see to the bottom. Your mother in a bikini, Tom. Yes, I was helpless after that, wanted her for myself, dreamed of us together and wrote lovesick poems with Susan as my muse.'

I was tempted to say, 'You got her to yourself in the end', but that would have been clumsy, even callous. He did get her, but it hadn't been the end.

I said nothing and the conversation lapsed. I was on my own again, with too many hours to Singapore and Susan wedged between Dad and me, as she had been so often since the Fitzgerald days in Brisbane.

And that was where my memories wandered next: Grandma Joyce died just as the after-wash of the Fitzgerald Inquiry was making itself felt across Queensland, and it was something of a renewal in my life, too. With Joyce gone, the Kinnanes no longer treated me like a living billboard of my mother's crimes.

I hadn't been the only one set free. At Grandma's wake, Aunty Diane downed two beers faster than the men and took me by the elbow.

'Come out into the yard, Tom,' she said. 'I want to tell you about your mother when she was a girl.'

I worried she would cut into Susan like a leg of lamb. But Diane wasn't like that. She was judgmental, just as Grandma Joyce had been, but there was no stiletto hidden up her sleeve.

'They fought like nobody's business, you know, specially after Sue left school,' said Aunty Diane, once we were far enough from the rest.

'Your mother was just so excited to be out there at St Lucia, free of all the petty rules and with a new bunch of girlfriends, because she hardly had anything to do with the old lot once she left Avila. The things she got up to . . .'

My aunt rolled her eyes as though she couldn't imagine half the things Susan did as a student.

'Drugs, you mean?'

'Oh God no. Tom, don't ever think that.'

I might have said leprosy!

'No, not drugs. Sue got drunk a lot in her first year and that was enough for Mum to start calling her wild. No, what I mean is, she just went a bit crazy with the freedom, stayed out all night and wouldn't say where she'd been, or who she'd been with. Drove Mum mad. It was a different world then, Tom, especially in our house. You didn't get a key until you were twenty-one. Mum was worried Sue was being, well . . . Do they still use the word promiscuous? That was what she called it, like it was the scandal of the century. Sue didn't tell me much. Worried I would tell tales, I suppose, but I don't think she got up to anything with those boys, not like Joyce imagined anyway.'

'What about my father?'

She stared at me and I quickly understood her confusion.

'I don't mean Dad, I mean Terry.'

She was still reluctant. Perhaps it had just occurred to her that she was talking about sex and even with a couple of beers on board, Diane was still her straight-laced self.

'Yes, well, I suppose she must have been sleeping with Terry.'

SUSAN
May, 1971

I held Terry's hand tightly as we walked, sometimes lagging to make him tug me along, not so much reluctant as coy. It was a game I loved to play and that helped to kill the faint vestiges of guilt. I should have been at a tute, after all. My tutor had seen me in the lecture, leaving me no valid reason to skip.

Terry was reason enough. He'd been at a meeting in the union building and just happened to pass the lecture hall as I came out. Had my tutor seen me kiss him? There was my excuse.

Tired of acting coy, I was soon taking the lead, pulling him across the lawn below the Forgan Smith Building and towards the hitching post on Schonnel Drive. Terry stuck out his thumb and within minutes a Holden stopped to pick us up.

'Thanks,' I mumbled, as we fell into the back seat, but the driver had recognised Terry. It was hardly surprising when his face had been in the *Courier-Mail* only days before, after a demonstration outside Parliament House. Terry's speech was the thing. A couple of Aboriginals spoke with an anger and conviction that only personal experience could fire, but among the whites who followed, none was a match for Terry as an orator:

The international community must stand shoulder to shoulder against apartheid with Australia at the very centre, the keystone and catalyst for action. It is up to us to confront this travelling bandwagon of propaganda. The reception the Springboks get here must show every South African what the rest of the world thinks of their apartheid.

No wonder the papers wanted him afterwards, and it was the

certainty he put into every word that claimed me then, and every time, whether he was talking to a thousand or to me alone. Whatever he called into being would live and thrive. Terry Stoddard would change the world and I was going to be at the centre of everything he did.

But for now we were in the back of a stranger's Holden, the driver resting one hand on an untidy pile of essays beside him as he switched between watching the road and glancing over his shoulder.

'Saw the interview you did. I doubt you'll stop the Springboks from touring, more's the pity.'

The stiff-collared shirt marked him as old-school, but he was a fellow traveller where it counted. Terry sat forward to speak more easily over the front seat.

'We're mounting a campaign. The unions are against the tour, too. McMahon'll be sorry he let those Boers into the country.'

Listening, I felt the thrill of the change we'd bring, which somehow folded itself into the joy of the wind in my hair and with every mile along the road, the anticipation that was building. Auchenflower wasn't far. We'd soon be there.

The man dropped us on Coronation Drive, half a mile past the Regatta Hotel. We rounded a corner to head away from the river and when Terry took my hand again, I tensed my fingers, trapping his.

'Ouch, you've got me,' he said, and laughed, kissing me above the ear. 'Never let me go,' he whispered.

'Well . . . not for the next hour, maybe,' I said.

He pulled me to him in front of a panel beater's shop and kissed me full on the mouth.

'Lucky bastard!' a grinning mechanic shouted from the darkness.

'Come in here and let me give you a kiss, too, love,' called another.

We ran off, laughing, towards the house, aware that this time it wouldn't be just for an hour or two. He didn't have anything planned for the entire weekend. He was all mine.

There had been others before Terry, boys with names I could barely remember, who'd fumbled in the dark as much as I let them.

Sex was like drinking, a heady rush, more enjoyable because it was forbidden at home, than for the pleasure it brought.

Then suddenly there was Terry; heart-thumping, loud-hailing Terry. He took me for a starry-eyed groupie at first and, besides, I wanted to be sure there was more to him than fine words on a podium. I went to meetings, made him notice me and, when I got him alone, measured him against the promise of the more public Terry until I knew there was only one face to the man.

'Don't you have a boyfriend?' he asked me finally.

'Would it matter if I did?'

'No, but I've got enough enemies as it is,' he said, then promptly took me to bed in the house in Auchenflower, a place where his friends let him crash whenever he liked, since his mother lived miles out on the southside somewhere. I wanted him all the time now, not for the sex so much, but for the way I felt when I was with him, every part of me alive.

We crossed Milton Road with the four Xs of the beer factory winking at us on the crest of the hill, urging us on towards the sun-burnt Queenslander with its peeling paint and badly built-in verandas. Terry felt underneath the top step until he came up with a key.

'Anybody home?' he shouted into the fog of midday heat and last night's mosquito coils.

No reply and immediately I began a familiar game. We both knew where we'd end up soon enough, but I headed for the kitchen and with Terry watching from the doorway, set about making a sandwich. The air moved languidly through the house. Above our heads the corrugated iron strained against its rusty fixings. Neither of us spoke. I was wearing an Indian cotton top and a wrap-around skirt, deliberately hitched low on my hips. I knew Terry's eyes were tracing the lines of my body and enjoyed the expectation it sent through me. I could feel my desire like a silken sheet gliding in waves around me, slowly, deliciously wrapping every inch of me inside it.

Terry moved to the bench and began to kiss me, on the back of the neck, on the shoulder, until I turned. Then we were in one of the bedrooms where anything on the mattress was swept aside with a scoop of his hand. I loosened the skirt and let it join the jumble of dirty clothes and half-read novels already on the floor.

There was a party at the house that Friday night, which became Saturday morning while I slept beside Terry, and finally Saturday afternoon. When I woke still beside him, I watched him sleeping with the fascination of a first-time mother. The contentment lowered me into sleep again, and when I woke a second time found him staring fixedly at the ceiling.

'What are you thinking about?'

'All sorts of things,' he said, without breaking his far-away gaze. Terry wasn't one for limits. He was staring straight through the roof, to the universe beyond. 'Getting support for this Springboks thing,' he confided. 'I've been to a couple of Labor Party meetings.'

I lifted myself onto one elbow to look at his face. 'How'd it go?'

Terry took his time over the answer, until I wondered whether he'd heard me. He sighed and said, 'They're not an inspiring lot. A mixture of socialist warriors and old-style head-kickers better at getting the numbers in a backroom vote than coming up with ideas. About the only one with any life about him is Tom Burns.'

'No women, I suppose.'

'As far as these guys are concerned, sheilas make the tea.'

'And root for the team,' I said, nudging him.

Terry laughed. 'Some better than others,' he teased, gathering me into the crook of his arm. 'The point is, though, what makes them any better than the other side? A wad of tired ideologies, rights for the worker, that's about all.'

'If you went into parliament, you'd shake things up.'

I meant it. I'd seen inside him more deeply than anyone, not just as a lover, but a believer. He carried the passion of his words in every breath and every twitch of his muscles. It was why I loved him.

'You're thinking about it, aren't you, going into politics?'

Terry shifted to kiss me softly on the forehead, then settled my head on his chest. 'What I'm thinking about is taking you to Paris.'

'Spending whose money? You're poorer than I am!'

'Who needs money? We can do it without leaving this bed. I'll be your guide.'

'You've never been to Paris.'

'Neither have you,' said Terry, undaunted. 'Just as well, too, because I haven't got a clue which end of the Champs Elysees they put the Eiffel Tower.'

'That's the Arc de Triomphe.'

'You're sure?'

'Get on with the tour.'

Terry put on a faux French accent and, without missing a beat, directed us through the Louvre, then a boat along the Seine to Notre Dame, a bird market he remembered from a picture book his mother read to him over and over, on to Montmartre, complete with eccentric artists in berets and finally the site of the guillotine, where he described Marie Antoinette proudly mounting the steps to her doom.

'Then it's back to our studio high above the Rue de whatever, where we make love all afternoon. We'll be hungry by then. Maxim's, I think . . .'

'Where have you been?' said Joyce, when I mounted the front steps on Sunday afternoon. It was almost dark by then, although I hadn't planned to be quite so late.

'Uni, mostly,' I answered, swinging my shoulder bag onto the sofa, where a heavy book spilled out on cue. Evidence.

'For three days!'

'I was studying. Stayed at Donna Redlich's both nights. Didn't you get the messages I left? You were down at the church doing the flowers when I rang yesterday.'

'As you knew I would be,' she said.

Of course I'd rung when I knew she wouldn't be there, just as I'd picked the busiest time on Friday, so one of the boys would beat Mum to the phone.

I looked away at the porcelain cats on the sideboard, each sitting demurely on its doily, at the photo of Diane on her wedding day and Dad in his army uniform. It was going to be like this, then. Had I really expected anything different? I'd had the best weekend of my life and now my mother was going to make me pay.

'Mum, why the third degree? I'm here now, aren't I, sober, all in one piece, no needle marks on my arms?' I presented them both for inspection.

She ignored the provocation. 'My daughter, not even twenty years old yet, leaves home Friday morning and the next I see her it's Sunday night. Of course I'm going to ask where you've been.'

'Why do you have to know where I am every minute of the day? You should have guessed, anyway. I was at uni, studying.'

But I'd made a tactical mistake. I wasn't a studier. I passed my subjects with last-minute cramming and assignments done the night before they were due. I wasn't the type to spend an entire weekend at St Lucia when exams were still a month away, and Mum knew that better than I did.

'You weren't at Donna's, were you?'

Had the bitch rung up and asked for me? I felt the blood heating up beneath my skin. But she was bluffing. Donna's place didn't have a phone, in any case.

'You were out with that one who's been in the papers.'

I could have denied it, could have stuck it out and gone off to my room with her suspicion sticking out of my back like an assassin's blade.

But I hated the lying. It made me feel dirty, petty, like my mother. It made the world narrow and mean when, for three whole days, it had been as broad as the sky with Terry and me floating about in the blue and wishing every day could promise such freedom.

'Terry, his name is Terry Stoddard and yes, I was with him. So what? He's my boyfriend. Why shouldn't I be with him. We're in love.'

Mum seemed startled. 'Love?'

'Yes, *love*. What's so unusual about that? Why can't you be happy for me?' I said, too loudly, and barely avoiding tears. I didn't fight well through tears and Mum was laying out her forces for a battle. 'At my age, Diane was in love with Jim and no one was happier than you and Dad. Why's it different for me?'

'They showed they were in love by getting engaged,' Joyce shot back.

'Yeah and Jim Wells had short back and sides and Diane slept in her own bed every night. That had a lot to do with the smile on your face too, didn't it?'

'Susan.' Mum drew out the name as a warning.

Which I didn't heed. 'But love doesn't count when Terry's a God-less long-hair with his picture in the *Courier-Mail*. That's it, isn't it, and because we don't need to be married to show how much we love each other.'

As battle strikes go, I'd scored a bullseye, but what was the point when the enemy was as unassailable as a fortress above the Rhine?

'You *were* with Terry then, and not out at the library like you told me. You lied to me. You were with him last night, too, weren't you?'

'Yes, I was with Terry. And since you think it's any of your business, we had sex, too.'

What did it matter if I told her so, and bluntly. It was only what she suspected. Let her have the moment of outrage her heart was so set on.

'I should throw you out in the gutter.'

'That's a change of heart then,' I said, baiting her openly now. 'Whenever I talk about moving out, it's over your dead body. Make up your mind.'

Mum was furious at the way her own words were being flung back at her. I pressed on, taunting her. 'I hope you do make me leave. I'll go and live with Terry.'

'I won't let my daughter be ruined like that.'

'Ruined! Will you listen to yourself? It's a bit late to worry about white weddings. Mum, all that hypocrisy's over with. You can't control my life like some dictator any more. As soon as I graduate, I'm going, and if I want to shack up with Terry then I will.'

I'd said 'shack up' on purpose because Dad used the same words when he listed the scandals among his young mechanics at work.

'I tell you, Mum, it's not going to be me who's thrown out, it'll be you who gets tossed out of *my* life – and I can't bloody wait!'

36

TOM

On a modest hill above Brisbane's CBD stands the oldest surviving structure in the city, an unremarkable windmill built of stone blocks in a style known the world over as a 'tower mill'. Rendered in white cement these days to stop it crumbling, it's a relic of the city's convict past, otherwise obliterated, and few miss what was little more than a footnote in the convict legend that took shape more memorably in Sydney and Hobart.

I have been to the Tower Mill many times since learning its significance in my own family legend, but I knew none of that on the day Susan asked to meet me there. I assumed it was simply a convenient landmark, since she would be in a courtroom in George Street all day and I was coming from school.

It wasn't the only assumption I got wrong that day. To begin with, we had different places in mind. To me, the Tower Mill meant the old convict thing, so I dumped my bag in its shadow and kept watch down Wickham Terrace, since that was the way she would surely come.

'Tom,' a voice called from behind me. When I turned, Susan was thirty metres away, looking surprised. I swung my heavy school bag over one shoulder and headed off to join her.

'You're crying,' I said, when I saw the panda smears around her eyes.

She offered an apologetic shrug, more a wince, really, and said, 'It's this spot, outside the Tower Mill.'

She was staring across the street now at a circular building, and I began to twig to some kind of mix-up. I didn't ask because we'd found each other anyway and, besides, her tears hadn't entirely ceased and I was quickly growing uneasy. I'd cried tears of my own after our last meeting, at the university, and this one was kicking off with hers.

I tried to break through the awkwardness. 'Where do you want to go?'

'I want to stay here a bit. That's why I said meet me at the Tower Mill. Do you know what happened here in '71?'

'No,' I said.

'Mike has never said anything?'

I shook my head, trying to make sense of where this was going. Whatever she was talking about, Dad must have been here, too. I asked her to confirm it.

'Both your fathers were here, Tom, placards and all. END APARTHEID NOW, RACISTS OUT. This was the hotel where they lobbed up.'

'Apartheid! I don't understand. Who lobbed up here?'

'The Springboks,' she said, spitting out the word. 'Don't you know any of this, how Bjelke-Petersen called a State of Emergency, all because we wanted to protest? Queensland was the laughing stock of the whole bloody country.'

Here was something, at least. Of course I knew who Bjelke-Petersen was. Old Joh had been premier for most of my life and the Springboks were the Rugby team from South Africa, except nobody would play against them any more. We'd studied apartheid at school.

'Okay, Joh and the Springboks. What have they got to do with this place?'

She blew a frustrated gust from deep in her throat, as though I'd forgotten the date of Australia Day. It wasn't fair! How was I supposed to know this stuff? I kicked at my bag and turned away so I didn't have to look at her face. 'What's Rugby got to do with it? You hate the game anyway. You said so, and the Springboks aren't allowed to play here any more.' That was it. If she was going to make me feel like a fool, then I wasn't saying another thing.

'They might be banned now, Tom, but they weren't in '71. We came here to demonstrate against apartheid, to show they couldn't go on like it was business as usual. Students like Terry and me, lecturers, union people. I even saw a teacher from Avila. There were hundreds of us.'

Years later, once the Tower Mill had come to taunt me as much as it taunted my mother, I found out all I could about that night, from old newspapers and the rest. What stunned me more than anything was the number of police. Extras had been ordered in from the country and the ring-ins weren't happy, either.

The warning signs were obvious if those wondrously naive protestors had wanted to read them. In their home towns, those country police dealt with boongs every day, and here in the city they were confronted by a bunch of hippy types and commos having a go at the South Africans for keeping their own blackfellas in line.

Those poor kids had no idea how much they were hated. There weren't enough thirty-six-inch batons to go around, apparently: that much was documented.

SUSAN
22 July, 1971

With the garage doors tilted open, cool winter light brought out the colours we were busily splashing onto cardboard – and the Rileys' unprotected concrete. The cans were all crusted around the rim and none had more than an inch or two of paint in the bottom, but that was all we needed. Six of us were hard at work, although, apart from Mike Riley, only Donna Redlich was a friend and I'd only come along because she kept me to a rash promise I'd made days before.

I was more interested in the granny flat that took up the rest of the ground floor. Mike had told me about it while we were down the coast at Christmas but I hadn't listened. Now that I'd seen it first hand, I was jealous. The lucky bastard had this whole space under the house as his private domain, yet he still got dinner every night and the use of his mother's car. What Terry and I couldn't do with that set-up.

I stepped back from my masterpiece. SMASH APARTHEID, it declared. I'd wanted RUGBY RACISTS but Mike had talked me out of it: 'It's not the game that's racist. You'll only alienate people who like footy for its own sake.'

I was quietly pleased that the first word retained the violence that seemed so much a part of the stupid game. What was it about boys, that they enjoyed smashing into one another like bulls in a paddock? Couldn't they just compare the size of their dicks? It was all the same thing, if you asked me.

'Time to get moving,' Mike called to the others.

With the signs done, he would drive us to the airport in his mother's car, which we all thought of as his, anyway.

'Do you mind if I don't come along?' I said, and immediately his face fell.

Oh shit, I thought. He wasn't still hot for me, was he? It had been obvious when I first started going out with Terry, but that was ages ago and it wasn't as if we'd had anything much going, just those weeks down the coast.

Mike was a nice guy, the organiser, the driver, but Terry was the one, and that morning I couldn't concentrate on anything until I'd talked to him. We had a problem.

Mike dropped me at uni and I walked up to the union building. The police had arrested some demonstrators outside Parliament House the day before and Terry wanted the details of how they were knocked about. The meeting was just finishing up when I found the room.

He was seething. 'The pigs confiscated all the film from the *Courier-Mail*'s photographers. Can you believe it? What ever happened to free speech?'

I didn't know if he was furious or just incredulous.

We bought burgers from the refec, but this conversation needed privacy and I led him down among the lily ponds above the river, to a bench beneath a poinciana.

'My period's never late, Terry. I can't go to the doctor, because he's a friend of Mum's and he'll be on the phone before I'm even out of the surgery. This could be serious . . .' I managed to get it out before the tears rained out of me.

If he'd started in with frantic questions – how could I be sure, why wasn't I on the Pill – if he'd shown any weakness at all, I might have hated him as quickly as I'd fallen in love with him.

Instead, he tossed his burger to the ducks and enveloped me in the comfort of his arms, his hand gently pressing my head against his chest.

'Cry all you need to,' he said. 'We'll sort this out. It's going to be all right.'

My tears were of relief then, almost joy.

'Whatever you want,' said Terry. 'We'll handle this whatever way you say.'

Yes, but even while he cooed such reassurance I needed more from him than 'whatever you want'. 'This is too big for me to decide on my own,' I said, standing back. 'I want to know what you think. Tell me honestly. If I *am* pregnant, what do *you* want to do?'

Terry's brows lowered, a sign that presaged his deepest thoughts and even without another word, he told me he would carry his half of whatever came our way. I could have kissed him for that alone.

'A baby's certainly not in my plans at the moment, Sue.'

'Mum and Dad would want us to get married, for God's sake, just so they can hold their heads high at church on Sunday.'

'Married,' said Terry, as though the word was new to him.

I didn't want to hear the word right then, either. Marriage was for the future – Terry and me, sure, that was my dream, but not yet.

'We've got so much we want to do,' I thought, and only afterwards realised that I'd said the words aloud. 'You know that tour of Paris? I want to do it for real one day, Terry, with you, but if there's a baby and the rest, it won't happen, will it?'

He shook his head. 'Suze, since you're asking me straight out, then I'll tell you. I think the best thing's an abortion.'

There it was, for only the ducks to hear, and the pair of us, too. 'It's such a big word,' I said, glad that it had come from his lips and not mine. It had been in my head for days, whenever I checked for signs that I would never have to say it.

'I know what you mean,' he conceded. 'Tell me how you feel about it.'

What did I know? I'd chanted slogans and marched for a woman's right to control her own body, but all I knew for certain was that there would be no baby afterwards, no pregnancy, finito. I just wanted things the way they had been these last months and once it was fixed, we'd be more careful. Maybe it wasn't so hard to go on the Pill after all. I'd find out.

'It's more than likely a false alarm,' I told him, forcing a smile. 'Every girl has them. But . . . but if it's for real, then we've made a stupid mistake, haven't we?' I shifted away from him a little. 'Shouldn't have let it happen, wasn't supposed to happen. Neither of us wanted it to happen, and it'll change everything, especially for me. Shit, Joyce will go off like Krakatoa.'

Terry grinned. He'd never met Mum but I'd told him enough about her to see the explosion. There wasn't going to be a volcano, though, was there, so we could afford to be flippant.

I looked at Terry, who seemed so steady, so sure. 'I just want to be unpregnant.'

'It'll cost. And we have to find out who . . . You know. That part shouldn't be too hard. As for the money, we'll just have to find it.'

He was smiling still, sheepishly. There was nothing we couldn't overcome, that smile was telling me. 'Guess you have to pay for your mistakes,' he said.

'I wish you'd paid for more condoms!'

I hadn't meant it as a joke, but we were happy to make it one. I'd thought it would take longer to decide, but there amid the shady chaos of the poinciana and with a view of the languid river offering a sort of peace, it seemed we'd already made up our minds.

That day turned into a farcical game of cat and mouse. When the unions refused to let the Springboks travel to Brisbane on commercial flights, a fleet of small planes was rounded up, and, instead of landing at Brisbane airport, they sneaked in through an airfield in the suburbs. Mike Riley and the rest missed them altogether. Only late in the afternoon did we find out they had gone to ground at a place on Wickham Terrace called the Tower Mill Hotel.

I hadn't counted on a vigil, not after dark and on a hilltop with a westerly wind raising goosebumps on my bare legs. Idiot. I should have worn jeans like the rest, but when I'd left home for Mike's place to help with the placards, the sun was shining and I'd simply thrown on a skirt and long-sleeved top. After an hour in the open, I was shivering.

'Like a plucked penguin,' I told Mike, who'd found me in the crowd. 'Wish I had Grandad's greatcoat.'

Mike had come better prepared. Typical.

'Here, put this on,' he said, and, before I could stop him, he'd stripped off his heavy woollen jumper and held it out to me.

'No, then you'll be cold,' I said, but it ended up around me somehow, still warm with his body heat.

I searched for Terry's shaggy head and found him at the edge of the footpath, conferring with three others as though they were generals laying siege to Rome.

Mike nudged my arm and nodded towards a broad-shouldered figure in front of us, noticeably older than the rest of the mob and dressed differently, too. He was inching towards the gutter, towards Terry.

'Hey mate,' Mike called, 'if you Special Branch shits want to know where the Molotov cocktails are, why don't you come straight out and ask?'

The bastard turned a blank shrug our way – who, me? But nothing much was happening, most of us were bored as well as cold, and this was all we needed to renew the chant in his face: 'Apartheid Out! Springboks Out!' Left in a circle on his own, the spy slipped to the edge of the crowd and disappeared altogether.

Watching him go, I saw that some of the protesters were drifting away, too. The South Africans had come onto their hotel balconies earlier to watch the ruckus, but when this only incited louder jeers, they withdrew. Maybe they'd been ordered to. For all we knew, the Boers were now feasting on some slaughtered bullock on the far side of the hotel, oblivious to our placards and the show of Queensland force assembled to protect them.

I couldn't really blame the deserters for heading out of the cold. I'd have gone with them, if not for Terry. It was all an anticlimax, really. We wanted to send the brutal pride of apartheid back home with its racist arse kicked but all we had to shout at were the ranks of our own police, who were no more than patsies sent out by our own geriatric regime. We were here for the Afrikaners who herded blacks into Bantustans and policed the Pass laws.

The front line of cops was assembled along the white line in the centre of the road, each wearing a motorcycle helmet, which seemed a bit ridiculous when there wasn't a bike for even one of them to ride.

'There's more than at parliament yesterday,' I said to Mike. 'What do they think we're going to do? Set fire to the hotel? Jesus, we could do with something to warm us up.'

I wasn't about to admit it to Mike, but the lines of police worried me, the way they marshalled like an army. That was just what those grandads in the government wanted it to look like, no doubt. First principle of the oppressive tyrant, I'd heard Terry explain at a rally earlier in the week, was intimidation through a show of force.

'Bastards,' I said out loud. 'A State of Emergency just because a few of us want to demonstrate.'

'Bjelke-Petersen's cleverer than that,' said Mike. 'All this makes him look strong for the by-elections next week. We're playing into his hands here.'

It sounded like a criticism of Terry. 'So you think we should pack up and go home because it *looks* bad?' I challenged him.

'No, of course not – but it's McMahon in Canberra we have to convince.'

Terry had said the same thing, in almost the same words. 'Yeah, Joh's a sideshow.'

The minutes ticked by coldly. Mike was shivering openly now and I felt a twinge of guilt; it wasn't enough to give back the jumper, though. I was bloody freezing and the sight of all those police didn't make it any easier. The fear fluttered again in my stomach when an officer walked behind the helmeted line only thirty yards away. Some kind of order was being shouted out, lost to my ears in the chanting and the gusty breeze.

'Why the motorcycle helmets?' I asked Mike.

'Oh, we're a vicious mob.'

He was closer to me now, although not intentionally. Despite the defections, the numbers were swelling again and the footpath was narrow. Even with bodies pressed unnaturally close, some spilled into the park behind us, where the ground dropped away, making it tricky underfoot in the darkness.

The restlessness had spread to the nearest row of coppers now. It brought a new edge to the night that I didn't like. I looked for Terry, but couldn't find him this time and the crush was too tight to go searching.

'He's over there –' Mike's voice was right in my ear – 'talking to the Aboriginal guy.'

Mike was watching me, aware of me and what I was thinking. I should have resented it, and if we hadn't been talking about Terry, I might have told him off.

'Terry never stays still for long, does he?' I said proudly. 'One minute he's revving up the crowd and the next he's conspiring one on one.' Was he really mine? There had to be a better word than boyfriend. Lover, maybe. There was an old-world daring about the term that appealed to me.

'Terry took me to a party last week,' I said. 'I couldn't believe who was there.'

'Yeah, you told me.'

Did I? 'Oh, sorry.' I'd mentioned it to a few people out of sheer wonder, really, that such company would open up to me. I hadn't sat in the corner like some decoration, either, while Terry worked the room. When he was drawn away from me, I plunged straight in and found myself talking seriously with people who'd only been exalted names around the campus until then.

Going home afterwards was like slipping through the gloomy gates of a prison, from freedom to the cage, from grown-up to child. That was when I saw what bound me to Terry: more than the sex and the laughter, he was my ladder over the wall.

That delicious thought was still in mind when the crowd's mood shifted, and things began to fly over my head onto the road, whatever lay at hand, even a half-eaten hamburger spilling out of its paper bag. The mess was a sign of the frustration we shared, a petty demonstration of something far deeper.

'Littering as public disobedience,' I joked. That was going to change the world, wasn't it? Yet the silly missiles somehow added to the anticipation and I was no longer shivering simply from the cold.

'They look more pent up than we do,' Mike said, and I knew what he meant: The police were arrayed with such precision along the white centre line.

Then the line began to move.

Everyone on the footpath that night must have seen it begin. What Mike picked out before the rest, though, was what it meant.

'I don't like this,' he said, and before I quite knew what was happening, he'd grabbed me by the sleeve of his own jumper and backed across the footpath towards the park.

By then the police were on the charge and already at the gutter.

I didn't resist Mike's tugging, not at first. I had no choice, really, because bodies were shifting around us, all in one direction, away from the helmets and batons. Screams shot into the night air, some so close they pierced my ear drums; people pushed and jostled to get away.

Only when Mike had us both ten yards down the slope could we think about turning one way or the other, although even that was limited. Downhill was the only escape.

But I didn't want to escape. Not yet. It was easier to stop now and I slapped at Mike's hand, trying to pull away. 'Terry, what about Terry?'

'Too late for that! Can't even see him. He'll be on the run like the rest of us.' Mike tugged my arm harder this time, and, confused, frightened, crying, I let myself be pulled along as we careered down the slope, blind to where our feet were landing. I would have fallen if Mike hadn't kept hold.

Bodies, feet, snatches of human form were all I sensed around me as everyone fled in the weakening light. We'd come so far now the blackness of the park seemed to swallow us whole. Others cried out, in shock, in outrage. I glanced over my shoulder and saw gleaming white spheres reflecting the light from street lamps: the police were still coming, herding us more deeply into the park. I could feel the fear around us now, the fear of falling, of being caught. Christ, we'd be beaten to a pulp.

I simply couldn't believe it. None of us had thought anything like this could happen. A confrontation, yes, the front rank – people like Terry – taken away, with arms wrenched behind their backs. But not a baton charge, not riot police, like Brisbane had suddenly become Paris or Chicago. I couldn't accept what was happening, but I kept on running because it *was* happening, and because Mike Riley held on with a grip that made my arm ache.

Then a sudden halt. 'We'll be trapped above the retaining wall,' he said, fighting for breath. 'This way.'

He veered off to the left, under a metal guardrail and we slid down the landscaped embankment behind the dental hospital, and finally we were in Albert Street. Behind us, we could hear the others screaming. I was terrified.

'Come on! We don't know how far they'll chase us,' he said, and pulled me sobbing and stumbling for another city block and into King George Square.

Finally I caught my breath. 'How could they do that?' I shouted at Mike. I was shaking, not with cold, but shock. 'We have to find Terry.'

'Not yet. It's too dangerous.'

Fuck him, he'd finally let go of me so I took off into Albert Street again and uphill into Turbot, forcing Mike to follow. Outside Trades Hall, which backed onto the park, police were manhandling a figure into their car.

When it pulled away, we ventured closer, asking after Terry whenever we found a familiar face.

No one had seen him.

'You can't go into the park,' someone warned. 'The pigs are still prowling.'

Wickham Terrace was cordoned off entirely. An hour passed while we skirted fruitlessly around the streets, jumping at every sound.

'They'll fucking pay,' I cried. 'They had no right. We were just standing there!

'Where's Terry?' I heard myself wail over and over. I felt wild and empty, like a drunk. 'There's a house in Auchenflower. Maybe he's gone there.'

*

48

Terry's friends in Auchenflower made us coffee and dragged out a blanket from one of the bedrooms so we were warm, at least. I sat with Mike, his arm around my shoulder and his voice in my ear saying that Terry would turn up. No need to worry. Someone went off to ring the watch house from a phone box on the corner.

'He's not there,' was the update. 'The smart arse copper said all the long-haired mob have been bailed already.'

Where else could he be? 'The bastards. They won't get away with it, you know.' I could feel hatred rising into a fog above my head. I was afraid to look up in case it was really there.

Then Mike went off without saying where he was going. It was almost three a.m. before he came back and, despite the worry, I was half-asleep and too dopey, at first, to guess why he was explaining to the others that his father was a doctor. I came awake quickly, though, when he got to the point.

'I asked Dad to ring around the hospitals, use his contacts. Terry's at the Royal. They brought him in unconscious. Some kind of head knock.'

THREE

TOM

During my year as an articled clerk, one of the partners sent me to track down some medical records for a complicated insurance case. It dawned on me afterwards that I could request my father's from the Royal Brisbane Hospital.

Terrance John Stoddard, aged twenty-three, was written at the top of each document. You only learn a person's full name if he appears in the newspapers, accused of a crime, or else among the death notices.

But my father wasn't dead. Mention of a cranial fracture first appeared in the notes of the emergency ward registrar, who described the trauma as being consistent with a high-speed car accident, probably because he saw cases like it every week.

I read down the dispassionate list of observations – *extensive bleeding in the frontal lobes, raised intracranial pressure, tissue dangerously swollen.* Someone had scribbled in the margin, *4hrs?* A different pen had underlined the same jottings. Later documents confirmed that four hours had elapsed between the injury and first examination in Emergency.

Other details came from the police report. Terry had been found beside a path that had a steel railing along one side. It seemed all too clear what had happened. In fleeing the police, he'd tripped and smashed his skull against one of the unforgiving uprights. I winced every time I thought about it.

Did the surgeon wince when he opened my father's skull to stop the bleeding? He could hardly have stood among the nurses shouting, 'Holy shit, look at this mess.'

No, most likely he winced, privately, invisibly, beneath his mask, whispering, 'You poor bastard. What have you done to yourself? Better see how much there is to save.'

My mother was told all these details at the time, I suppose, but while Terry lay in a coma through that first week, all she would have cared about was that he held on to life. If he died, she would die with him, she told Dad, who sat with her through the worst of it.

SUSAN
26 July, 1971

'I'm his girlfriend!' I shrieked at the nurse. 'You have to let me in.'

Raising my voice got me nowhere. I would go for her throat soon. The hospital had been stonewalling for days and I was fed up, desperate, exhausted beyond tears.

'Please, Sister,' said a voice from beside me, 'if you let us see him, just for a few minutes, it will give Sue something to hang on to, might help her sleep.'

This lame plea came from Mike Riley, who'd driven me to the Royal and come in with me, even though I'd told him not to. I didn't want to sleep, I didn't want anything to hang on to except Terry's hand, but if this silly twaddle got me to his bedside, I'd go along with it.

The nurse went off to ask, again, leaving me to walk the corridor, again, until the heavy doors swung aside and the nurse was back. 'One of you, only. You'll have to suit up.'

Mrs Stoddard was beside the bed when I was finally allowed in. We'd only met twice before and a hug seemed too intimate for where we stood with each other. With masks over our mouths we couldn't do much more than mumble a greeting and it didn't help that a rosary swung from the woman's hand.

Bloody witchcraft. I wanted to snatch it out of the old girl's fingers.

'Oh Terry, look at you,' I whispered. He lay on his back, his head a ball of white gauze and with a mask over his nose and mouth. The parts of his face I could see were stained yellow by whatever they used to ward away infection – a bit more scientific than rosary beads.

His exposed arm belonged in a Hollywood morgue. Around him machines puffed and clicked, screens blinked, drops fell into a bag suspended from a pole until I had to turn away out of fear that this was where his life existed, not inside his sallow skin.

'It's my fault. I shouldn't have left you there. We should have run down into the park together, all the way to Auchenflower.'

I knew he couldn't respond, but that didn't mean he couldn't hear me. If Mrs Stoddard hadn't been watching, I'd have kissed his cheek and stood back to watch him rise out of the coma, like Lazarus, or Christ himself.

Later, in Mike's car, I couldn't stop myself. I smashed my fist against the door, making Mike jump in the driver's seat.

'I shouldn't have let you drag me away like that. If I'd gone back for him, this would never have happened. It's my fault. I didn't think fast enough and you were pulling me down that hill before I had a chance to do anything else.'

'They were on to us too quickly, Suze. You're forgetting what it was like, all the people—'

'I should have gone back for him!' I shouted. 'If you'd left me alone I would have found him and he wouldn't be in that hospital bed.'

When the Cortina pulled up at home, I fought my way out as fast as I could and headed for Mum, who was waiting with the front door open.

'Did they let you see him this time, darling?'

'For five bloody minutes.'

I took refuge on my bed and raged that all I had were prayers I didn't believe in and calls from friends like Donna who were sure he'd be all right, even though they knew even less than I did. I lay face down and wept in fear and frustration even when the door opened and a weight pressed down on the bed beside me. I didn't have to look to know it was Mum's soft hand on my back.

When the grief became unbearable, I wrapped myself around her, hugging as fiercely as I'd ever held Terry. 'Oh Mum, what am I going to do if he dies?' I kept saying, and she held on to me just as strongly, saying, 'He's not going to die, darling. He'll come through.'

A weekend passed and on Tuesday morning I went to uni, to a room I'd sat in a hundred times, listening to a lecturer who always managed to draw a laugh or two, no matter how dry the topic. I needed distraction, a moment's respite, but I didn't hear a word, and when it was over I fled from the claustrophobic walls.

Mike was crossing the Great Court. 'Have you got your mother's car?' I demanded, and when he nodded, asked, with only marginally less aggression, 'Will you take me up to the hospital?'

He came in with me again, and annoyed the crap out of me by insisting I sit with him in the cafeteria, first.

'Mike, I just want to see Terry.'

'You're shaking. I'll bet you haven't eaten properly for days, have you?'

'Mike . . .'

He pushed a tray into my hands and loaded it with two sausage rolls, a bucket of chips and a chocolate bar. Only when the first of the chips slid down my throat did I realise how famished I was. My mood improved enough to offer thanks, which he waved aside as he filched another chip from the bucket.

By the time we reached ICU, I'd stopped shaking and the urge to cry that had lingered like a persistent cold had left me at last.

'Okay, I can handle it from here,' I told Mike, once my jeans and jumper had disappeared beneath the green surgical garb. As I pushed through the heavy doors, he called something about a lift home, but the mask was over my mouth and I didn't bother with a reply.

Terry was better; not so many tubes and the nurses didn't visit his bed as often. Mrs Stoddard stayed in her seat in the corner while I had my turn. It had been like this each time I'd visited and even the greetings we exchanged were repetitions. The surgeon came by on his rounds and accompanied us both into the corridor, where Mike was scribbling on some scraps of paper; poetry, I was pretty sure, after he'd reluctantly shown me a few lines during our weeks together on the Gold Coast. He stuffed paper and pencil hastily into his pocket and came to join us.

'Mrs Stoddard tells me you two are her son's closest friends,' said the surgeon, a pale man with fingers like a pianist's.

57

Me, yes, of course, but Mike? It didn't seem important enough to correct him.

The surgeon continued: 'The last twenty-four hours have seen significant improvement. He's out of danger, no doubt about that.'

'How long before he wakes up?' I asked immediately.

'Days rather than weeks, I'd say, but you must remember—'

'How long will he need to stay in hospital, once he's awake?'

The surgeon's face said he wasn't used to being interrupted.

'Going home is getting a little ahead of ourselves at this stage,' he said slowly. 'I've already explained this to Mrs Stoddard. Terry will stay in ICU for up to a fortnight, yet. We'll know more about the long term when he regains consciousness. I don't want to speculate until then. It wouldn't be fair to his loved ones.' He managed a gracious nod towards both Mrs Stoddard and me that warmed my soul in a way I hadn't known since the accident.

'There'll be a lot of rehabilitation needed, but some of that might be possible in the home. Depends on how much executive function he's lost.'

'Function!' said Mike, from behind my shoulder. 'You mean he . . .'

Whatever he was going to say died when I turned a for-Christ's-sake-shut-up look on him.

But the surgeon had guessed his question and used terms I barely understood. 'Neural signs . . . post-traumatic amnesia . . . apraxia.'

What the hell was apraxia? I didn't care. The doctor expected Terry to wake up soon and things would be different then, even if Mike didn't seem to think so during the drive home in his mother's car.

'His poor mum,' he said. 'I drove her home a couple of nights ago and she talked about him the whole way. I don't think there's anyone else, no one she can talk to. Terry's all she has.'

Hadn't he listened to the doctor? Terry was on the mend.

'He's awake,' I called through the house, before the telephone had settled back into place. 'Mum, Mum – Terry's woken up! Can you drive me to the Royal?'

As we crossed the Story Bridge I warmed myself with a vision of Terry sitting up in bed, smiling weakly, pleased to see me, and with so much to tell me that one thing would get jammed up with another as he fought to get it all out of his mouth. Would I be allowed to hug him? Gently maybe. The touch was what mattered, the press of his skin on mine.

Mrs Stoddard was there when I arrived, withdrawn into her corner as always, only this time she didn't seem to notice me.

Terry was on his back as ever, head and shoulders slightly elevated this time and with the mask gone from his face. His eyes were open, focused on the ceiling as I crossed from the door to his bedside.

'Terry.'

He didn't turn his head, didn't smile, didn't respond at all.

I squashed the disappointment and leaned over him, pushing my face into his line of vision. 'Terry, it's me. Susan.'

I was looking down into empty eyes.

The shock snapped me to attention. His face seemed made of plasticine and not a muscle moved beneath the skin. But the movement had attracted his attention and, slowly, his head turned so that his eyes could follow me. They stared at me, seeing nothing. Then his jaw moved up and down once, twice, in a parody of speech, but no words came out. The only sound was the dull flap of meeting lips, amplified grotesquely by the hollow mouth behind.

'What's going on?' I demanded. This wasn't how it was supposed to be!

I turned towards Mrs Stoddard, seeing her properly for the first time and found her weeping quietly, her rosary beads nowhere in sight.

In ICU, I hadn't been aware of other patients. Even when they'd moved Terry to this ward in the Rehabilitation Centre, I'd had eyes only for him. That morning, for the first time, I began to examine this new world he'd been brought to, made up of bodies beneath white sheets, mostly, no different from his own. Many were old, grandad old. Some stared into the same space above their beds, mouths open and slack on one side. Stroke victims.

A man was being helped from his bed, his scrawny legs barely able to support his body. He leaned on the wardsman, utterly dependent and with every ounce of concentration devoted to this simple task.

'That's it, Mr Pendlebury. Much better than last week.'

The patient's reply was half-moan, half-whimper like the cry of an animal left to die slowly in a forgotten snare.

The cold winds of August gave way to the cloudless skies I'd always loved. There was no joy in them that year, and no change in Terry's condition, despite what the doctors said. On an afternoon in mid-September Mike Riley drove me home once again, following a familiar route through the Valley, across the Story Bridge and along Main Street. At an intersection near the cricket ground the light was red, but I kept right on going.

'That bloody hospital, the nurses, the whole fucking lot of them. They're not doing anything. Last week the doctor tried to sell me some bullshit story that Terry would have to walk with those metal rod things on his legs. Can you imagine? They've given up on him completely, just shove food in his mouth like a baby in a highchair and his useless mother stands around crying, bamboozled by the whole doctor-knows-best routine. I won't let it happen. He'll get better, I know he will. He'll be like he was before.'

The light went green, signalling Mike's turn.

'You have to face facts, Suze. There's only so much they can fix. I mean, it's the brain.'

'So you've given up, too. The hospital can go on treating him like a vegetable and you don't care, either.'

He sighed as though he'd expected me to go at him like this, no matter what he said. So why did he say it? It seemed he'd appointed himself the voice of reason in all this but that wasn't what I wanted.

'I didn't say we should give up,' he continued, in a level tone that irritated me even more. 'I'm saying we shouldn't get ahead of ourselves. If you expect too much, you're going to end up disappointed.'

He'd flogged the same caution on me a dozen times already and looked pissed off that he wasn't getting anywhere. That was when he said, 'You know, Sue, I saw this movie a while back, about a skier who broke her neck. She wanted to ski again, and of course she couldn't, but the movie was about how she came to appreciate the things she *could* do. It was a triumph, really. If you're in a wheelchair, then walking with callipers must feel like flying.'

'I don't believe this! Now you're quoting some feel-good movie at me. I'm not listening to this crap. Stop the car. I'd rather walk home.'

Mike ignored me, which was a red rag to me. 'Stop the fucking car!'

He began to pull over and I wrenched opened the door before he'd even stopped the car. But I didn't get out. I didn't want to get out and I felt stupid because I'd known as much even as I was shouting at him. I just wanted to shout.

'Don't get out,' he said.

That made it easier for me. I closed the door, relieved. 'I don't want to hear any more about Terry in a wheelchair,' I warned. 'I don't want to hear about how they'll teach him to talk again, to say 'water' when he's thirsty, or say my name when he sees my face. He's going to talk to me like he always did.'

'Do you really believe that, Sue?'

'I have to,' I said, too quickly.

'You're fooling yourself and you know it, don't you? I've stood beside Terry's bed, too. I can see how bad it is. It's not a bunch of broken bones that mend themselves good as new, it's brain damage. He'll never be the same, never, and you have to accept that.'

'No!' I slammed my clenched fist down on the Cortina's glove box and when the violence of what I'd done made no difference, I found myself rocking forward and back, forward and back, suddenly helpless.

'It's horrible, Mike,' I heard my voice say. 'I can't bear to see him like this. I can't look at the others in the ward, dribbling, pathetic, their minds gone. He's just like them.'

I looked across at Mike, my eyes surprisingly dry because this wasn't a play for sympathy. I was just so desperate.

'The way his mouth opens and closes . . . it's disgusting. I wish they'd tape it shut. And his eyes, they just stare at me, with no idea who I am. I want to put dark glasses over them so I don't have to see. He doesn't even know what a human being is,' and this last was a terrible lament I wrenched from so deep within myself it might have brought blood.

'I feel so guilty that he does that to me, Mike. I loved him so much and now I can't stand to be near him. I can't tell them at the hospital, can't tell Mum. Bloody Mum, she goes on like this is a trial sent to test me and all the time I can see behind her eyes how relieved she is that there'll be no more Terry, not the way it was before.'

I stopped, expecting Mike to be angry with me, yet what I saw in his face was pity, not for Terry but for me, his eyes like outstretched hands and then I was launching myself across the seat, latching on to him.

'Help me, Mike. I'm so ashamed.'

TOM

All children are suckers for the story of their own birth: they are fascinated by pictures of a mummy unaccountably younger than the one who now tucks them into bed, her hands resting on a watermelon that's been shoved up her front. She's invariably smiling. Maybe that's the attraction. *That's you inside my tummy, darling. I'm smiling because of you.*

Some must ask how they got out, I suppose, and are told it happened at the hospital, which isn't the answer they were looking for, but distracts them enough to avoid the need for diagrams and blushes.

'Did you ever take a photo of Susan while she was pregnant?' I'd asked Dad when the fascination overtook me years ago. I guess I must have been sixteen, maybe seventeen.

'A few,' he said. 'They're at Grandma's, in with the other albums,' and the next time we visited, he hunted them out.

Did he save them for me? He didn't keep the wedding photos – I asked about those, too, soon after, and was told they were gone, not destroyed, just let go, left behind and best forgotten, like the marriage itself, I suppose.

If it took me longer than usual to show any interest in my genesis it was because I'd always known the mum in my daily life wasn't the one who'd carried me around like a melon. But I'm not that different. I did gestate inside my mother for nine months, like everyone else.

Susan was pregnant right through those terrible weeks while she waited to know whether Terry would live or die and once that was no longer her fear, while she suffered assaults of grief, anger, shame and finally despair. I was with her through all of it.

That's you inside my tummy, darling, even though you are too small to see, too small to make my dress bulge outwards, too small even to remind me you are there.

SUSAN
Late September, 1971

'Judging from the dates you've given me, Susan, I'd say you're thirteen weeks.' She was the first woman doctor I'd ever been to, and worked at a place I hadn't known existed until a few days before. Not that I would have made an appointment at the UQ clinic any earlier even if I had known she was there. My head was too full with other things.

Afterwards, I sat alone in the refec, with a coffee going cold in front of me. I wasn't afraid of public tears; I'd shed so many over the weeks since the Tower Mill that I knew the signs, but this time they didn't come, even as I made myself think of Terry.

'He's dead. It's all gone,' I muttered. I simply couldn't make a connection between Terry Stoddard and the baby inside me, as though it had lodged itself there spontaneously. It didn't seem anything to do with me, either. It was just there. A decision had already been made before . . . before, before, before. Oh fuck!

How would I go about it? Abortion had only ever been an abstract thing, an issue, condemned at Avila without discussion, debated hotly at uni, but never as an act that had to be arranged.

For weeks I'd lain on my bed without a reason to do anything, yet that wasn't me. I'd been waiting for a life that was never coming back, floored by my own powerlessness. It was time to break out.

I stood up from the table and found myself oddly galvanised by what I was about to do, by my own efforts and however hard it might be, it was a challenge I was up for.

At a phone box on the ring road, I called a number I still knew by heart, even though I hadn't dialled it for two years.

'Mrs De Jong, it's Susan Kinnane. Could you please give me Karen's number at work?'

I met my old school friend the next day in Anzac Square, finding a bench below the cenotaph away from the paths and prying ears and there I laid out the problem, tearlessly and in a voice that didn't waver on a single word. It wasn't heartlessness, I told myself, it was the need to feel in control at last.

My composure broke a little, though, when Karen started talking about money.

'Where did your sister get that kind of cash?'

'Mum and Dad, of course.' When I looked stunned, she added in a sardonic tone: 'Oh, they're good Catholics on Sunday, but Barbara was pregnant on the other six days as well.'

Karen promised to ring that night with the phone number. I would take the call in the lounge room, with Mum and Dad watching television only a few feet away. There was nothing suspicious about copying down a phone number, and when I made my own call I would go to the phone box on Logan Road.

'Shit,' I said under my breath while I waited for the bus in Queen Street. I had no idea where I was going to get that kind of money.

And money was the biggest hurdle. Friends came good, without asking why I needed whatever they could spare, or when I could pay it back. Others said they couldn't help, sorry. In the week after meeting Karen, I must have asked a dozen people. Then I came home one afternoon and found Mum sitting on the sofa.

My wariness flared. A silent television was the clue I'd picked up without realising. She never sat in the lounge room by herself, unless the television was on.

'Come and sit down,' she said. 'I want to talk to you. Or maybe there's something you want to tell me.'

My mouth was instantly dry. 'What makes you think that?'

'Because I do your washing.'

'My washing! Mum, what are you on about?' I managed a laugh. This might not be the moment I'd dreaded after all.

But it was.

'There hasn't been any blood. You've never been careful with pads and things, have you Susan? I have to soak your underwear, only there's been nothing to soak for months.'

'My period's playing up because of what's happened to Terry, that's all. It's stress.'

'When you've been sleeping with your boyfriend there's a more common reason.'

'That's none of your business.'

'You think it's not my business if my daughter's pregnant?'

'I'm not.'

'Aren't you? I should have guessed weeks ago. Your face has been white as a sheet every morning.'

'Mum, my boyfriend's half-dead in hospital! Why wouldn't I look pale?'

'You're anaemic, like I was every time, and Diane's the same. I've made an appointment for you with Doctor Tunbridge. If I'm wrong about this, you'll have my sincerest apology.'

That was it. She got up off the sofa and went into the kitchen without another word.

I struggled through a sleepless night, but in the morning there was no point holding out any longer. After Mum was done with the rush of getting men out of the house, I sat down heavily at the kitchen table and ended the pretence, expecting Krakatoa to flatten half of Holland Park.

It didn't happen, and once I saw there weren't going to be any pyrotechnics, I almost convinced myself the baby was gone, too.

Phone calls were made. Diane came round with her little Rosanna, gave me a hug and told me it would be all right, *really*. The boys were left in ignorance, but Dad certainly knew by the time he came home. The anger was there in his face, but he said nothing, his eyes flicking towards Mum.

My stomach tightened. There was something going on here. By now the house should have been echoing with shouts of 'slut, promiscuous little fool, family disgrace, brought shame on us all'. The only conclusion I could draw was that Mum was still wearing the kid gloves she'd donned after Terry's accident. I wasn't convinced by this, though, and spent a second night dreading the day to follow.

'Susan,' Mum called through my bedroom door about ten the next morning. 'Come into the lounge room. Your father and I want to discuss your situation.' 'Situation' was the word my parents had assigned to the news.

They were sitting side by side on the sofa when I arrived, leaving me the overstuffed chair that faced them. I slumped into it, my body to one side, resting my weight on an elbow. I dared to look across at them, still certain it would turn hostile at any moment.

'The baby is due in March,' said Mum.

'The nineteenth,' I confirmed. We'd been over this yesterday.

'The situation has to be faced. You are going to have a baby.' This from Mum, also, as though she were measuring out her words by the ounce.

I didn't interrupt. I knew there would be no drive down to Tweed Heads, no need for the hundreds of dollars I hadn't yet raised. That was a relief of sorts, at least.

'It's terrible what's happened to poor Terry and we don't doubt that you loved him, and still do. The fact is, though, he can't help you with this child. Instead, your father and I must step in, and that's exactly what we're going to do. You're our daughter and we love you – you shouldn't doubt that for a minute. We'll support you one hundred per cent.'

It all came out so neatly, a speech – no, a tutorial presentation that showed they'd already thought much further ahead than I had. Until I'd come home to find Mum waiting on the sofa, the 'situation' wasn't going to exist much longer, so why would I have thought any further? Even last night, with the landscape changed dramatically, all I could think about was how my parents were taking the news. Their disapproval hadn't materialised and now that was making me uneasy in itself. Mum was practically measuring me up for maternity clothes while we sat there.

'I might give the baby up for adoption,' I said solemnly.

'No, no, darling –' this time it was Dad who spoke up – 'your baby will be our grandchild.'

That was the second time I'd heard them say 'your baby'. It disturbed me, made it harder to concentrate.

'A cousin for Diane's little girl, a Kinnane. There's no need for adoption. You and the baby will have everything you need, a home, a loving family to care for you both . . .'

Mum stayed mute while beside her Dad laid out how it would be, but it was in her face that I found the real story. I would raise the child myself, in this house.

No wonder there had been no tirades. Mum was quietly over the moon, and even though she hid behind her silence while Dad delivered the lines she'd primed him with, she couldn't quite keep the delight from her face. Her wayward daughter would be tamed after all; I would be dependent on them, on her, for everything. The only money I'd have would come from them; when I left the house, Mum would want to know where I was going and when I'd be back, for the baby, of course.

While I tried to fight off these horrors, Dad canvassed my prospects as a woman. 'There are plenty of blokes who'll take on a wife when she's already got a kiddie. Happens all the time these days. Got a fellow in the workshop now who's just married a divorcee with two little ones.'

Divorcee. I had joined the ranks of those my parents gave labels to, looked down upon, patronised. I was to be an Unmarried Mother whose loving parents were guiding her back to respectability, which meant that all the battles I'd fought over the past two years were null and void. I'd lost the war.

I stared, disbelieving, across the room at Mum's magnanimous smile, and knew it was all she could do not to dance a victory jig around the room.

Days passed without interest or meaning. I became aware of the daily rhythms in our house that I had never noticed before – the regular phone calls, visitors at the door, Mum's trips to do the shopping. That's what you get when you mope about the place too much, I scolded myself when I realised what was happening, but without enough passion to feel guilty about it. Or to do anything differently. I was just grateful the morning sickness had eased. I'd let it debilitate me more than it should have and couldn't muster any guilt over that, either. The house had been remarkably quiet concerning my 'situation', which had settled seamlessly into fact, and we were all simply getting on with it.

Then, a fortnight after my parents had laid out the future for me, Diane arrived with Rosanna perched comfortably on her hip and a lighthouse glow in her face. With the one-year-old playing happily on the carpet and a cup of tea in her hand, she said, 'I've just come from the doctor's. I'm having my second. In May. Our babies will be only months apart,' she said, beaming at me. 'We'll pretty much be pregnant together, Suze.'

I hugged her and said all the right things.

'Three grandchildren in two years,' said Mum, as though it was all her own work. It damn well was!

I made an excuse and went up to the phone box to call Donna Redlich.

Donna had come to the hospital with me more than anyone else from uni, except Mike, of course. None of them had been close to Terry in the way I had, but they came to support me. Now I was discovering how even the steadiest of friendships fade when you don't see people every day. Donna was frantic with exams and as gently as she could, put me off. I would have done the same, and with considerably less grace.

I called two more lapsed girlfriends and met with similar regrets; then I dialled Mike's number.

He sounded weary as he asked how things were going with the baby. His sister, Jane, had suffered terribly from morning sickness, apparently.

'Listen, Mike, what are you up to at the moment?'

'I'm under three feet of notes. Haven't seen daylight for a week. My last exam's the day after tomorrow and that's it for my arts degree. Just have the Dip. Ed. next year, then look out world.'

My weariness was lifting. I allowed myself to hope. 'You wouldn't be able to come round, would you? I've got to get out of this house before I go mad.'

Oh God, he was hesitating. 'It's that last exam, isn't it?' I sounded pathetic and hated myself for it.

'Look, give me a few hours to get on top of this. Is after lunch okay?'

Mum hovered by the front door when the Cortina pulled up. I was about to assure her we'd only be an hour or two but stopped myself. That was what she wanted. I kept quiet, but there was no way to stop Joyce Kinnane from running an eye over Mike to see if she approved. The door swung back to reveal a young man in tailored shorts and brand new Dunlop Volleys, his hair washed that morning and shorter than last time I'd seen him, even if it did fall halfway to his shoulders. He was tall, like my brothers, whom Mum always stared up at with pride.

'Hello, Mrs Kinnane,' he said, with a tentative smile.

And Christ, Mum was smiling back at him and suddenly I wished he'd turned up hung-over and scratching at a three-day growth.

But if he had, Mum would have jacked up and then where would I have been? Shit, shit, shit! I was losing control of my life and the baby wasn't even showing yet.

Mike held the gate aside for me then hurried across the footpath to open the car door. The chivalry was overdone, a signal, maybe, that he wasn't thrilled to be hauled away from his books.

'I'm sorry about this. You'll still pass, won't you?'

'Pass! It's Twentieth-century Poets, Sue. Eliot, Hughes, Larkin. I'm hoping for a high distinction.'

'I'm sorry, Mike. I was desperate.' Surprising myself, I reached up and kissed him on the cheek.

'You can play me like a fish, Kinnane,' he said, laughing. 'All right, Larkin and the rest can wait. Do you want to visit Terry?'

'No, I went last week and it was awful. I just sat there crying like his mother with all the other human wrecks around us. I don't care where you take me, as long as I'm out of the house.'

Then I was crying again, as bitterly as I had on the night of the Tower Mill, and I didn't care. 'They're manipulating me, the pair of them. Mum can't get over herself. She waltzes around the place like the most forgiving, caring mother on the planet. If they loved me, they'd help me get on with my life, but she's keeping me helpless. I'm scared, Mike, really scared that I'll end up like Terry, with what I used to be lost somewhere inside me and gone forever.'

Mike listened, said nothing, a witness to my misery as he guided the car wherever he'd decided to take me.

'McLean's Bridge,' he said, when I asked, and it instantly became just the right place. I knew it from childhood picnics, carefree games with Ritchie, and my dad in a playful mood. On Beaudesert Road I began to escape my self-pity while the warm breeze toyed with my hair.

Mike had brought a rug and a sticky bun and shared similar stories about his own family, who'd come here so he and his sister, Jane, could swim in the shallows.

'I guess I'll bring my baby for a paddle in a couple of years,' I said, patting my stomach. It was the first time I'd spoken about it with any affection. I saw myself in the water up to my knees, holding a one-year-old's arms as the river tickled her feet.

We played on the sandbanks and splashed around like a pair of kids while my shrieks bounced off the gum-lined banks above us.

'Thanks for bringing me here,' I said meekly, then folded myself into him while we stood with our ankles still submerged in the chill water. 'You've been very good to me, Mike, taking me up to the hospital all those times. I haven't shown it, maybe, but I appreciate it, really I do.'

He held me until I'd had enough then took me home along the same route, where my melancholy returned as we grew closer to Holland Park. I felt myself diminishing and fell silent.

'I wish there was something I could do,' Mike said, before escorting me formally to the front door and accepting a second kiss on the cheek for his pains.

'Good luck with the exam,' I said, but he didn't seem to hear, as though Larkin and his mates were already displacing me in his mind. Later, I would realise what was really swirling in Mike Riley's head as he drove away that day.

TOM

My Riley 'grandparents' tried to talk Dad out of marrying Susan. I certainly would have, if I'd been in their position. Dad couldn't support a wife and child and still finish his Dip. Ed. unless they helped with the money, but, when they pulled this lever, Dad said he'd ditch his Dip. Ed. and find a job in the public service. Mike Riley as a graduate clerk? He was born to be a teacher and his parents knew it. They caved.

For a few years, Rob and Helen Riley were the only grandparents I knew, even though they were nothing of the kind if you're a stickler for DNA. Helen was both wonderful to me, and the slightest bit reserved. Her reserve was hardly surprising, when you consider what happened a couple of years later. Even then, she was never less than welcoming, attentive to a fault, yet I didn't feel she loved me the way Grandma Cosgrove did, and Grandma Cosgrove had no more blood connection to me than Helen Riley. Helen was Mike's mother, though. She loved me because she loved her son, which gave the pair of us solid ground beneath our feet when we needed it most, but I was never going to earn the same love in my own right.

SUSAN
Middle week of
November, 1971

I felt Mike's unblinking eyes stare into my own. 'You can't be serious,' I said.

'That's not quite the answer I was hoping for.'

'But Mike. Marriage!'

'Sue, I love you. I've loved you almost from the day I met you.'

Oh Jesus, he *was* in love with me.

'But I don't love you,' I said, and watched Mike's face slowly fade to a blank. He wasn't defeated, he didn't seem hurt, despite what I'd just said. I searched for something that might end the embarrassment without sounding cruel, and snatched too quickly at the first thing that sounded heartfelt.

'Mike, there's no love in me for anything right now, not even for Terry. I don't think he exists any more, and every part of me has gone numb because of it. Please don't take this badly.'

I could feel myself about to launch into a consolatory list of all his good points that would end with words like, You're the gentlest, most caring person I know. I killed it off before more damage was done.

After a tender kiss on his lips, because he deserved that much, I walked away across the grass of the Botanical Gardens where he had brought me for his proposal.

I took the bus straight home, where Mum didn't quite jot a time down in a log dangling from the fridge, but the effect was the same. Diane came round. They spared me a repeat of last week's fashion parade of Diane's loose-fitting skirts and dresses. As long as I kept to my room, the scream stopped clawing its way to the base of my throat.

Mum and I had taken to sniping at each other again. Her sympathy over Terry seemed to have run its course, especially now that I could ward off thoughts of what he had become. The pain was there, though, whenever I remembered what he had been, yet even that was fading and I was afraid my life would fade to black along with it.

I had to get free of this house, I'd told Mike when he took me to McLean's Bridge, but how far could I get with twenty dollars in my bank account? I'd read of girls who did it anyway, thumbed a ride far from home, but the stories didn't make comfortable reading: before the halfway happy endings, there was sex with truck drivers, nights with dope fiends, bruises, loneliness and childbirth in a Salvation Army shelter. I was trapped, but I wasn't crazy.

Mike rang two days after we'd met in the Botanical Gardens and for almost five minutes we each danced skilfully around the issue. Then, from him: 'Have you thought any more, about what I said?'

'Nothing's changed, Mike. I'm sorry.'

I was close to five months' gone and resigned to the tightening at the waist of my skirt when, in the last week of November, a letter arrived from uni.

Dear Miss Kinnane.

The officialese detailed my crimes. This moment had hovered in the back of my mind for months yet I'd done nothing. It was time to change that. I found a photo of myself with Terry on the front steps of the house in Auchenflower, and collected newspaper clippings from the *Courier-Mail*. *Student Radical in Coma* was one headline.

The dean was sympathetic. He could not reinstate my scholarship, but he would let me finish my degree without penalty.

I took the happy news home to Mum, who was cooking tea.

'Darling, you won't have time for that.'

'Not in first semester, no,' I conceded, 'but I thought I'd try a subject in second semester.'

With the potatoes on the boil, Mum dried her hands and sat down with me at the kitchen table.

'Susan, I'm surprised you're even thinking about this. Raising a baby is harder than you think. You're going to feel like you don't have enough time anyway, let alone study as well. And you can hardly take a baby to lectures.'

'I thought you could mind it while I'm out at uni. Only be one day a week, and only for a couple of hours.'

Mum shook her head. 'It's not how long you're away from the baby, it's leaving the little thing at all. You'll be a mother soon. When I said you won't have time for study, I meant, ever.'

'But I want to finish. I want to graduate, get a proper job.'

'Your job is being a good mother to your baby.'

If I'd kept up the argument, we would have been at each other's jugular in no time. I couldn't face it. I regrouped, strategically, as I was learning to do, and spoke to Diane instead.

Yes, she would mind the baby while I went to lectures, as long as I took care of Rosanna and her own newborn in return. She quite fancied the idea – until her enthusiasm mysteriously evaporated. I suspected heat from Joyce Kinnane.

Even if I could get to lectures, there were still the fees to pay and Dad simply refused outright: 'You had your go at university, and I can't say it did you much good.'

At last I'd glimpsed the future they were planning for me. It wasn't just my body they wanted to imprison, and not just until the baby arrived. They wanted all of me, forever. Mum was set on total victory.

FOUR

TOM

I was present when each of my mothers married. As a six-year-old, I stood in Wanganui Gardens with Grandma and Grandad Riley while Dad was out the front with his bride, Lyn Cosgrove. At Susan's wedding, I was even closer to the action, inside the white gown.

For years I harboured an entirely egocentric interest in whether a bump was in evidence at the church. The only picture I've seen, snapped by Aunty Diane's husband and preserved in their family album, was taken straight-on and leaves the matter inconclusive. The photo is interesting for another reason, though – the biggest smile undoubtedly belongs to the bride's mother, which seems a little ironic in the circumstances.

'Joyce, oh she was delighted,' Dad had told me brightly, when I asked him about it years ago. 'I was a good Catholic boy, soon to be a teacher. Her daughter was saved. She practically said that much to me outside the church, although she had the good sense to make sure Susan didn't hear, or they'd have had a barney in front of the guests. Our first argument was over Joyce, actually.'

'I thought married couples fought over money,' I said, trying to sound more knowledgeable than the schoolboy I was at the time.

'Not us. Never a cross word on that account. We were always a bit different. No, she took me to task for being too pally with Joyce –' and, putting on a high-pitched voice, he'd mimicked Susan in full flight – 'You don't know what she's like, you just see the smiles meant to draw you in. She'll use you to control me!'

The exchange left me with visions of a paranoid mother, which I knew to be unfair, because the performance Dad had just bunged on for my benefit was only one side of her.

Susan's view, Dad's view – the subtle differences posed an interesting conundrum. Most of what I knew came from two people unashamed of their own bias; their stories, their excuses had to be weighed and sifted, and by what, if not my own bias, because I had ways of seeing things, as well. That became worse, years later, when I knew more, knew more than even Dad about certain things; by then objectivity had become impossible, as it always is when you're angry with someone, or for someone, when an injustice sticks in your craw, when you can't forgive.

Marriage. My mother used it to escape, something she's been entirely open about since I was old enough to discuss such things with her. In 2003, when I made that long flight from London with Dad at my elbow, marriage was on my own radar. At thirty-one, I was in the zone, you might say. Hilary and I had certainly discussed it; we'd discussed it in half of the restaurants around London and in the flat we shared in Kennington before she went home to Australia.

Did I ever ask her straight out, 'Will you marry me?'

I can't have, because she would have said yes and that would have demanded that one of us make the compromise we were each hoping the other would make. The shift wasn't coming from me and since she wasn't yet ready to force the issue, for a long time she took the soft route.

'You've got to get over it, Tommy,' she'd say, knowing damned well how much I hated the diminutive. 'You don't belong over here any more than I do. Let's go home, and Brisbane's not so bad, really. It's certainly got a better climate than London. You can hardly argue about that.'

I wasn't the commitment phobic of popular cliché – quite the opposite – and if I needed reminding of the joy marriage can infuse through a man's life, like the rosy glow of a Renoir, I only had to look at Dad. Mike and Lyn Riley were quite a canvas and I wanted that painting on my own wall one day.

They stayed with me in Kennington for a week before Dad started a stint as poet-in-residence at East Anglia University. Hilary had gone by then, though. They knew about her, of course, and were clearly disappointed to have missed her.

'Her visa ran out,' I said, and left it at that, although I could see they expected more. Thankfully, they were good enough to leave the questions unasked.

It struck me, afterwards, that I had envied them since I first became aware that love was not automatic or forever, and that a long-haul marriage wasn't the only kind. How old was I then? Mid-teens? Later than some of my friends, who learned this truth at a younger age, and with a hell of a lot more pain.

Considering the pain Dad's first marriage brought him, it was hardly surprising he gave few details away. It was only through an unguarded moment on his part that I found out where he and Susan had lived straight after the wedding – a house in Taringa close to the route I took each day on my way to uni.

I didn't take much notice, at first. It was only later, when I wanted to know all I could about my mother, that I went back for a closer look. It also held a significance for me, I realised, since it was my first home, the place they must have brought me to straight from the hospital.

SUSAN
1972

Barefoot, and sweating beneath an old shirt I used as a painting smock, I crossed a floor carpeted with newspaper. The shirt, one of Mike's father's, had turned up in Taringa among the drop sheets and brushes borrowed from home. Mike was stripped down to even less, just a pair of football shorts.

'Here,' I said, handing him a glass of cold water. 'Could it be any hotter, do you think?'

'How's your back?'

I made a rather deliberate face and with a hand over my kidney, stretched a little to test it, making the bulge in the shirt more pronounced. 'Better than yesterday. Will the undercoat hold out?'

We looked together into the near-empty can.

'Should be enough for the windows,' he said. 'I'll start on the yellow this afternoon.'

I backed away to the single bed Mike had covered with drop sheets and lay on my side, the only position left to me by then. From there, I watched the muscles of his back working and the way the sweat formed beads that trickled in little rivers all the way to his waistband.

He'd been so good about everything – so good to me. Better than I deserved, because, try as I might, I couldn't always keep my mouth shut when he niggled me.

'There, finished,' he announced, standing back with the brush still in hand and thoroughly pleased with himself. He looked so hot.

A bucket of water stood close to the bed, in case of spills and rogue strokes from the brush. I sat up and drew the bucket across the news-paper, until I could reach the rag floating on top.

'Come here. You've got paint all over you.'

He sat on the edge of the bed and watched as I wrung out the rag and then made him turn away from me while I wiped away the broad smear where he'd backed into the wet wall. It was a powerful back, muscular.

When the paint marks were gone, I went on washing the sweat from his skin.

'Lie down while I get the paint off your stomach,' I said, and once the dabs of undercoat were gone, I went on smoothing the cloth gently, up over his chest and shoulders, too.

He'd closed his eyes to enjoy the sensation, but when I kept it up, longer than needed to wash away the perspiration, he opened them and watched me expectantly. He'd always been slow on the up-take.

He drew the shirt over my head and helped me slip off the sensible bra. He liked my hair to fall over his face, although he'd never said anything.

My briefs followed, then I stripped off his shorts and for a few sweaty minutes, we bucked up and down until he spent himself with a final grunt. The facial contortions had disconcerted me on the hon-eymoon, but after three months I'd decided they were the sign of a job well done.

'That was fantastic,' he said, still out of breath.

I lay down beside him, panting myself and put my head on his chest.

'You can see why they call it making love,' said Mike. 'We made more of something, out of nothing. We're Gods.'

'You're full of shit, Mr Riley,' I said, laughing.

He seemed to drift into sleep then surprised me by speaking almost into my ear. 'Have you thought any more about names?'

'Well, Riley as a surname cuts out Kylie and Wendy, anything end-ing like that.'

'You don't really like those names, do you?'

'No, I hate them, but I'm just saying . . .'

'Any boys' names yet?'

'It's a girl, Mike,' I said, with a certainty that made him snort.

'I don't imagine the name Joyce is likely to get a guernsey.'

I slapped his chest, making him jump at the sudden pain.

'If it is a boy, will you call him Terry?'

'No,' I said instantly, and the reason came out too quickly: 'I'd think of his fath – of the other Terry every time I said the little thing's name.'

My mind still went to fuzz whenever Terry came up between us. Not Mike, though. Things were already settled on that score, as far as he was concerned.

'When will we tell her, or him, whatever. Do you want her to call me Daddy or Mike?'

It was a surprise then that I answered immediately and with the same certainty that I was carrying a girl. 'Kids should have mummies and daddies. We'll stick with that, except this one –' I dropped a hand onto my belly – 'will hear about two daddies. It'll be like Santa Claus. Kids don't question contradictions until they're ready to know the truth.'

'S'pose you're right,' he said, as though he couldn't be bothered to put his own view. That annoyed me.

'You don't have to agree with me on everything,' I said, raising my head so he'd see I was serious. '*You're* going to be this thing's father, Mike. What are you painting this bedroom for if you're not?'

Settling back into the crook of his neck, I couldn't see his face, but the silence showed he was thinking about what I'd said.

'When I was little, they used to call me Thomas because I wanted to see things with my own eyes. I quite liked it. When I needed a confirmation name, that's what I picked.'

'Thomas Riley.' I tried it on my tongue. 'A bit formal.'

'Everyone will call him Tom.'

When he didn't say any more, I moved to get up.

'No,' he said, drawing me back to the bed. He squeezed out the rag and began to sweep it slowly over my belly. He'd told me that my body was the most beautiful thing he had ever seen, not a bad thing to hear when you're feeling every ounce of the extra weight.

Mike refreshed the rag and went on soothing my back, slowly, from under my hair all the way to my ankles. When it was done, he put the rag aside and ran his open palm over the slippery skin, into the cave of my back and over the outward curve of my bottom.

'Up at Cedar Creek, and even when I saw you walking across the Great Court, I dreamed of doing this. The gods have whispered magic among the planets, just for me.'

'Is that your precious Larkin?' I asked. 'Sounds more greeting card to me.'

He laughed and put his shorts back on.

TOM

I was born on 31 March, 1972, twelve days later than predicted. The obstetrician planned to induce me if I hadn't appeared by the following morning, and, considering the baggage attached to my very existence, a birthday on April Fool's would have been no joke at all.

Susan was going spare, apparently, until Aunty Diane told her babies were more trouble out, than in. The birth required four hours of painful pushing on the part of my mother, who screamed every curse known to woman and invented some new ones the midwife hadn't heard before. That was one piece of news she was happy, even proud, to tell me. Dad had been sent home: no husbands present in those days.

'What did you think when you first saw me?' I asked Dad once, when I'd pestered him for every baby photo he could find from among the boxes still stored at Grandma Riley's.

'Your head looked like a sucked mango seed.'

'Love at first sight then.'

He nodded and blessed me with one of his unrestrained smiles. 'All babies are beautiful to their parents.'

'Even Mum?'

That was the first time I'd referred to Susan, and not Lyn, by that fraught word. Dad stared at me for a long moment and said, 'She loved you then, she loves you now, Tom. No matter how you ask the question, my answer will always be the same.'

'Sorry, Dad. Stupid of me to say anything. Did *she* think I looked like a sucked mango?'

He went on checking me over as though he didn't trust my instant capitulation, then told me things I had heard before: 'She searched for Terry in your little face. She didn't say so, but I could see her doing it. You had Kinnane colouring, though. I don't know whether that made it easier or harder for her. But you've quizzed your mother about all this, I know, because she told me last time she rang up to check on you.'

'But you were there, too, Dad. Just trying to get another angle. It's hard sometimes to sift the truth from the myths and the bullshit. She says she wouldn't relive the day you brought me home from the hospital, not for a bucket of gold.'

'Ah, that was Diane's fault. Told your mother to stick with four-hourly feeds like you were a robot. You started yelling the house down ten minutes after we walked in. She walked you, I walked you, we changed your nappy and still you cried. After an hour we were out of our trees, and, of course, Susan would rather cut her tongue out than ring Joyce for help.'

'So you rang a neutral party.'

He laughed at that. 'An interesting way to put it, but yes, I rang my own mother, who said, "For God's sake feed the little thing." You were fine after that.'

'You kept going into the room to check on me, didn't you?'

'Ah, I see more myths have been embroidered.'

'But it's true.'

'That one, yes. You were the most wonderful thing I had ever seen. Worth a few lines of unpublished poetry, too. How did it go? *Dependent flesh, with eyes and waving hands alone to conjure love.*'

Alone in my room afterwards, I wondered whether my mother was ever truly happy as Dad's wife. She had given me conflicting answers over the years. The older she grew, and the greater the lapse of time since those short years, the more inclined she was to say yes, or perhaps it was simply because by then she *was* happy. It wasn't a topic we discussed in the Fitzgerald days, when I was a teenager, and more fragile inside my First xv jersey than I wanted to admit. Any version of her marriage she might have given me then would have been distorted by the rollercoaster of the Inquiry.

It was later, when I started spending time with her in Sydney, that I worked up the courage to ask whether she'd been happy with Dad, and for my pains received a curt 'no, not really'.

Was it the truth, though?

She brought the matter up herself during my first year at university: 'If I had days, even whole weeks when I was happy, it was because Mike ticked all the boxes for what a husband's expected to do.'

'That's not exactly a heartfelt endorsement,' I said.

At the time, I was sitting with my first glass of Scotch in hand and gaping at the view of Sydney Harbour behind her. Perhaps it was the alcohol, but I suddenly pictured her with clipboard and pen, marking Dad on his performance.

Yard kept tidy – tick
Helped with the housework – tick
Got the baby up so I could sleep longer in the mornings – tick
Came home on time, never raised his hand to me, marshalled our money
prudently, remembered my birthday – tick, tick, tick, tick

'The best thing Mike did was get me back into study,' she declared, after she'd poured me another centimetre. 'I'd had this idea that I would do a subject part-time in the semester after you were born, but well . . . you proved more of a handful than I'd bargained on.'

She stopped there and smiled to herself, some private joke I guessed, because she looked down at her wine glass for a moment before speaking again.

'You didn't sleep through a single night until you were six months old.'

'Dad says I was a tyrant.'

'You just weren't your cousin Rosanna, that's all, and I'd assumed all babies would be like her. Christ, what did I know, and the way Diane talked, you'd think it was a piece of cake. Anyway, I wasn't in the best frame of mind, but Mike said I had to have a degree. It's the only time he pushed me into something, or the only time I let him.

Since you're asking, Tom – yes, I had a life. Best of all, I was out from under my mother and at the end of that year, the ALP swept into office. God, those were fabulous days. Mike started teaching soon after. First time he got paid, we sat on our bed with you in the middle and spread the notes out like Bonnie and Clyde.'

She didn't have to tell me there were happy days, not when she let stories like that slip out.

'It was a bit like an arranged marriage,' she said another time, when she was in a more thoughtful mood, and entirely sober. 'You don't have to be in love to feel affection for someone. Mike tried so hard, and look at him now, with Lyn. All he needed was someone who loved him back.'

There was more, then and afterwards, when I coaxed her into grinning anecdotes for those years, yet, in the sensitive and intensely personal stories of her happier days, I didn't seem to play any part at all. I realise now I was waiting for it, I was waiting for her to look straight into my face and say, 'Tom, I had you, and you made me happy, no matter what else was going on in my life.'

She never did.

SUSAN
1973

I knew what the doctor was going to say from the complacent way he'd gone about the examination.

'Nothing to worry about, my dear. Your GP was quite right. Be patient a couple of years and his eye will straighten. Perfectly normal.'

My dear! Where did he get off, patronising me like that? It had been Mike's idea, anyway. He'd insisted I make the appointment with a specialist, which meant taking Tom into the city when I didn't have the car because Mike drove it to work.

The damage began earlier when we were too late for the bus because Tom had dirtied his nappy just as we were heading out the door. That meant a taxi if we were going to make the appointment on time and money was tight.

'I'll have to drop you up a little further,' the cabbie had said when there were no spaces at the kerb in Wickham Terrace, and, in the fluster of payment and extracting Tom, I hadn't realised where we were until I looked up and found myself standing on the very spot where those bastard police had charged onto the footpath.

Then the doctor was running forty minutes late, so I could have waited for the next bus after all. Did the receptionist apologise? Don't be stupid.

The coffee table offered only tattered copies of *House and Garden*, and *Women's Weekly*.

'Bloody garbage,' I said, loud enough to make the receptionist look up.

I retrieved the *Courier-Mail* from a seat opposite, and, in a sign that my day might be picking up, I found a picture of Donna Redlich on page five. Hers was one of four faces, all women, and all looking dreadfully important despite the obligatory smile for the camera.

Team to Establish Shelters said the headline. The Federal Government was setting up a women's shelter as a refuge for battered wives and Donna was to be assistant to the group's leader.

A women's refuge was just the kind of work I would have thrown myself into, and I immediately pictured myself arguing our case at meetings, defying public servants twice my age to demand justice for disempowered women. The film in my head rolled on until I glanced down at the newspaper, still open and with the familiar face staring up at me. It wasn't *my* face. If things had been different, if I'd been able to apply, I would have landed that job ahead of Donna.

I brooded all the way home to Taringa, even though I scolded myself for being so childish with every lurch and turn of the bus. Tom was fractious on my knee and it didn't help that the bus was crowded with boys in the red and black of Mike's old school. They'd surrendered a seat to me but with nowhere else to go, they hung from the straps directly above. There was no ill intent, but I felt intimidated by their size, their proximity.

Closer to the driver and well out of earshot, a blond All Hallows' girl talked with another Gregory Terrace boy. His mates had noticed and began to make adolescent comments, all bluster and ribaldry.

'Do you reckon she's a natural blonde?' said one.

'He'll never find out.'

'Neither will you.'

From the rumble of sniggers, it dawned on me they were discussing the girl's pubic hair.

My mind was still planning refuges where women could escape from the misogyny that fed such jokes. Tom began to whinge. By the time our stop was close, he was whimpering with tiredness and drawing the eyes of other passengers.

'Excuse me, I've got to get off at the next stop,' I told the closest boy.

'This is my stop, too,' he said. 'I'll carry that for you,' and he'd picked up the bag at my feet before I could decline.

So there I was on the footpath, having to say a polite thankyou to a smiling schoolboy, who only moments before had been making sexist remarks about the girl I could still see now, oblivious to it all, through the bus window.

I wanted to scream!

At home, I'd just got Tom off to sleep when Mike pulled into the driveway. I hurried to meet him at the front door with a finger to my lips and led him through to the kitchen where it was safe to talk.

'Hey, I had a breakthrough today,' he began immediately. 'I finally connected with the too-cool crowd in Year Eight. I've had them reading—'

'I don't want to hear about it,' I said.

He stopped, but couldn't hide the mild offence.

'I'm sorry, Mike,' I said quickly. That was all I needed to say, but my bloody tongue had a mind of its own. 'It's just that you come home every second day with a story like this and I'm a bit tired of it, okay?'

I should have stopped at the apology.

His eyebrows lifted. He shrugged. 'Okay, I'll give it a rest.'

No, that wasn't what I wanted, yet I couldn't name what I did. No wonder Mike looked mystified.

'When you get all excited about your work, it reminds me that I'm a million miles away from having a job myself, one I can throw myself into the way you do,' I said, knowing that this was reasonable, an explanation that made sense and at the same time didn't really tell why I was angry.

'Tom's a job on his own. You've told me often enough.'

'Don't, Mike,' I warned, and he let that angle drop, thank God.

I told him about Donna Redlich.

'Yeah, I saw it in the staffroom copy. Isn't it great?'

'Yes, it's fucking great – for Donna!'

Now I'd raised my voice. For fuck's sake, shut up, Susan! 'I'm sorry, Mike,' I said again, determined to leave it at that and then said, 'It was a pain getting Tom into town for the eye specialist.'

'That was today? What did he say?'

'That it's nothing to worry about. All a waste of time,' I couldn't help adding. 'The doctor treated me like a moron because we didn't believe the GP.'

'Doesn't hurt to get these things checked out.'

'It does when it's such a hassle getting there and back again.'

I could feel the heat under my skin. Stop now. It's over, no harm done. Just shut up.

'It would have been easier if I'd had the car.'

I knew what reaction I'd get and I hated myself when the despondency appeared in his face. 'It's hard enough getting a lift one day as it is, Suze. Frank never says no, but the signals are always there about how far out of his way he has to come.'

I began to cry. The car wasn't important. My tears came from disappointment that I'd even brought it up.

'I can try taking the bus again,' he said.

'No, no, no!' I wailed. 'That's not it. I could have the car every day but I'd always have to take Tom with me and I'd always have to come back here afterwards.'

Mike shifted uncomfortably. 'We can't afford a better place yet. I'm sorry about it, but—'

'I'm not talking about this place. I mean I have to come back to you and Tom all the time.'

'Don't say that. You're tired from going into town. I'm sorry it was all for nothing, and I wish there was something I could do about the car . . .'

He kept talking, but I was thinking about what he'd muttered a few moments before. *Don't say that.* Why not? Why couldn't things be said? Why couldn't I say them?

'I know, I know,' I shouted, 'but none of that's the problem. If this was a proper marriage it wouldn't matter, but I only got married to get away from my bloody mother and now I'm trapped all over again with a husband and a bloody baby.'

I'd said it. I had felt it there, lurking beneath everything else, a boil too sensitive to lance. I'd known these words would end up running out of me like pus. I collapsed into a chair at the table and sobbed into my hands.

When I looked up, Mike was gone.

I called his name. No response. I went looking for him but he was nowhere in the house. Christ, what had I done?

'Mike!'

I found him at the bottom of the stairs, sitting hunched over on the lowest step. His shoulders jerked a couple of times then fought to stay still. Did he know I was watching?

I despised myself, felt sick to my bones. 'Mike, I'm so sorry,' I called down the steps.

He didn't turn around, didn't acknowledge that he'd heard me at all even when I started down the stairs and stopped two steps above him. I sat and put a hand tentatively on his shoulder. He flinched.

'I should never have said those things. It wasn't fair. If I could scrub them out of your head, I would.'

I tried my hand on his shoulder again, the same place. This time, he left it there.

'I can't do any more,' he said, still looking away, still struggling with tears.

'You don't have to. I'm just jealous of Donna, that's all. Schoolgirl stuff.'

I lowered myself to the next step and pressed my face between his shoulder blades. Put my arms around him.

'I didn't mean it. I didn't mean that bit about our marriage. I do love you, I do, I love you, I love you, I love you.'

I wasn't the first to hope a mantra would bolster belief.

TOM

I could never bring myself to ask Dad, 'When did things go wrong between you and Susan?' even though the question itched like a scab right through my teens. There was no doubt what he would have said. Bindy – their marriage fell apart in Bindy – and he'd have been right, but not for the reasons he thought.

For a long time, Dad didn't know about Barry Dolan. I could have changed that once I'd learned of the part Dolan played in our lives, but convinced myself the story was Susan's to tell, not mine.

What difference would it have made for the three of us, if Dad had known – what if Susan *had* taken the last of the anonymous letters to him on the day she first read it – her hands shaking in outrage as they must have been? I know Mike Riley. He would have given even more of himself to Susan, instead of making the stand that he did. He might have saved his marriage! But then what? If he had, there would be no Lyn Cosgrove in his life, as there is today, no daughters named Gabrielle and Emma and I doubt there would have been an invitation from East Anglia University to be its poet-in-residence in 2003.

Would Susan's life have been any better if they'd stayed together? Less pain perhaps, or would there have been a great deal more? It's impossible to say. And what of little Tom who grew into big, tall Tom? The same words apply, I suppose, although they never stopped me wondering.

What *did* happen was Dad's transfer to Bindamilla for the start of '74.

Although it was my home for eighteen months, my only memories of the town have been fabricated from the stories of others. My mother hated the place, and if, in contrast, Dad managed to salvage one of his proudest achievements out of his time there, it was misery that let him drill down to words he hasn't matched in his poetry since then.

'Why didn't you try to get out of it?' I asked Susan, when I was twenty and finally understood the importance of what had happened in Bindamilla.

'I did,' she said, reasonably.

'Not until the second year,' I pointed out. But I meant why didn't they get out of the posting altogether. When I said as much she had to give me an answer, and obviously didn't want to.

'It was the Aboriginal thing. Bindy had a sizable black population and Mike wanted to teach disadvantaged kids. It was the Whitlam years. I could hardly renege on my principles, could I?'

By that time, I'd long since found the tiny dot on the map of Queensland, a full day's drive from Brisbane. On the edge of the Outback, the town spread out across the black soil, making it seem bigger than it really was, according to Dad. 'A bacterial maw', he called it in a poem from his first volume, *The Unquiet Landscape of Silence*.

Later, I rummaged through the folders where Dad kept early drafts of his poems and found the photo of a grand Queenslander, which had seen better days, certainly, but, since my mother stood on the veranda with a baby in her arms, I realised it must have been where we lived. It was the only proof that I had ever lived in Bindamilla because the rest was all stories.

Just beyond the edge of that photo must have been the vacant block where I ventured one morning to begin the downward spiral of my mother's standing among the locals. I climbed out of my cot, the story goes, doing fatal damage to the kilter of my nappy and finding both Mummy and Daddy asleep still, and a door onto the veranda unlatched, I went exploring. My nappy finally slipped free at the bottom of the steps and with my little willy pointing the way, I walked along the footpath to where a scrum of Aboriginal kids was playing *brum-brum* games in the dirt.

I still have clear images in my head of every moment, right down to the strange lady who picked me up some time later and took me home. Except I was barely two years old on that day and I've surely embroidered such memories from the stories Dad told me later. Dad, not Susan.

SUSAN
May, 1974

'Oh my goodness, look at you,' I said to the little monkey who'd lurched from the stranger's arms and attached himself to me. I hugged him tight, then jumped at how cold his bare bottom felt to my hand.

'What happened?' I asked the Good Samaritan who stared at us from the top of the staircase.

'I found him playing with some Aboriginal children on the corner,' she said.

I should have asked her name straightaway, but the whole thing was such a hoot. Instead, I raised Tom in my arms to see his face. 'How did you get out? Quite the little Houdini, aren't you?'

To the stranger, I said, 'He scoots around so quickly these days, I can hardly keep up,' and laughed at how true that was, all the while jigging my son up and down. 'Yes, you're a proper Burke and Wills.'

Embarrassment didn't kick in until I looked again at Tom's rescuer. No mirth in that face. What was she, sixty-five? A grandmother out on her morning constitutional in a faded dress and leather shoes with closed-in toes to keep out the gravel. A Bindy local from better times.

'You should think about locking your doors at night if your little one likes to roam,' she said. 'Then you can sleep in all you like.'

Oh dear. I glanced at Mike, who was thinking the same thing. But it was a sunny autumn morning, the air was invigorating in a way it hadn't been through the hot and wretched months after we first arrived, and I wasn't going to let the old biddy dump any guilt on my doorstep.

'I don't think I've met you before,' I said.

'Mrs Shepherd. I live a few doors down the street.' She pointed. 'I've seen you walking with the little boy. That's how I knew where to bring him.'

No first name, I noted. We were from different generations, and some of the older types were sticklers for convention, even in Bindamilla. Come to think of it, especially in Bindamilla.

'Well, we really can't thank you enough, Mrs Shepherd. You've certainly lived up to your name this morning.'

I was hoping for a smile, but no, my lame joke had gone the way of a lead balloon.

Mrs Shepherd wouldn't stay for a cup of tea, thank you all the same. She was just pleased to see the baby safe with his parents, a sentiment she delivered with the formality of a speech.

Mike escorted her to the gate, and, even though I didn't hear what was said, I could tell, from the way he bent over her deferentially, that he was grovelling over our negligence as Mrs Shepherd seemed to expect.

'That lady thought the wolves were going to eat you,' I told Tom, while he splashed in the blackened bathwater. 'You didn't see any wolves, did you, Tommy, or I suppose it would be dingoes out here? Dogs, any doggies?'

Tom stopped playing and looked at me. It was a word he could put a meaning to and so he repeated it: 'Dog.' He checked behind me to see if there were any in evidence and seemed disappointed when there were no doggies to be seen.

I still felt a thrill when he responded to words, and loved to name things for him, like Eve in the garden. No *bow-wows* for my boy.

When he was dry and dressed I took him to the bedroom where Mike was settling back under the blankets with the Sunday paper he'd been down to the main street to fetch.

'It didn't go as well as expected,' he commented, showing me the headline. 'Gough's back in, but with a reduced majority.'

'Let me see.' I swapped Tom for the newspaper and, while the bed shook and the room filled with a two-year-old's squeals, I read the results from the federal election. 'Geez, we lost more seats than I thought we would.'

Mike had given away the tickling and the two of them now lay panting beside me, with the smaller body enveloped in his daddy's arms. 'Do you want a baby sister to play with, Tommy?' said Mike.

I stopped reading and looked down at them both, certain now that the hokey pose was chosen for the occasion. 'Are you asking him or me?' I said. 'He'd get more fun out of a dog.'

Mike said no more about it, and when Tom became restless I took him into the kitchen, slotted his expeditionary legs into the highchair and tied a bib around his neck.

A second child. 'Only it will really be your daddy's first, won't it?' I said to Tom, posting the first spoonful of cereal into his eager mouth. 'Do you want a little sister? Will you two be like Ritchie and me, making mischief together and driving your mother mad? It would serve me right.'

It's time. I smiled ruefully at how Labor's slogan from the '72 election was being turned on me. If I fell pregnant soon, there'd be three years between my firstborn and my second. Just right, like Goldilocks' porridge.

Tom thought only of porridge, and of stairs to climb down and new places to explore. A baby's privilege. Despite his presence, I felt alone in the kitchen – alone in the house, too.

Mike was slow on the up-take, as ever. Mum and Diane had been building their case since before Christmas, with unsubtle references to the best gap between children. In their opinion, I owed it to Mike because he'd ridden so valiantly to my rescue. Even if neither one of them dared to say so, the insinuation lived in every glance, every half-smile sent my way, while Diane fussed over her pigeon pair.

I didn't want another child. There, the truth was easily said. It was much harder, though, to fend off fears that to feel that way loosed my claim on the title 'Loving Mother'.

'I do love you, Tom,' I said to the self-absorbed figure in the highchair, 'I do, I do.' But I only managed to dredge up memories of an afternoon at the bottom of the stairs in Taringa.

I was resisting a bigger truth that morning: a second child would change the dynamic between Mike and me. Two years ago, I'd been vulnerable, losing the shape of my life. I'd needed an ally, so in front of that priest, Mike and I had struck a deal: I escaped my mother's deadening hand, and he got his dream girl.

I'd fought against such thinking since that afternoon on the back stairs, but truth was a persistent bugger and it was whispering again as I wiped Tom's mouth and set him down on the floor. Things were different now. I wasn't pregnant and powerless. If I had a baby with Mike – and why just one? – I was choosing to be his wife in a way I didn't when Tom was the size of a plum inside me. I would become Mrs Riley at last, wife to a loving husband and mother to our brood of children. A second baby was my choice, a free choice.

'Free,' I said, as Tom rushed away like a possum springing from a trap.

Yes, I was free, all right – except for ten thousand years of social norms and the burden of biology.

Mike came home with the first stories on Monday afternoon.

'They knew all about Tom at school,' he said. 'Before I was even through the gate, Marg Hackworth said she'd heard how he'd gone walkabout. Then Mr Verity called me into his office to ask if Tom had suffered any ill effects. You'd think he'd been kidnapped by cannibals. Even the kids got in on the act. That little shit Rodney Acres pipes up in class, "Hey Sir, your little boy got a bit black in the dirt yesterday, eh? Hope it all came off," he says. Even the black kids were sniggering.'

I thought he was overreacting until I copped the same at Millers' the following day: 'Good to see your son got his nappy back from the blackfellas,' said the woman behind me at the checkout.

'And his nose wasn't running all over his lip either,' I shot back at her. She had to wipe the snot off her own little darling, then. Wiped the smirk off her face, too.

It was the way of small towns, I told myself on the walk home, although I didn't have to like it. And there was a deeper issue to grapple with. It was all very well to score points in a checkout queue, but I needed people, a few new friends. The women on Mike's staff were mostly our age, but they were single and partied hard. To them, I was a matron they deferred to because of my status as wife and mother. As if!

'Come on,' I felt like saying, 'let's get drunk,' but if we had, or even if I'd suggested it, my impropriety would have wrinkled the corners of their eyes.

Still, I saw more of them than the Bindy women. I'd heard so much about the hospitality of country folk and somehow imagined it would simply fold me into its bosom. There'd been plenty of smiles from the locals – just nothing behind it.

'We're transients,' Mike explained. 'When our two-year stint is up, we'll scuttle back to where we came from. Out here, friendships are for life.'

We had one like-minded soul, at least, in Louise Moriarty, a nurse with the Aboriginal Health Service. Overweight and not one to give a damn, she came round on weekends to talk politics and drink beer and invariably left me happier than before she'd arrived. Unfortunately, she also pointed out the unofficial apartheid down at the movie theatre. Only 'friends of the manager' were welcome upstairs, where the seats were more comfortable; curiously, the manager didn't have any Aboriginal friends. Mike was outraged, and when the local paper ignored his letter to the editor he insisted that we join Louise's silent boycott.

One less thing to do in Bindamilla, one more way to stand apart. If it had been up to me, I'd have ignored the discrimination and gone to the movies with everyone else.

FIVE

TOM

By the time I left school, I was five centimetres taller than Dad and had a voice like Rocky Balboa, which I like to think I put to better use than the mumbling boxer. I was never sure whether it was the voice or my size that convinced Dad of my maturity, but he began to discuss the issues of the day with me more. We were on the cusp of a new decade and the tension between Hawke and Keating in Canberra had the media enthralled, my mother as much as anyone.

'I'm surprised Susan never had a go at politics,' I said to Dad one night after the television news.

'She writes headline articles for a national broadsheet, Tom. Would you not call that having a go at politics?'

'You know what I mean. As a candidate. She's got all the skills.'

To my surprise, he laughed openly, leaving me to feel insulted on her behalf.

He saw my confusion and said, 'Skills, yes. In parliament she would have been an asset to any party.'

'Only one, surely. She's Labor through and through.'

He made a face at this. 'She's what you'd call *of the left*, same as me. Comes with the times we grew up in, I suppose, but in her articles she dumps on either side if the evidence is there. Couldn't be so good at her job if she went easy on one side. But as a candidate . . .' He chuckled again at the thought. 'Not Susan. The American's have a nice way of putting it, Tom. Couldn't get herself elected dog catcher. Anyway, she did have a go. If we hadn't been out in the bush, she might have done well.'

'You mean she actually had a go in Bindamilla?'

'Yep, good old Bindy. Not as a candidate, though. It was the state election in '74, the cricket team election. Your mother got all fired up. It was a sight to behold, I can tell you. She drove two hours up the unsealed road to a branch meeting and met the Labor candidate – a bloke named Dowd, if memory serves. Came back as his sub-branch organiser for Bindy, although I don't think there'd ever been one before.'

'She never told me any of this.'

'I'm not surprised, Tom. It didn't go well. It was the wrong time, the wrong place and your poor mother was a babe in the woods.'

'What happened? Labor didn't win the seat, I take it.'

The laughter almost choked him this time. 'Win! Christ, no. Bindy's heartland for the old Country Party. Labor couldn't even take that seat after the Fitzgerald Inquiry, when the stink of the Joh years was up everyone's nose.'

SUSAN
October, 1974

I was more nervous than I'd been since my first seminar at uni.

'Can you see her yet, Mike?' I called through the front door.

He was watching the street from the veranda, which had come to feel like the ramparts of a castle in recent months, or the watchtower of a prison.

'Not yet,' came the reply.

'Shit,' I muttered, careful that Tom didn't hear. I checked myself again in the mirror, and liked what I saw. Miniskirts had given way to the maxi and that suited my plans for tonight, for I wanted attention on my words, not my legs.

'How much longer, do you think?' I asked, walking onto the veranda, as though harrying Mike would make Muriel turn up sooner. She was great with Tom but she was prone to turning up whenever, and I didn't want blackfella time to make us late.

'She'll be here. It's just gone seven now,' he said, defending Muriel as though he'd guessed what I was thinking. Shit, I was so on edge.

Muriel emerged beneath the weak street lamps and mounted the stairs. 'Sorry, Mr Riley, doing my English homework, eh,' she said, with a wicked grin.

'Liar,' said Mike, enjoying the game. She was his favourite.

Muriel chortled deep in her throat, then followed me into the house for last-minute instructions. 'Tom can stay up for half an hour, but then it's into the cot. The meeting shouldn't go much past nine o'clock.'

Muriel waved us off from the veranda as though she owned the place. What had seemed like a prison earlier now afforded safety.

'Maybe we shouldn't go,' I said suddenly.

Mike took my hand. 'You'll win them over. Think of the way Terry could move a crowd.'

There it was again, the way he could speak that name with ease while I was forever cautious, just in case it hurt him. It wasn't a bad piece of advice, though. Terry had been fearless; he would stride into a meeting like this, up for the fight and with words his only weapon. I put one foot in front of another.

'We haven't been to anything political for ages. Feels good,' I heard myself say.

The shire hall was just beyond the strip of shopfronts, its generous glow drawing figures towards it.

'Geez, look at the numbers,' said Mike. 'I didn't think there'd be this many.'

Neither did I. The electorate was safe for the government, which bred complacency among supporters and indifference from the rest. Eric Morris had been warming a parliamentary seat in Brisbane for twenty years.

We slipped inside the hall unnoticed by the locals, who greeted one another with masculine growls and grasps at weather-leathered hands.

'They're all wearing the uniform,' I said, unconcerned that they'd hear me. 'You should give up teaching, Mike. There's got to be a fortune in akubras and moleskin pants.'

He found two seats at the end of the third row and commented again about the numbers. 'Some of them must have driven sixty miles to be here.'

The rest took their seats, more than a hundred, less than two, and fell silent when the shire chairman walked to centrestage. 'Tonight we're honoured to have our local member visiting. After so long, there's no need to introduce Eric Morris to this audience, I'm sure. He's been Bindy's man in state parliament for as long as any of us can remember—'

'Speak for yourself, Jock,' came a good-natured interjection that matched the tone. This was a homecoming, a low-key triumphal.

'Well, if you're a youngster like me, it's hard to remember anyone else.' There was more ribbing from the audience. 'And if the turn-out tonight is any indication, he's doing a great job. He's graciously agreed to come here tonight and keep us all abreast of what they're up to down there in Brisbane, so please welcome Eric Morris.'

The man hadn't even opened his mouth yet and the audience was cheering. When Mike turned my way, infected, now, with my earlier apprehension, I winked. Let Morris enjoy the adulation because I'd have him by the balls soon enough.

Morris spoke in an excruciating drawl that on any other occasion would not have held anyone's attention for long. I'd heard true orators at work, Terry among the best of them; young, lively men who took possession of an audience with the energy in their voices and the fire of their words. Yet, as I marked him down for his droning ways, the faces all around us seemed enthralled.

The spellbinding topic was fertiliser: 'Stopping the super phosphate bounty was a criminal decision and one that I have dedicated myself to seeing reversed,' said Morris.

Mike leaned close and whispered, 'That's a federal issue, state MPs can't do a thing about it.'

But Morris had moved on: 'The worst thing those city folk have done is re-value the dollar. How can farmers like you compete for overseas markets when an overvalued currency makes your produce so expensive? It's all right for the city types importing their shiny Japanese cars 'cause a high dollar makes the damned things cheaper, but who pays for them in the end? The blokes in this room pay this country's bills.'

More federal grievances. Where was the shopping list of local achievements a backbencher rolls out like dodgy fabric to be sold off as the finest silk? I couldn't wait to have a go at him.

'Eric will now answer questions from the floor,' said the shire chairman.

A couple of Dorothy Dixers followed, which let Morris repeat whole gobs of his speech, especially about the socialists down south. 'You'd think Canberra was a shrine to Karl Marx,' said Mike. He said something else but I missed it because the chairman had finally given me the nod.

'Mr Morris, everything you've talked about this evening is a federal issue,' I began. 'Surely the federal election was back in May. Now it's time for voters to turn their attention to state issues decided up here, not down in windy Canberra. That's why I'm so pleased to see you in Bindy tonight, especially when you are a member of the ruling party in Brisbane.'

I'd rehearsed this opening. I'd never stood on the podium and harangued a crowd as Terry had done, but all those years of tangling with Sister Bernadette had given me a voice that demanded engagement. It was paying off, too. Faces turned my way and the occasional solemn nod showed they'd picked up the cues in my careful wording. 'Up here' meant Queensland, God's own earth, and the line about windy Canberra mocked the capital's legendary chill and, at the same time, slipped in the boot about windbag politicians. Perfect preparation for a right to the jaw.

'And so, Mr Morris, I would like to ask you why it is your government's policy to deny Bindamilla a bitumen road between here and the Warrego Highway.'

No one saw it coming, and certainly not Eric Morris, who looked stunned that anyone would want to take a swing at him in a meeting of his own kind. In the throat-clearing, chair-scraping silence after I landed my punch, serious glares were directed at the local member.

'A sealed road to Bindamilla is a priority,' Morris said quickly, 'and I'm able to tell you that it has been slated for commencement straight after the election. In fact, once the government is returned, it will be among the first projects announced by the premier.'

Morris knew how to spar and he'd scored a point with the judges from Bindamilla, if the murmurs were any indication. I'd expected nothing less.

'Mr Morris, I guessed you would say that. Do you know how I guessed? Because you say it a lot.'

That earned a chortle. They knew it was true, as I quickly reminded them. 'I checked the newspapers, and you made exactly the same promise before the last election. You are getting a lot of practice at saying it,' I pointed out brightly, and immediately felt the heady rush of watching an entire audience laugh at my victim. I paused to let it go on, at the same time judging the precise moment to start up again.

'But no matter how much you say it, the people of Bindamilla still don't get their road. I checked *Hansard*, too, Mr Morris. You haven't asked a single question in parliament about our road in all your years as member for this area. The government might show more respect for Bindy if they weren't so cocksure of winning your seat.'

A sheen of embarrassment broke across Morris's brow and the skin of his flabby throat flushed red all the way into his flannelette collar.

'You know so much about politics, do you?' he said, the drawl gone. 'I don't know your face, to be honest. New in the area, are you? Well, if you were a local, young lady, you'd know who's really to blame for the dirt road. It's those socialists in Canberra. For years it was the Liberals who ignored our needs, and then when it looked like the funds would be available last year, Whitlam and his mates took the money for some pinko project down south.'

It was bullshit, but how could I prove it? For the first time, darkened looks came my way. They didn't know my face any better than Eric Morris did. Doubt had been sown and it was a hardy truth that could stare down the suspicion of outsiders, especially in Bindamilla, it seemed.

The chairman looked away from me then, but when my hand was the only one left in the air he let me have another go.

'Mr Morris, funding for Aboriginal housing has seen families become more settled in towns like ours. In other electorates, members have pushed for truant officers to make sure black children come to school. Why haven't you sought similar improvements for your Aboriginal constituents?'

It was true. The money was there but Morris had sat on his hands. It was more outrageous than the neglected road, yet this time my question was greeted with open hostility. From the row behind us a man muttered 'sit down', and from the back of the hall came a louder call: 'Don't answer such a stupid question, Eric.'

Don't answer! Morris couldn't believe his luck.

'Aboriginal families are well catered for in Bindamilla. They wouldn't have the houses they do if the government hadn't bought up the properties for them. As for truant officers, if a few black parents keep their kids at home, that's their business.'

'Hear, hear.'

Mike was trying to get my attention. Something about 'the black thing', but I couldn't pick up what he was saying and the interjections made it hard to think.

'My husband here is a teacher at Bindamilla School, Mr Morris, and he'll tell you that the greatest frustration teachers have is lack of regular attendance. Are you suggesting that black children don't need an education?'

'Never did me much good,' a voice called over mine, earning an easy laugh.

'Turned you into a snooty bitch,' called a second heckler in the row behind.

Mike was on his feet looking for the culprit, but the hall had dissolved into laughter more than jeers and there would be no punches thrown.

Other hands went up; more body blows to the devils in Canberra.

By then I was playing a farcical game with the shire chairman, who wouldn't look my way. In the end, I had to interject.

'Staff at the hospital, there aren't enough nurses.'

Faces glared at me with contempt. I didn't notice a figure making his way up the side aisle until he stopped a row or two in front of me. I was trying to make a point and then – flash – he'd snapped my picture.

Mike was tugging at my sleeve. 'Sit down, Suze. You're only making things worse.'

I snatched my arm away, but it was hopeless and I slumped into my seat, arms folded until the meeting ended. Mike was quickly on his feet and eager to be out through the wide double doors and into the street.

'I'm not going to run like a scared rabbit,' I told him, loud enough for half the hall to hear.

When we did make our way towards the exit, we had to cut a path through milling bodies. Most of the faces wore complacent smiles, like footballers who'd had an easy win and could afford to offer gratuitous pity to the vanquished.

That changed when a voice said, 'You should keep your wife at home, mate. Teach her some manners. This is the bush out here, not a tea party for prissy women.'

The words weren't even directed at me. It was Mike they were having a go at, as though his cattle dog had let the team down.

A few paces ahead, one man stood his ground rather than shift to let us pass. Mike stared him down, but once we'd passed out into the night, the same man called, 'Go home to your little nigger boy, lady. Be a decent mother like you should be.'

And if the hilarity had shaken the floor minutes earlier, this time it brought the house down.

I wasn't going to let the slip-up with Morris discourage me, and the following Saturday I set up a table and chairs on a street corner near the Bindamilla Hotel. Locals, townies all of them, gave me a fair hearing and went away perusing the leaflets I'd handed out. This was better. I felt like I was getting traction.

On Monday, the first letter turned up wedged in the cyclone wire of our front gate. Unsigned, of course. I don't know what made me laugh more, the four-letter words or the spelling.

'You should correct it in red pen and pin it to the notice board outside the post office,' I said to Mike.

He didn't crack a smile, though; instead, he read the letter again and again for the least hint of a threat.

'Don't worry about it,' I told him. 'Just proves we're getting under their skin.'

'Will getting under their skin win votes?' he asked.

I snatched the letter from him and threw it into the bin. 'Where it belongs,' I snapped.

His comment had hurt, because it was true. But stirring people up was part of politics and if you wanted to change minds, first you had to engage them.

When the election was announced for 7 December, I rang the local Labor candidate, Alan Dowd, who'd impressed me at the branch meeting weeks before.

'Alan's doing a sweep through the area next week,' I told Mike. 'We'll turn things around, cut through all the bushy bullshit and show the town which candidate deserves their vote.'

Unfortunately, the turnout was poor for the meeting I'd arranged in the shire hall – barely twenty and that was counting three Rileys.

'Better than I had up the road,' said Dowd. 'All I hear is stuff about Whitlam, like it's still the federal campaign.'

Afterwards, Dowd unloaded official posters of his sombre face from the boot of his car, and Mike spent the afternoon nailing them to pickets hastily bought from the hardware store.

'Alan's younger, more dynamic, don't you think?' I said, as he hammered in the first one.

He laughed at me. 'He could look like Robert Redford and still go down to a fogey like Morris.'

At the post office a second letter turned up, from out of town and sent care of Mike at the school. There was no return address. This one had been prompted by an article in *Queensland Country* that had been accompanied by the photo of me from the shire hall.

Susan Riley, wife of a Bindamilla school teacher, questioned whether local MLA Eric Morris was doing a good job in his electorate. She criticised state government policy towards Aboriginal welfare, claiming more needed to be done. In reply, Mr Morris . . .

'No mention of my question about the road,' I complained to Mike later, but the telling thing was my face in the picture. To me, it told of my frustration but Mike saw something else.

'You look like some nutter escaped from the asylum. You're a scold, darling. Three centuries ago they'd have put you in a ducking chair.'

Mike slipped his arms around me but I wriggled free, in no mood for his sympathy and stung by the way I'd been identified as his wife, as though I had no legitimacy on my own.

Both the campaign and the year ticked languidly towards their ends. I couldn't wait. Through much of November Mike was submerged beneath piles of exam papers and stayed awake until two in the morning writing meticulous reports half the parents couldn't read. The Year Tens celebrated their early freedom in the milk bar, and at the pool where I took Tom to cool off. Christ, it was hot, and I couldn't remember what rain felt like on my skin.

On a Saturday evening we pushed Tom's stroller to the principal's house for an end-of-year barbecue, where I consigned myself to the circle of fold-up chairs with the women drinking Moselle or sipping beer from a glass.

Tom was the only toddler. In minutes he was wound up like a clockwork train and racing from smiling face to smiling face. I let the girls demonstrate their maternal skills and drifted to the covey of men around the barbecue where Don Murchison, the district union organiser, was holding court about next week's election.

'About as much chance as this bit of steak here galloping round the paddock again.' Already charred, he tortured it with another pass over the flames.

'Will it really be that bad?' asked Mike, who was on to his third stubby.

We all knew Alan Dowd would go down in a screaming heap and I was quietly resigning myself to this sad fact when I found Murchison staring at me through the wavy heat of the hotplate. What was that about?

When the steaks were ready, we shuffled to the tables to load up our plates while slowly the sun disappeared and darkness dried our perspiration.

'Can I have a word, Sue?'

I looked up to find Don Murchison hovering.

'What about?'

He walked off a few paces, inviting me to follow. 'The election,' he answered when we were out of earshot. 'I ran into Alan during the week and he asked me to pass on a message. The truth is, he'd prefer you didn't hand out How-to-Vote cards on Saturday.'

'But the cards are all ready. Of course we'll hand them out.'

'Yes, yes, there'll be someone on the booth to do that. Alan just doesn't want it to be you.'

If I'd only looked into the man's face I'd have sensed his embarrassment, but instead I was forcing him to spell it out.

'The feeling is you'll drive away Alan's votes in Bindy. God knows, he's not going to get many in any case. Best if you stay out of the campaign from here on in.'

TOM

I had to keep at Dad, listening for crumbs and at my mother, too; I had to keep nudging, cajoling and all the time conscious that I was stirring painful sediments that they would have preferred to keep as impermeable rock. But I wanted to know; I wanted to know everything, whether I had the right or not. It was my life, too. I had grown out of them – Susan especially.

What Dad had told me filled in a gap that I somehow knew was there. My mother is far too political an animal to have stayed out of party politics entirely. She'd picked a bad time, though. I knew my ALP history and 1974 was as dire as it got for the party in Queensland. *They make 'em different north of the border*, goes the saying. You heard that a lot back then, apparently. It is still said today, although always with a wry grin because the sting has gone out of it. The points of difference between Queensland and the southern states aren't a call to identity in quite the same way, and certainly not with the same intensity. But in the mid-1970s, the dictum became a proud declaration on the lips of Queenslanders themselves, and a knowing smirk when muttered by the rest of Australia.

As well, Dad's story about Susan's political exploits shed light on something that had niggled at me for years. Yes, the result of the '74 poll was abysmal – Labor became a parliamentary rump bounced around on the shitting end of a rampant bull named Bjelke-Petersen. Why it was so significant to me, though, had nothing to do with numbers in parliament. Rather, it helped explain my mother's state of mind when the last of the anonymous letters turned up in Bindamilla during their long absence for the Christmas holidays. It must have sat there for weeks, in the way a landmine lies patiently for its singular moment.

I have often pictured Susan pushing my stroller to the post office on the first day of school in 1975.

'Mail for Riley,' she would have asked at the counter, or perhaps after a year there was no need to give her name. If the postal clerk had been a true believer like Susan, they might have exchanged a few words of commiseration over the election result while the clerk shuffled the envelopes. After their long holiday, there must have been quite a bundle, and among the bills and tardy Christmas cards there was one bearing unknown handwriting with no address on the back.

She wouldn't have read it there in the post office, with others milling around and the gossip vultures not afraid to pipe up, 'Not bad news is it, dear?'

She would have gone outside, bumping me down the steps because there were no ramps for the child-encumbered in those days. My personal picture of Bindamilla's post office has a park bench under an awning on the footpath outside, and so the scene, invented in my mind entirely and revisited more times than I can count, has Susan sitting on this bench to tear open the envelope.

Yes, I was close by in the stroller but Susan was alone when she read that letter. I've come to believe that my mother remained alone from that moment until she showed it to me in Sydney, and I was at uni by then. That's a long time to be alone, a long time to be so angry and with no one else to share the weight of it. And anger is the heaviest emotion. I know that as well as anyone on this earth.

It didn't have to be that way. She could have pointed the stroller towards the school straightaway and simply turned up at Dad's classroom door. He would have dropped everything to help her get over the shock.

She didn't, though.

What was in her mind? Why did she keep it to herself? It would be years before she told me, leaving a silence between us that shaped my life in ways I couldn't see. At first I assumed this was because she genuinely didn't know, but as I grew older I became less tolerant of my mother's evasions. I loved her, but I didn't trust her. Susan did know, and simply wouldn't tell me, because to do so would be to tell herself. It would have been a confession like none she had ever made to a priest, a cleaving open with the same knife that severed her marriage to Dad.

Oh Mum, I could only imagine. Terry was my father, but I never knew him as you did.

The letter was anonymous, but it did contain a name, even if the letter writer hadn't intended it to. It was a first name only, for a man she would take some time to identify, but that name became both her torment and her lifeline. It drove her from Queensland and it brought her back, which meant it brought her back to me, too, to take me out to the university and make me smoke a cigarette with my feet up on a chair, to meet me outside the Tower Mill with tears in her eyes that I mistook for grief and pity, when in fact they were tears of vindication and the very human satisfaction one feels in revenge, even when that revenge has not come by your own hand.

SIX

TOM

It's difficult to place precisely in time when a particular conversation with my mother occurred. Many took place in Sydney and she has lived in the same Rose Bay apartment since her stint in London. There was one conversation of more significance than most that began on her balcony in Rose Bay. It must have been after Susan took me to France in 1990, because she'd shown me the Bindy letter by then, but before the Bjelke-Petersen trial, so it can't have been much later.

The important thing is I was older and felt this should be recognised with something deeper from her, even if I couldn't name quite what I wanted. I was prepared to be more daring, too.

'Grandma Riley has never forgiven you for the way you treated Dad,' I told her bluntly.

'Doesn't surprise me,' she retorted. 'If a woman treats *you* like that, Tom, I'll cut her off at the knees.'

'So what are you saying? You're putting your hands up? "I'm guilty. Drag me off to bad girls' gaol?" I'm not sensing a lot of remorse.'

'That's unfair, Tom,' she snapped, and immediately the nonchalance was dispensed with. 'You've seen the letter. You can work out what was happening to me. As for Mike's mother, yes – Helen has every right to judge me, but it's not as though she asked me what was going on.'

'Would you have told her?'

There was a long pause, then, 'No.'

'It might have helped Dad if you'd explained. You could have shown him the letter, at least.'

'Fuck you, Tom.'

She went inside, leaving *me* feeling remorseful, and angry, too.

This was a problem I ran into occasionally in those days, when my allegiance as loving, loyal son was prone to unpredictable swings from one parent to another. When you love someone, it's difficult to understand how they can hurt others, especially when the victim owns your love in equal measure. I just wanted Susan to explain herself, to let me know what was in her mind. I don't know why it meant so much to me, but my new-found confidence wasn't done with yet.

I left my remorse with the million-dollar view of Sydney Harbour and went in pursuit of my mother, who was making busy in the kitchen to no real purpose.

'Wouldn't it have been easier for Dad if you'd told him? I mean, he stuck it out in that hole for an entire semester without you, but he must have known it wasn't so you could be back at uni six months early. The letter would have explained what was driving you, but instead you made him jump through hoops not many men would have stood for and you didn't give anything back, not that I can see. Wasn't there another way?'

'You think you deserve an answer, do you? I didn't explain myself to Mike, but you're different, is that it?'

'You can't divorce me,' I said curtly.

'No, but I can show you the bloody door!'

She was pointing with an enormous kitchen knife and rather than back down, I left.

We laughed about the knife later that night, when she announced there was even more of her in me than she'd realised, and we got drunk over a second bottle of wine, but at the time I felt stupid marching away in high dudgeon, not least because I was staying with her, and had nowhere else to go.

I took a bus into the city and wandered around Circular Quay to the thump and whine of amplified didgeridoos and the foreign patter of tourists. That was the day I discovered the bronze disks set into the paving stones, an odd kind of manhole cover I thought at first, until

126

I realised they carried quotations from Mark Twain, Joseph Conrad and a demilune of home-grown writers.

Would Michael Riley ever get a guernsey among such company? He was starting to be noticed by then: *A late bloomer with an original eye and a sensibility to match*, declared one critic. Another thought he possessed *more intrinsic honesty than any living poet in the country*. But Dad didn't belong among these luminaries, especially when each quotation was a paean to Sydney. He'd never felt comfortable here, and for good reason, it had to be said.

My hour spent moving from disk to disk was a calming pleasure that finally drew me to the water's edge to admire its colour. Poor Brisbane. Its river was the colour of army fatigues and no match for the harbour's rich emerald, churned to turquoise by departing ferries as I watched. Yet, poor Sydney, too: no amount of colour and life would change the place it held in the history of Mike and Susan Riley.

But then, Sydney was simply the end point for what had started in the park below the Tower Mill and was later made unbearable by a letter read in solitude outside Bindamilla's post office while I squirmed in my stroller.

That was as much as I knew on the afternoon I stood dazzled by the harbour, with a homage to the world's best writers underfoot. I pointed myself back towards the apartment in Rose Bay, apology at the ready and resigned to making do with what I had.

Susan opened the door quickly when I knocked, as though she'd been listening for me. 'I'm opening a bottle,' she said, more as a question.

I nodded and followed her out onto the balcony, where her first words were, 'I'm sorry about the knife.' That was when we laughed, although there was real contrition in the way she'd spoken.

'I know exactly what my journo friends would do with that kind of scene,' she said, and in a masculine tone she drawled, 'The female offender threatened her son with a knife. Police consider Ms Kinnane dangerous and warn the public to approach her with extreme caution.'

'I always do,' I said, leaving her with no option but to laugh again, to counter any fear I might have meant it.

'Tom, I do want you to understand the things I did back then. It wasn't like I treated Mike so badly on purpose.'

Was she going to open up at last? I sat forward with the glass of wine left untouched between my knees.

'The letter changed everything, of course, but I didn't think of going back to Brisbane straightaway. Didn't think I'd need to. I started with letters to government departments, but they were too easy to ignore so I tried calling from the phone box outside the post office, with you threatening to run onto the road at any moment. Even when I got through, the bastards stonewalled me while the meter ticked at trunk-call rates. Being so far from the people who could give me answers was just too frustrating.

'By Easter I knew I just had to be in Brisbane if I was going to nail the bastard. I nagged Mike to get a transfer, but he was worried about what it would do to his career and he wouldn't apply for private schools because he'd have to refund his bond – thousands of dollars – just because I had the shits with Bindy. That's what it looked like to him. He was calm, sensible, typical Mike and all that did was wind me up even more.

'On top of that, I had Bindy pressing around me like a vice,' she said in a softer voice. By then she was leaning forward in her chair, as well, as though this news needed to remain between the two of us. 'The more time I spent among them, the more I saw their narrowness, the chip on the shoulder about city know-it-alls like me. They were the very people who sneered about demonstrators deserving everything they got. You've seen the letter, Tom. You can imagine how that made me feel. In my mind, Bindamilla had become Queensland.'

Yes, I'd seen the letter. So why not Mike? I wanted to say. But Susan was talking freely so I held back, hoped the answer would come without anything more from me.

'Mike guessed how I felt about the Bindy mob,' she said, leaning back now, our conspiracy loosening. 'He kept making excuses for them. "It's a country town," he'd remind me. "They're always suspicious of outsiders, but they're good people at heart." He said that over and over. They were good people. It was just that new ideas, new ways of doing things made them uneasy. It was all about Whitlam and the change he was putting us all through.'

'But he was wrong, Tom. It *was* about Queensland back then, about the soul of the place. They were afraid of anyone and anything different from themselves and when they shoved their ballot paper into the box, they were voting for people who feed on those fears. Without telling Mike, I filled in application forms for UQ and when confirmation turned up at the post office, I simply told him. "I've enrolled at uni for second semester, full-time, back in Brisbane." I was going and that was it. He was angry, but more than that, he was frightened of losing me. Christ, I was a bitch. I played on that fear, you know. Made him talk his parents into letting me live in the granny flat beneath their house. But I had to. I had to be in Brisbane if I was going to get the rest of the name in that letter.'

'Me, too, though. You took me with you.'

Susan looked at me. 'Yes, of course,' she said, as though there was no need to confirm it. 'Helen agreed to mind you when Diane was too busy. Through gritted teeth, I might add.'

'And Dad? He had to finish out the year in Bindamilla without us.'

She nodded, but said nothing more about him. 'You have no idea what the politics was like back then, Tom. It got in the way of everything.'

Maybe it did, but that wasn't what I'd hoped she'd talk about. What were her reasons for keeping the letter from Dad? I was still no closer to understanding that, no closer to understanding her.

SUSAN
1975

'Sue, I don't know how you can say that,' said Diane.

I saw instantly that I'd made a mistake in letting my thoughts become words. It was because I was stuck in the granny flat with only Tom for company and, in fact, that's what we were talking about, really. I'd made new friends at uni, but they all had part-time jobs, leaving Diane as the only option on weekdays and, much as we were growing closer, there were times I wanted to stick my head out the window and scream.

I was annoyed with her about other things that morning, as well. She'd been too obviously fishing for news of a second baby, 'a brother or a little sister for Tommy to play with'.

She was plump with her third and seemed to think the melon-humping should be shared around more evenly among sisters.

And then I'd let my honesty get too cosy with my tongue and said, 'I'm not a natural mother like you, Di. I love Tom, of course I do, but it's not like I can't imagine a life without him.'

That was too much for Diane: 'I'd die without my kids.'

Not far away on the new carpet, Rosanna was exercising her right, as the big girl, to engage both brother and cousin in a game of house, which involved entirely too much sitting still. I could see the boys about to rebel. They could easily be brothers, which was what had set Diane waxing on in the first place.

And separate from what was going on in my sister's lounge room, I was wondering how I could call the number I'd already tried twice before leaving home. When the boys broke up Rosie's domestic idyll, I said, 'Why don't we go outside and play in the sandpit?'

That way, I could duck back inside to make the call.

I'd found John Obermayer's name in the *Courier-Mail* while researching the Springbok protests, and immediately detected a sympathy in his reporting. He was the only one; all his mates seemed to have relished what had happened to the demonstrators. When I called the paper, they told me Obermayer had moved to Melbourne and the girl on the switch didn't know how to contact him. But I'd been lucky – he was on staff at the second Melbourne paper I called.

'I'll only be in Brisbane for two days and Friday's out of the question,' he said, when finally I got through at Diane's. His nasal drone, which I'd become used to, seemed harried and I had to be careful not to press too hard.

'When do you fly back to Melbourne?'

'Sunday morning, early. If you want to meet, it has to be Saturday.'

'No, I can't. My husband's coming home for the weekend.'

Mike and I hadn't been together for five weeks. The weekend was off limits.

John was firm. 'I can't change my plans. Do you have anything new since last time?'

'Very little.' I sighed into the phone. 'The police are a closed shop. Won't even talk to me now. Ignore me at the counter if I go to Makerston Street.'

'Did you expect any different?' said John. 'They're hardly going to let you see personnel files. For all they know, you're an ex-wife chasing maintenance from one of their own.'

'Yes, it's a boys' club all right. I *was* able to confirm that Dolan's in north Queensland, Townsville, in fact. He's in the CIB now.'

'How'd you find out?'

'Rang every police station until he turned up,' I said proudly.

He laughed. 'I've done the same thing myself. Sometimes there's no other way. Not something they tell you at uni I'll bet. Are you getting much out of what they're teaching you?'

I had switched my degree to Arts, where I could major in journalism, something Mike didn't know about yet. I was planning to break the news on the weekend.

'I still can't confirm where Dolan was posted in 1971,' I said, 'or even that he was one of the country coppers bussed in for the protests. All I've got is the letter that doesn't even tell me his full name. What I really need to know is who wrote that letter 'cause he's the only one who can give evidence.'

'Evidence. You're getting well ahead of yourself, lady. Your chance of seeing him charged is next to Buckley's.'

'Did you bring your notes with you?' I asked.

'Yes, but I thought you said Saturday is no good.'

'It's not,' I confirmed quickly. 'Look, John, do you think you could—'

'They're not leaving my possession. I'm sorry, some of what I have isn't legal, the way I acquired it, I mean. I can't take any chances.'

Obermayer had been a treasure trove, especially when I'd struggled at first to uncover anything on my own. A contact in that file had led me to the name Dolan. Without quite knowing how, I made a decision.

'I'll meet you on Saturday then. Is eleven all right?'

'No, make it noon, in the foyer of the Tower Mill Hotel.'

Mike left Bindy on the dot of three that Friday, stopped only for petrol and even then it was after ten before he arrived. In the morning, I woke to find Tom already crawling over his daddy, who had miraculously turned up in the night. Later, he sat like a prince between us while we shared breakfast in bed. Helen brought the weekend papers down for us, and between the talking and the tickling, Mike's mouth must have grown tired of smiling.

I felt awful, even as I played the good wife. And it wasn't an act, in any case, but all the while I kept wondering how I was going to tell him I had to duck off for an hour. I gave in to cowardice all morning, and more than once decided to skip the meeting with Obermayer.

Then Mike piped up, 'How about a picnic in New Farm Park?'

and I was telling him it was a special thing for uni, had to be that day, it would only be an hour. Still plenty of time for New Farm Park.

It didn't sound so bad when I couched it that way and he waved me off with Tom in his arms and no more than a bemused look on his face.

But John was late at the hotel and made up for it by replaying the police charge in forensic detail. I showed him the route Mike and I had followed, guided by the garden bed we'd scrambled through to escape the batons.

'It was utter panic.'

'I know,' said John, who hadn't been at the demo but had interviewed many who had. 'Your lot fanned out. Any direction that let you get away.'

Eventually, we reached the path and the rusty handrails. I'd been there many times, but I still didn't know exactly where Terry had lain for so many hours in the darkness.

We returned to the foyer of the hotel, where John opened the file of photographs he'd collected. I pored over pictures that hadn't made it into the *Courier-Mail*, scribbling note after note onto a Spirex pad. I'd been among the crowd that night and had my own pictures filed away within synapses and ganglions, but they were nothing like these. The photographer had snapped shots from among the police lines and regularly aimed his camera across the road at the protestors, showing me for the first time what bystanders might have seen, had there been any.

And of course there were, thousands of them, who opened their newspapers the next morning to see photographs carefully selected to suggest it was the protesters who'd turned violent.

I lingered on images of the stark police lines. 'So many. I don't remember there being so many.'

John rifled through until he found one in particular. 'You must remember these ones, though?'

It showed the rank of makeshift riot police in motorcycle helmets. Their uniforms appeared black in the monochrome, which made the helmets stand out even more under the street lamps. They were assembled shoulder to shoulder and gun-barrel straight as though lined up for review, each solid, tall and deeply menacing.

'Why weren't we more afraid?' I murmured.

'Because you never thought they'd charge, that's why. You'd come to shout and wave your signs, part protest, part street party. Everyone I spoke to had the same story. You hadn't read the tea leaves, any of you. Overreaction. The whole week was an overreaction. That was going to be a chapter heading in my book.'

'Book?'

'I thought there might be a book in it. That's why I did the extra interviews. Same with these photos and all my notes.'

'Are you going to write it?'

'Bit late now,' he said, sounding defeated. 'And besides, in Melbourne nobody gives a rat's arse what happens up here.' He held my gaze for a moment and I sensed a decision being weighed behind his eyes.

'That's not the main reason, though, is it?' I said, hoping he'd come out with it.

He shook his head. 'The political climate isn't right. I thought it would work because there was a shift going on and any fool could see Whitlam was going to win in '72. Time for a change and all that. It was a good slogan, so I thought it was time for a book that showed up the old crowd as out of touch, and those Springbok protests were a classic example. My book would sell all over the country to people hungry for change and maybe it would get a healthy political cycle going up here again.'

'You're forgetting about the gerrymander. The cards are marked against Labor.'

'You can't blame the gerrymander for what happened last December. Labor would have been trounced anyway. As for my book, well, I gave it away because I couldn't get to the heart of what's going on up here.'

'What do you mean?'

He glanced at his watch, prompting me to do the same.

'Shit! I have to go,' I blurted out.

He shrugged and said, 'If you're interested, there's a lecturer at UQ who can explain better than me. Talking to him I realised I was on the wrong track.'

'Would he talk to me?'

'I could take you to see him now, if you like.'

No, I was late already.

'He might not talk to you alone. Has to be careful, poor bastard.'

'What do you mean?'

He waved a hand with a wince and a frown. 'It would be easier for him if I was there with you. Look, he doesn't live far from here. Auchenflower.'

Any other suburb and I would have gone home, but Auchenflower . . . We were there soon after and when the lecturer found John Obermayer at the door, he spread his arms wide to embrace him.

I was expecting the absent-minded professor and a moth-eaten sitting room lined with books piled in precarious stacks. I couldn't have been more off the mark. The timber floors gleamed, a skylight flooded the hall with bright welcome and the room he showed us into was a Scandinavian cliché.

A second man appeared, a little older and dressed in slacks with knife-edge creases and shiny brogues. 'Would your friends like a cup of tea, Trevor?' he asked, with such grandeur he might have been butler to the queen.

Queen was right, I decided, as the tumblers fell into line. No wonder John had spoken of reticence.

There was more delay while the tea was poured, but once we got talking, I forgot the watch on my wrist.

'The Springbok protests were old-fashioned dissent, a bit of street theatre that points the way ahead,' said Trevor. 'Every society has similar moments. The Moratorium marches were much more significant, of course.'

'But they were mainly in Sydney and Melbourne,' I pointed out.

'Exactly,' said Trevor. 'As ever, Queensland needed something different to turn the wheels. It was the same thing, though. John here wanted his book to be about how dissent is forcing change in public policy, but the Springbok protests showed that public policy isn't really the main game, not up here, anyway.'

'The Queenslanders are a different thing again,' I said, hoping he had more for me than platitudes. 'If that's not the main game, then what is?'

He made a face, not unpleasantly – more in the vein of a man who enjoyed subtlety. 'It's about how dissent is tolerated. No government enjoys criticism, but they don't normally see it as a personal affront to be silenced by every means available. At least not in a democracy, and certainly not in Australia, not until now, anyway.'

I listened for half an hour, which became forty-five minutes while I scribbled frantically in my notebook. When, finally, I hurried out of the house it was after three-thirty, which blew out to four o'clock by the time I arrived home.

'I'm so sorry.'

Mike said nothing while I stumbled through my excuses, which sounded even more feeble now that I was actually mouthing the words I'd made up in the car.

'Can we still go to the park?' I said brightly.

'Bit late for that,' Mike said, and taking Tom he went upstairs to his parents, forcing me to join him.

In my Year Nine history book at Avila there had been a woodcut showing the French ambassador entering Elizabeth's court after the massacre of the Huguenots. The looks I got from Helen Riley were no less poisonous. What had seemed like the sensible thing to do, the essential thing to do, when I was in Wickham Park, now seemed unconscionable. Mike had driven seven hours to be with me, and he faced another seven to be back again in time for school on Monday morning. I was close to tears with the weight of my own folly.

'I'm sorry about this afternoon, really I am.'

What else could I say, and keep saying, until I could escape down to the tiny kitchen and get busy with dinner.

When Mike brought Tom down soon after, I had a beer ready for him and threw down two glasses of wine myself, eager for the alcohol to kick in, and by then Mike had opened a second stubby and was talking more freely.

Dinner wasn't as awkward as it might have been, and, with Tom delivered upstairs to sleep, I took the lead in bed, letting Mike have my body to look at and touch as I'd stopped doing in Bindy. Yet his heart didn't seem in it any more than mine was. I'd mucked it up.

When I woke on Sunday morning, Mike was playing noisily with Tom upstairs. Departure already loomed. It would have been better if he'd exploded as his mother so clearly wanted to do. Then I'd have had a chance to cry and beg forgiveness and admit how stupid, how thoughtless, how hurtful I had been. I deserved his anger, and I would have willingly copped it, I might even have told him about the letter and the whole story of who I'd been so desperate to meet instead of going to New Farm Park. I could have told him how John Obermayer had introduced me to a man who saw the politics of it all more deeply than anyone else I'd come across so far.

Why couldn't Mike do that, instead of offering up more wounded understanding? I was beginning to hate him for it.

TOM

How did Dad survive those months when my mother abandoned him to finish out his Bindamilla posting alone? Whether he wanted to admit it or not at the time, those months were the harbinger of his marriage's end, but at least they left a legacy of a different sort that he's rightly proud of. He let slip occasional snippets over the years, enough for me to assemble a vague picture of those lonely months – and then there are the poems, some of the most heart-searing verse I have ever read.

On weekends, he would take sheets of scrap paper into the sand hills beyond the southern edge of Bindamilla and scramble his way to the single tree that clung stubbornly to the crest. Here, he was far enough from town to hear none of its slow breathing, as he described it to me once, and when the wind dropped, there was a silence like he had never known. That was why he came. The house, for all its size, was claustrophobic.

'At school, did they teach you about Wordsworth's emotion reflected in tranquillity?' he asked me once, and we'd shared a good laugh then because those were the very words my English teacher had used. 'Nothing much changes, then. I was told the same thing. Except it's bullshit and I needed Bindamilla to teach as much.'

I heard then of how he'd despaired at the trite lines he came up with. There was no poetry in those tranquil sand hills and no poetry in him, either, it seemed. He stared out at a landscape utterly devoid of human presence and only became more aware of himself as an alien amid such emptiness. Mike Riley belonged where human beings crossed his view, he belonged among houses and streets and the hum of traffic and the shadows cast by office towers.

'The silence, Tom. You have to experience it to know how all consuming it can be. Even the scratching of pencil on paper was carried off into its vastness,' he told me. '*I wandered lonely as a cloud*,' he'd called once, at the top of his voice. There was no echo. The silence devoured Wordsworth, too. He tried Larkin, then Shakespeare. *Shall I compare thee to a summer's day?*

'I could feel the horizon laughing at me,' he confided. 'Especially after I made a rushed visit to Brisbane to spend time with your mother. I was lonelier than ever after that weekend and walked out to the hills, to no avail, it seemed. But one day when I stood up and turned around, there was Bindy. At my back all that time, I'd forgotten it and taking it in suddenly, like a slap, I felt my own revulsion and at the same time my need. It was my wife that small town had rejected, not me.'

So he sat down again, at the base of the same tree, facing the town this time. He said he could feel the weight of the landscape against his back, but it was Bindamilla that jerked his pencil into motion. 'Forget Wordsworth,' he told me. 'Tranquillity was no mood for the poetry in me, Tom.' And with the town stretched out before him, he'd listened at last to a landscape that was anything but silent, and began to write.

SEVEN

TOM

In my twenties a certain rhythm worked its way into how I built a picture of Susan's marriage. I would talk to her, winning precious nuggets, assay them in my own good time then go digging for more from Dad. That was why, soon after my solo tour of Circular Quay, I found myself saying to him, 'It must have been hard living in Bindy by yourself.'

By then he was used to such questions popping out of the blue. 'You can put up with anything when you know how long it will last,' he said, 'and there were some compensations. I wrote all the Larkin and Eliot out of myself and started hunting around for an original way to say things.'

'You found your voice.'

He shot a dismissive breath down his nose. 'Don't get wanky on me, Tom. Anyway, much as I missed your mother, having some space between the two of us brought its own relief. Looking back on it now, I can see how unhappy she was married into a compromise and stuck out there among people she didn't understand. At the time, it seemed like an emotional flu that never went away, and I was the one she wiped her nose on. What I missed wasn't Susan so much, it was marriage, the partner thing. And I missed you, too, more than I'd bargained for.'

'Who's getting wanky now?'

'No, it's true. I guess that had a lot to do with what happened afterwards.'

'In Sydney?'

'Yes, in Sydney. Susan's told you about the rows we had, I suppose.'

'She thinks she was half-crazy, should have been on something to calm her down.'

'Your Riley grandparents would agree,' he said, then making a face he tilted his head to one side as though considering this idea as a work of art. 'The result would have been the same, though. Had to be. We were growing apart too quickly and you can only follow someone a certain distance before you realise she's not leading, she's running away. And then, of course, there was the Dismissal. That seemed to stir her up even more than the state election where it all started.'

No, Dad, I wanted to say. It started at the Tower Mill when the police charged into the crowd with thirty-six-inch batons in their eager hands. You were there, Dad. You saw it begin.

Instead, I said, 'She still gets hot talking about what Kerr did to Whitlam.'

'Yeah, well, I was just as angry at the time. I was still in Bindy when it happened, a Tuesday – I remember because we were setting up for a staff meeting when someone came in with the news.'

'Susan was visiting Diane at Mater Mothers',' I added. 'Said she came out onto the footpath afterwards and saw the headline at a newsstand. She started to shake.'

Dad's face went heavy with an odd solemnity as he listened. According to them both, the death of John Lennon wasn't the where-were-you-when-you-heard moment for their generation, it was Whitlam's sacking by the governor-general.

Poor Dad. He was wrong about the Dismissal, too. Yes, Susan was outraged, but it was the phone call she'd received the weekend before that did greater damage.

I was in a privileged position again, where I knew more than he did, and once more had to convince myself that silence wasn't treachery. He had never heard of a journalist named Obermayer and he didn't know that Susan had received an unexpected call three days before Kerr moved against Whitlam.

The caller was Barry Dolan.

'You've been asking around about me,' said the voice in her ear.

There was no name, but Susan's mind was so full of Barry Dolan by then that she immediately made the connection.

'How did you get this number?'

'I'm a detective. It's what I do,' he told her calmly. 'Wasn't hard, the way you've left such a trail trying to track me down. Now what's this about?' he demanded. 'Why so interested in me?'

She wasn't prepared and desperately tried to bluff her way through: 'I'm a reporter. I want to interview you about—'

'No, you're not. You're a student.'

Her mouth went dry. He'd done his own checks, probably knew where she lived.

'It's about the Tower Mill,' she said, hoping to put him off balance and for a few moments it worked. A long pause followed, and when he spoke he was wary rather than belligerent.

'What about it?'

'You were there, you chased the demonstrators down into the park.'

'There were hundreds of coppers that night. Our orders were to clear the public footpath.'

'You know what I'm talking about.'

Silence from Dolan, then the predictable: 'Haven't got a clue. You must have me mixed up with someone else.'

'There was a witness,' said Susan.

'Bullshit. It was pitch black in that park. No one saw a thing.'

Those were his words, Susan insisted whenever she told me about this telephone conversation. *No one saw a thing.* To her it was an admission of guilt.

But she was on dangerous ground. The witness was the letter writer, and she didn't know his name. But Dolan certainly did. She kept quiet about the letter and the vacuum this left was quickly filled by Dolan's reborn confidence.

'You've got nothing, lady. And seriously, do you think you could get anywhere with this, even if you did? How old are you, anyway? A fucking girl by the sound of you. Do you think my mates are going to investigate, no matter what you turn up, do you think the government's going to let one of us go down for that, just when things are getting cosy? Try all you like, but before you waste your time, take a look around. Does the man in the street give a shit? Or the papers? Of course not, and without them you'll get nowhere.'

I don't know if that's really how he said it, but Dolan had challenged her, openly, contemptuously and for all the steel in her soul, she knew he was right.

That call settled something that had been growing in her, a new pregnancy for the womb she wouldn't fill with a brother or a sister for me.

'I'm getting out,' she told Obermayer on the phone afterwards. 'I can't stand living in this state another minute.'

Getting out. She swore to me that was the first time the idea had taken form in words and I believed her, but she'd already got herself out of Bindamilla. Did she ever join the dots, as neatly as I did so many years later?

Another time I asked Dad, 'What was the summer course that caused so much trouble between you and Susan? The one she went to Sydney for.'

Mum, Lyn that is, had taken the girls somewhere and he was marking papers at the dining room table, as he often did on a Sunday afternoon. At this new assault on his history, he stared at me as though I'd enquired after the secret of life. Then a memory of my earlier questions about Bindamilla seemed to build context around my question and his face lost its confusion. 'Ah, you're thinking about 1975 still.'

'Well, technically it was '76. The summer school was in the new year, wasn't it?'

He stared at me a moment. 'You know a lot about it. Since you're asking, it was called 'Media and the Feminine,' he went on, as though the memory lay on his tongue as easily as the names of his daughters.

'She wanted to move down there, didn't she?'

'She talked about going overseas, actually. She started on at me about it as soon as I finished my time in Bindy. Christ, I felt like I'd been spun around in a clothes dryer. I wanted to teach overseas at some stage, in a good school if I could swing it, but she kept on about it, all because Whitlam had been chucked out, as far as I could see, and before I knew what was happening, we were shouting at one another.'

Dad paused there and it wasn't hard to guess why.

'You hated it, didn't you?'

'Fighting's not me, is it, Tom? Yet I could feel the missiles primed at the base of my throat. Shit, I'd been transferred to Kenmore High School and I didn't want to swap that for some London slum. That was all I'd get if we turned up out of the blue. I shouted those very words in your mother's face. She backed off, about England, at least, but then she started on about a summer school she wanted to do in Sydney. I said yes just so she'd stop ranting about how she had to get away.'

'She used those words, did she? She talked about getting away?'

He stared silently at me again, considering his answer, making me aware of how earnest I sounded. 'It doesn't matter,' I said, before he could respond.

'It does, or you wouldn't have asked.'

'I'm sorry. Really, forget what I said.'

He went back to his assignments and I wandered into the kitchen to check whether the fridge held anything more interesting than it had ten minutes earlier. As I closed the door in disappointment, he called through from the dining room.

'For the record, yes, she talked about getting away, or getting out, actually.'

I was quickly through the doorway to hear what else he might add.

He looked up at me again and in a tone that still held the faintest twinge of hurt, said, 'Fool that I was, I didn't realise she was talking about our marriage as much as anything geographical. I doubt she realised it herself.'

What I really wanted to ask couldn't be asked. Did she want to get out *with* me on her hip? The question would have sounded too pathetic.

SUSAN
January, 1976

Fate loves irony. Ask the Greeks, who laced their dramas with both to torment their protagonists more cruelly. Should it be any surprise, then, that the days Mike and I spent together in Sydney started so well? With Tom in a space-age safety harness strapped to the back seat, Mike drove the Holden down the Pacific Highway to collect me from the summer school, and, after some days in Sydney, we would make a leisurely return north, stopping for a swim at every beach that took our fancy. That was the plan, anyway. It didn't even matter that the hotel he'd chosen out of the phone book turned out to be a down-at-heel pub with rooms above the bar.

'Mike, Sydney's so alive,' I told him when I joined them there on the Thursday night. '*I* feel more alive.'

I kissed him, nuzzled Tom then pushed them both onto the ill-sprung bed for a tickling game, or was the game called 'mother and wife'?

I'd already decided on a place to eat and all the way there gushed about Sydney and what I'd been learning. 'There's a lecturer called Rhonda Nicolson. Oh Mike, you should hear her. She sees things so clearly. And, God, the university makes UQ look like a blockhouse. I could be walking around the cloisters of Oxford. Sydney's such a fantastic place, so much fun. Thanks for letting me do this, Mike.' And like the schoolgirl I no doubt resembled, I kissed him again, impetuously.

The next morning, while I went off to the last day of the summer school, he took Tom for a baptism at Bondi Beach and then a picnic by the harbour.

'There's a party to celebrate the end of the course,' I told him when we were together again in our room above the bar. 'Linda's place. Surry Hills somewhere.'

'What about Tom?'

'We can take him. Linda says he can sleep in her bed.'

He had a good laugh at that. 'I'd hoped my boy would be a bit older before he got offers like that.' He hadn't stopped smiling since he'd arrived. What a relief that was. I let myself believe things were on the mend.

When we parked the Holden at Linda's, the sky was on fire, and as a reminder of the sun's largesse my face was covered in a sheen of sweat before we could reach the door.

Linda's place was as ramshackle as our hotel, which only made it more appealing to me, a reminder of student days with Terry. I no longer dodged such reminders; I was eager for them, in fact, and it didn't seem to matter that I'd once had to carefully segregate my husband from the man who lived in those memories. The letter had changed that, and Sydney seemed part of the same renewal.

I held Tom tightly to reassure him among so many strangers, but unlike the teachers in Bindy, these girls didn't put on faux displays of mothering and they spoke to him in sentences, without the self-conscious cutesiness that annoyed the crap out of me. It made all the difference, as though I was home at last.

Mike tagged behind us, meeting Linda and her housemate, and with them the only male member of the summer school, Derek someone.

'God, I haven't been to a party like this for years,' he said to Derek, who shrugged.

'It's what students do.'

'Yep, and I partied with the best of them,' he tossed back lightly.

Good on you, Mike, I thought. Let's party. Tom will be right once he goes to sleep in the back room.

Polite questions followed as my new friends welcomed Mike among them yet all too obviously he answered like a teacher who'd been out in the real world for three years now, his student days already in past tense and tinged with nostalgia. He spoke about buying a house and how hard it was to get a loan from the bank, as if students gave a shit about things like that. Couldn't he step across the distance that his plans hollowed out between them, even for one night? I felt like calling to him, Mike, I'm over here, on this side of the ditch, come and join me.

The bundle in my arms was part of what separated him, as it separated me, now that my husband and my son had come to Sydney. Only in the smoky lounge room did I finally see what a holiday the past fortnight had been. The others in the room were entirely free in a way the Rileys were not, something Mike would have agreed with, devoid of the least resentment. To him, the freedom of youth was a currency you used to purchase your future, and, with me filling his eyes and now Tom, who'd somehow transferred into his arms, Mike obviously considered his wisely spent.

Derek produced a roll-your-own from his pocket. 'You want a toke?' he asked us both.

I'd taken him up on the offer more than once in recent days, but this time folded his fingers back over the joint and, with another shrug, Derek went off to find someone else to share it with.

I caught Mike's eye and grinned. 'Hey, they're students. We passed plenty of joints around in our day.'

'True enough. Doesn't feel right, though, kids and dope.'

No, it didn't, when he put it that way.

Tom grew limp in his arms and I took him in search of the untainted air of Linda's bedroom. There were more bodies when I returned, all contributing to the thickening smoke around the single globe. Mike was caught in the crush near the makeshift bar, where he listened to a half-circle of girls, the most vocal a leggy thing who was braless in a way that skinny girls could get away with. She hunched her shoulders, accentuating the bones, and blew smoke in a confident stream into the cotton wool cloud above her head. The music and the distance meant I couldn't catch what she was declaiming, but she was certainly having a go at another girl. Poor thing, the victim didn't look happy, especially when laughter broke up the circle.

Mike was still smiling when he extracted himself at last and came to my side.

'You happy?' I asked.

'Yeah, fine.'

'Great people, aren't they?'

'If you agree with what they're saying, yeah,' he said, looking over his shoulder at the girl who'd been the butt of the joke. Beetroot red with indignation, it seemed her opinion had been sliced through and left to bleed.

We fell into a group including the helpful Linda.

'Happy to oblige,' she said, when Mike thanked her for the use of her bedroom. Linda wore a loose-fitting dress, as well, although hers flowed gracefully to the floor, accentuating a long face that was framed by honey-blond hair in the hippie style that never quite slipped out of fashion. 'What did you do with your little fellow today?' she asked.

'We played the foreign tourists, never out of sight of an iconic landmark, two at once if I could manage it,' said Mike.

He listed where he'd taken Tom: Mrs Macquaries Chair, across the bridge just for the fun of it, a ferry ride to Milsons Point.

'Seems strange to go out of your way for them,' said Linda. 'They're just part of the landscape to us. Tom's lucky that one of his dads can show him around. Never knew my father, and Mum didn't find any-one else.'

Before Linda could say anything more, a new face become part of the huddle, through no deliberate choice, I thought, more in the way a pip is squeezed from an orange and has to land somewhere.

'Hello, Rhonda,' I said. She'd been coy about coming and I was suddenly delighted to see that she had.

'You're the lecturer,' said Mike quickly. 'Susan was raving about you last night.' He offered his hand.

Rhonda ignored it. 'Ah, the husband from Queensland,' she said, looking at me.

Undaunted, Mike pushed the usual pleasantries her way: 'Sue's really enjoyed your course.'

'Escape is always a joy,' she shot back at him.

Again she was looking straight at me, and this time so was Mike, clearly bewildered. He expected people to like him and couldn't work out why Rhonda was being so curt. I could have bloody killed her!

Mike turned full on to Rhonda, who offered no ironic smile to accompany her little barbs. Her silence seemed to offer him a free swing, as though she were saying, Come on, mate, your turn to slip in a witty riposte. What was she up to? Was she stoned already?

Rhonda didn't explain herself, and didn't hang around, either, leaving me to field my husband's questions.

'What did she mean by that? Escape from what? What have you been saying to these people?'

'Nothing, Mike. She wasn't having a go at you.'

But that's exactly what Rhonda had been doing. With help from the satyr-eyed Derek, Rhonda and I had got off our faces on the third night of the summer school and I couldn't stop leaking my unhappiness onto her sympathetic shoulder. I'd said more than I should have, heard myself say things that until then I'd stomped on whenever they tried to sprout in my mind.

'That other girl seemed to know that I'm not Tom's father, too,' Mike added. 'You've been pretty quick to tell them our history.'

'It came up in something we were discussing, that's all.'

I didn't want to stir up the rawness of the weeks before New Year. Not tonight; we were in Sydney to start over.

Mike went off, only half-convinced, to check on Tom, leaving me to fold myself into my classmates. The next time I saw him he was laughing with Derek, his humour apparently restored. I didn't see Rhonda until she was beside me.

'Look, I probably told you too much last week. Things aren't as bad I made out. Mike's been good to me, really.'

Rhonda shrugged, without offering any apology. 'They're all good to their wives as long they get things their own way. Believe me, Sue. I had a husband of my own once.'

I could have asked her to back off, could have *told* her to piss off for that matter, but Rhonda, this whole fortnight, had been so important to me, I didn't want it to end sourly.

Later still, Mike joined me. 'That Derek fancies you,' he said, laughing. 'What a hoot!'

He'd been enjoying Derek's generosity by the look of things, too. I took the joint from his fingers and held the smoke in my lungs while it passed to a waiting hand. Too late, I saw that it was Rhonda's.

Mike was watching her with open belligerence. Oh, would you give me a break.

'How did you spend your day?' asked a girl who hadn't been there earlier.

He started at the top with the swim at Bondi.

'Oh, I was there tonight. It's so easy now with daylight saving.'

'S'pose it is,' said Mike. 'We don't have it in Queensland.'

'Don't have what?' said the girl, confused.

'Daylight saving.'

'Bloody ridiculous,' snapped Rhonda, who'd closed in a step to claim a place in the circle. 'Typical dog-in-a-manger attitude of the ruling junta up there. Worried it's against God's law or something.'

If it had been anyone else in the room, Mike would have joined in her contempt. Ruling junta, hypocritical God-botherers; he liked to bang on about Joh and his cronies in the same words.

'Actually, daylight saving doesn't suit Queensland,' he said instead, rolling out an attitude he'd never mentioned before. 'Summer days up our way are hotter for longer. We look forward to the sun going down so the temperature will drop and give us a bit of relief.'

'And all that extra daylight fades the curtains, too, doesn't it?' said Rhonda.

Ah, that old chestnut. Someone was sure to bring it up. I laughed with the rest, even Mike.

'But it's true, what I said about the heat,' he lunged on, his serious tone out of kilter. 'The best part of the day in Queensland is the morning, when it's cool. Personally, I like it being light nice and early, lets me take Tom out in the stroller and get things done before it's too hot.'

They stared at him, perplexed; they were all young, single, they stayed in bed as long as they could in the mornings, just as Mike and

I had done once, ourselves. They didn't give a damn when the sun came up.

'Sounds like you're worried about the curtains,' said Rhonda.

There was no laughter this time. We'd done that joke. She seemed to realise and, holding Mike's eye deliberately, came up with a fresh dig. 'They should change Brisbane's name to Johannesburg after he bunged on a State of Emergency for those footballers. You know they're putting a new sign up at the border, don't you?' She raised her arms with fingers splayed wide to mimic a lavish billboard: *'Now entering Queensland. Turn your clocks back an hour and your mind back a hundred years.'*

It was so bloody true, I thought, and I couldn't help smiling with the rest, all except Mike. What was he upset about? Having a go at Queensland? Oh, come on, Mike. It's just a bit of ribbing, I wanted to say, and to be honest, the place deserves it. They could be such yokels. Even in Brisbane they went on like bushies, and the place was all the more backward because of it.

Mike would work his way out of his funk now, I thought. The jibe about the Springboks was an easy opening. Shit, none of this lot had been chased into a park by riot police in the fight against apartheid. All he had to do was say as much and he'd take the smirk off their faces.

I waited for him to bring Rhonda down a peg or two with the story, but he didn't. It was the petty stuff about Queensland that was getting his goat and, at that moment, I felt the gulf between us like the slash of a knife.

'Look, you don't understand what you're making fun of here,' he said, using his teacher's voice, the one he used on dolts who needed things laid out in simple lines. 'I spent two years in the bush. Daylight saving makes things harder for farmers.'

'Upsets the cows,' said Rhonda. 'They get to vote in Queensland, don't they? It's the only way Bjelke-Petersen can get elected.'

'Donkey vote,' said another voice.

'They're all donkeys up there.'

Everyone laughed.

'At least try to understand,' said Mike, louder now as he became more annoyed. 'When I was teaching out west, some of my kids rode a bus for an hour each day just to attend school. With daylight saving, they'd be waiting at the roadside in the dark. Why should they do that just so uni students in the city can go for a swim after lectures?'

He'd made it personal now, drawn a clear line of demarcation, him and them.

Rhonda didn't bother with him, but spoke directly to me. 'I didn't realise you were married to one of Bjelke-Petersen's mob.'

'Me?' cried Mike, appalled.

But they weren't interested in his indignation, they weren't interested in how ridiculous Rhonda's last statement was. He might as well have been wearing a t-shirt with STUPID emblazoned across the chest and an arrow pointing to his face, and he had no one to blame but himself.

Other conversations had faltered. Every eye in the room was on him, while beside him I just couldn't stand it any more.

'What are you defending Queensland for?'

'Because there's nothing wrong with the place.'

'There is, Mike. It's full of fucking Queenslanders.'

TOM

Not long before I graduated from uni, Dad's sister, Jane, split with her husband. She came round one evening to announce the separation to Mum and Dad and, to my surprise, she asked me to stay while she explained herself. At almost twenty-three, I was old enough to be part of such things, apparently, and I came to mark that day as the first time I was truly seen as an adult by others.

There was nothing salacious behind the decision in any case. She just needed us to understand that they hadn't been happy for years and it was better this way. It was hardly news, when even I had guessed as much.

What it did do, however, was get Dad talking. The following day, he said, out of the blue, 'Poor Jane. At least with Sue and me the agony didn't linger for years. S'pose there were cracks right from the start and it just needed a final deluge to breech the wall.'

I don't remember where Mum was during this conversation but since there was just the two of us, I pushed for more: 'She told me about a party in Surry Hills.'

'Oh Christ, that party. All I wanted after that was to load up the car with my little family and go sit on a beach somewhere. Would have been a great way to end my country service and you would have gone brown as a berry.'

'My mother had other ideas.'

'As I discovered straight after that party, yes. "Why don't we stay in Sydney over the weekend and start out on Monday?" she said, and when I pointed out that the grubby hotel wasn't good for you, she already had an answer. There was a spare room in Surry Hills.'

There was no bitterness in this telling, more a sigh for what he hadn't been able to avoid.

'What could I say? Seemed petty to argue over a couple of days, but once we had our bags inside, Susan settled on the sofa with a leg folded beneath her and a mug of coffee she'd made for herself and I thought, Shit, she's moving in. And if that wasn't enough to piss me off, her lecturer came around.'

'Do you remember her name?' I asked, curious to know how deeply the incident had taken root.

'Nicolson,' he answered, without hesitation. 'I'd tangled with her at the party and here she was again looking over from the sofa like a crocodile ready to munch me up anytime she chose. No doubt she could have. God knows, I'm not a hater, Tom, but I despised that woman with an intensity that scared me. I deliberately put you down on the floor, knowing you'd run to your mummy, just to wipe the reptilian smile off her face. Susan is mine, I want to shout. We're going back to Brisbane and you can find some other marriage to fuck with.

'The lecturer stayed for lunch, all those women around the table and me at the end, like a sore thumb. Then, while Susan was feeding you, she says, "What do you think about moving down here to live?"

'Guess I got a bit short with her about that, which helped to enhance my status as resident ogre. All a bit different from the way it's been for Jane. She was Eliot's whimper. Sue and I were the bang.'

SUSAN
January, 1976

I'd hoped Mike would pick up on the Sydney idea just from the way I talked about the place.

He didn't seem to, though: 'Living down here in Sydney, Suze. The answer's no, all right?' he said in the room we'd borrowed in Surry Hills.

He'd managed to cajole Tom into an afternoon nap while I helped with the lunch dishes, and to avoid waking him now that I'd joined them we were sitting on the floor with our backs against the wall.

'If we do make the move, it can't be until next year,' he said in a whisper. 'I'm not even certain I'd want to live down here at all, anyway. I feel out of place.'

'Why? Because you made a fool of yourself last night. Daylight saving, for shit's sake. What did you want to argue over that for?'

I didn't know how angry I still was over that whole debacle until the words were out there, more a hiss than a whisper.

He grimaced and nodded at the bed as a warning to keep my voice down, but his reply wasn't exactly a model of restraint.

'I didn't want to argue about it. I don't give a damn about daylight saving. I just couldn't stand the way they were bagging everyone north of the border, like we're all one bunch of hillbillies, and as for that Rhonda and her bloody smirk . . . All right, I made a mess of it, but I could have done with a bit of wifely support, you know.'

'What, you expect me to agree with you because I've got a ring on my finger?'

'Wouldn't have hurt,' he said, and then seemed to regret it.

I'd made it clear often enough that I wouldn't play the loyal wife out of some kind of duty, and to be fair I didn't expect the loyal husband from him.

He let out a long, weary breath through his nostrils. 'It's not just the party, anyway. I'm tired of Sydney already. Maybe I'll feel different tomorrow, when we head north.'

Tomorrow! I didn't want to go back to Brisbane so soon. The girl who rented the room wasn't due back until uni started. I'd already talked about it with Linda and now my eagerness was somehow escaping into words: 'There's plenty of time, yet. We don't need to leave tomorrow, and I'm serious about making the move, Mike. It's not like going overseas at all. You'll get a job, no trouble.'

'I've got a job, a good one that I want to keep. We're staying in Brisbane.'

I could feel the vice cranking in on both sides. 'So you've decided. The man of the house has spoken. No discussion.'

'Whenever we discuss things I end up losing. I'm sick of it,' said Mike, in just the tone to challenge me but without enough conviction to warn me off.

'I haven't even started yet,' I shot back at him.

Our voices were rising. We'd wake Tom and, of course, the girls were only a thin wall away.

He didn't seem to care: 'Fair's fair. I let you have your semester in Brisbane. I didn't spit the dummy when you switched to arts without even telling me. Better than that, I've encouraged you, I let you have this fortnight in Sydney, even though my own parents think I was nuts to say yes. When is it going to be *my* turn?'

In his mind the question was purely rhetorical. It was there in his face to see. He really believed it was all about turns and the things he'd let me do, like a child indulged by an exasperated daddy.

'Bullshit! I've given up much more than you, Mike, and you got what you wanted, anyway, right from the start. Don't try to blackmail me now with this crap about wifey knuckling down so her beloved can get on with his career. Our marriage is different. I don't owe you anything.'

159

'More than me! What have you given up? Let's have a tally, if you're so keen. Listen, Sue, I've earned that posting to Kenmore.'

The patience was gone from his voice entirely now. There was an anger in him I hadn't seen, so much so I might have been sitting beside a different man, a man who'd lived inside my husband for three years and never let me know he was there.

And, as quickly as this other man had appeared, he was gone again behind the cheery Mike I was used to.

'It's going to be a great year, I can feel it, Sue,' he said, almost brightly. 'We're going to get out of Mum and Dad's place, maybe buy a house once you see what sense it makes. It will mean our lives can finally get started, instead of just being on hold.'

Was it then or had I known for weeks, even months, or from the beginning, that the Mike Riley I knew was as frightening to me as the stubborn steel I'd glimpsed a moment before.

'No, Mike. If we do those things, it will *put* my life on hold, just when I feel I'm ready to take off. This time in Sydney is what I've needed, this is where I want to be,' I said, throwing my arms about to mean the entire city. 'I feel alive for the first time since UQ, for the first time since Terry and the Tower Mill.'

But our voices had finally woken Tom and I had to rock him on the edge of the bed to stop his crying.

At the same time, I admitted it to myself: this was serious, and Mike's leopard pacing around the too-small room showed that he knew, too. I wasn't going back to Brisbane to live. That part of my life, of *our* lives, was over and he just had to see it.

He agreed to stay another day, but that was it. He had to be in Brisbane on Friday for a meeting with his new principal and his heart was set on the beaches as we made our way up the coast. Weren't there enough beaches in Sydney?

On Monday morning, he unfolded the stroller from the boot of the Holden and pointed Tom ahead of him on a long walk, leaving me to Linda's sympathies.

'Sorry,' I said. 'We're going through a bad patch, that's all. You shouldn't have to hear it, I know.'

Mike's absence gave me a chance to ring the university about my course, but he was back before I'd finished on the phone. 'So I'll definitely get credit for what I've already done in Queensland?' I was asking as he walked in. It was all rather obvious.

He let Tom roam the house and went into our room to wait for me. Oh God, here we go, I thought.

'We haven't agreed on anything,' he told me, before I'd even closed the door.

'I was just finding out where I'd stand.'

'No you weren't, Susan. You're making plans as though we've already decided to move down here. I'm getting tired of this whole thing. I want to leave Sydney, today, this afternoon. If we don't start now, we'll hardly have any time for a holiday on the way.'

'I don't care about the holiday.'

I came to the edge of the bed where he was propped up on all the pillows, but didn't slide over beside him, even when he made room for me. Didn't sit on the edge, either. Stayed on my feet. The distance, the height above him gave me an advantage.

'Mike, I'm not going back to Brisbane. As far as I'm concerned, I never want to go back, ever. It's a bloody police state up there, if you get in the way of the government you have to watch your back . . . and your head, too, especially in the dark when there's no one to see.'

'What are you talking about?'

'The Tower Mill, the way the police came after us.'

He stared at me as though he still hadn't made the connection. And why should he? That had all been years ago, and he had no idea what I knew. So he plunged on with what he did know.

'You want us to leave Brisbane because you don't like the politics? That's just plain ridiculous. It's not Russia. I don't understand what you're so angry about, why you're so desperate to get out of Queensland. If we do move down here, you'll just have to wait a year or two.'

He'd been going to say more, but stopped, suddenly frustrated with what he'd said. His face hardened, as it had so briefly yesterday. I didn't like what I saw.

'Forget what I just said, Susan. We're not moving down here, not now, not in two years' time.'

I backed away from the bed and threw my arms wide, this time in supplication to a God I didn't believe in. 'Haven't you been listening to me, Mike? Haven't you heard me say how I feel alive for the first time in so long?'

'Why don't you say it, Susan. You feel alive for the first time since we got married, that's what you mean, and it's happened because you escaped from me again, like you did last year.'

He'd said it too openly to believe it. It was a taunt meant to draw me back to my senses, make me admit that I had more invested in *him* than my new Sydney friends.

I wouldn't let him get away with it. 'It's true,' I said. 'I should never have married you. Rhonda said as much.'

'What business is it of hers? Sounds like you've spent more time discussing our marriage with other people than you have with me. And it seems you were all too happy to tell them Tom is not my son.'

'It's nothing less than the truth.'

Mike was off the bed now. I backed away, to make space for him in the tiny room, but he was a big man, a full head taller than me.

'Tom *is* my son!' he shouted. 'I don't care about the biology of it all. He's every bit as much mine as he's yours and I won't put up with anyone saying otherwise, especially not you.'

'Tom wouldn't be yours if it wasn't for the fucking police that night at the Tower Mill,' I reminded him. 'And I wouldn't be, either.'

He'd frightened me with his sudden movement, but now that he was on his feet I knew he wouldn't hurt me. He was angry, though, in a way I'd never seen him, and ready to do damage.

'If it hadn't been for the police charge, Tom wouldn't have been born at all,' he said.

'Too damned right,' I screamed at him. 'He wasn't supposed to be born, he wasn't supposed to *be* at all. If Terry had stayed his old self, he wouldn't have been, and I wouldn't have married you.'

Mike reeled backwards and sank onto the bed, elbows on his knees, head down.

I couldn't help myself now. I advanced on him, close enough to anoint his bowed head. 'I don't want to play families with you any more, Mike. If I didn't have a baby, I certainly wouldn't have a husband. Then I'd move where I damn well like, instead of having you like a ball and chain round my ankle. I hate Brisbane, can't stand it, can't stand Queensland, the way they cheer that mumbling thug while he sneaks around snipping away at their freedom. I'm not going back. Do you understand me? Do you get it now? I don't want anything from you, no money, nothing, but I have to get out.'

'How will you take care of Tom?' he sobbed into his hands.

Even through his tears, he came up with the practical questions. It only made me want to scream all the more.

'I don't care,' I shouted. 'Maybe it's not too late to have him adopted. I need some air, Mike. I can't breathe with you two around.'

He wouldn't look up; he hadn't moved since he'd slumped onto the bed. What more was there to say, in any case? I left the room with barely a thought for what I was doing, and, in a faraway voice I didn't quite recognise as my own, asked Linda to look after Tom.

Moments later I was out on the footpath, heading in whatever direction my feet decided, as long as it led away.

EIGHT

TOM

I was told as much as I ever dared ask about the breakup and the arguments that Mike and Susan had in Sydney. Their separate accounts matched remarkably; it was in the nuances that the difference appeared. Neither knows what the other did once Susan left the house in Surry Hills and, in fact, I became a conduit between them, as much as either wanted to know, many years later.

Dad had always thought Susan went to see a lecturer named Rhonda Nicolson. He was wrong, though. For his part, he waited until noon, but with no sign of Susan, and the other women in the house skewering him with foul looks whenever he came out of the bedroom, he packed up and went back to the dingy hotel, taking me with him.

'Was that when I broke the cow?' I asked, when we spoke about it years later.

I remember Dad sniffed, then smiled. 'It's funny, the things you can't seem to lose, no matter how much you'd like to.'

We were talking about a porcelain cow that the Sydney publican's wife had given me to play with when Dad ran out of games to keep me occupied. It was black with white polka dots, not quite a Friesian, even if I always thought of it as one. I broke off one of the horns and Dad insisted on paying for it. That Friesian was still in the house somewhere, offering a crude metaphor – the fragility of porcelain, a marriage that broke as easily, although not at a child's hands. I've never carried that guilt.

I've pictured Dad and me in that hotel room many times. He was surely dreading another confrontation with Susan because neither of them could back down. He confided to me once that if he'd heard Susan go on about feeling alive there in Sydney one more time he'd have slapped her. I was shocked. Mike Riley lashing out? It told me how hurt he must have been and how fed up with Susan closing him out. You can't take back a comment like Susan's, not when it meant she'd felt half-dead in all the years they'd spent together.

But then, was I being too harsh on my mother? It took a certain courage to come out with something so honest, and much as it hurt Dad, it released him, as well, it let him admit how he'd been slowly dying throughout that second year in Bindamilla. In Sydney, in that sad hotel room, while I played farmer on the floor, he made himself imagine a life without my mother. I guess he never thought he could bear it until then, but now that she'd forced him to it, there was a kind of freedom. He *could* live without her, he *could* start a different life.

'The problem was, that life wouldn't include you,' he told me, laughing at the tears these words drew from him. 'Sucker for sentiment,' he said, scolding himself. 'Death for a poet, of course, but I cried in that hotel room, Tom, and I'm not ashamed to say it, cried for a marriage that was crumbling around my ears and cried for me without you.'

'You were still in love with Susan, Dad. That doesn't stop overnight,' I replied, surprising myself, but I already carried a scar from a girl who'd dumped me before I saw it coming. And I'd been no more than a love-struck boyfriend.

It was after this that he got to the heart of what happened, of how I ended up in Brisbane rather than Sydney. He sat back in his old cane chair that creaked whenever he moved, a sound he enjoyed.

'Waiting for Susan,' he chuckled. 'Beckett understood how it felt, anticipating the death of what you know, whether it's worth keeping alive or not. I waited until Wednesday morning when the publican wanted to know if I was taking the room for another night. "No, I'm going home to Brisbane," I called through the door and was relieved to hear myself say it. I packed everything into the car again, strapped you in the back seat and went round to the house expecting to give you up. It could well have been the last time I saw you. I mean, what legal rights did I have?'

'What did Susan do?' I asked, trying to hide how much his answer meant to me.

'Nothing. She hadn't come home the night before. The girls in the house thought she'd gone to have it out with me. So there I was with a car loaded up for the drive to Brisbane and you already in the harness, staring at me while I sat at the wheel with my hand on the ignition key. I turned round in the seat and said, "What do *you* want to do, Tommy?"'

'What did I say?'

'You didn't say anything, of course. I turned back to look through the windscreen, furious with myself. Why was I asking a three-year-old what to do? I didn't need anyone's permission, I just had to ask what *I* wanted for a change. That settled it. I turned the key and drove you home to Brisbane. Bloody scorching it was, too, and we didn't stop at a single beach.'

SUSAN
January, 1976

I hurried away into the streets of Surry Hills without a care for where the pavement took me. In Paddington I stood at an intersection, paralysed by choice, until an old man spoke to me. I thought he wanted directions, at first; when I realised what he *was* asking, I swore in his face and ran across the road against the lights.

I was crying violently by then; a fizzing beaker, a witch's brew. The dirty old man was lucky I hadn't turned him into a toad. If there was such a thing as magic I would learn its arts, not for turning toads, but to fold back the mechanics of time to the instant the police had charged outside the Tower Mill. I would break Mike Riley's grip on the jumper, lunge forward against the tide until I found Terry, then run down the hill with him instead, frightened and furious, until we emerged, chests heaving and light-headed with relief, into the streets of a different future.

The nuns had taught me white magic – prayer, they called it – and if it had proved any more effective than witchcraft I would have used it then. I walked on, instead, my mind full of the letter left behind in my handbag. A map of sorts, it showed Queensland, its coastline encoded in the scrawl of an anonymous hand. I couldn't go back within those boundaries. He was there, *both* hes, Dolan and Terry Stoddard. I couldn't go back to the house where I thought I'd found refuge, either, because another pair of hes guarded the way.

I needed some air, I'd yelled at Mike, but now I had it, the sky overwhelmed me.

I got lost, which delayed my return, and by then the Holden was blessedly missing from the street outside the house.

'He's gone back to where you were before,' Linda called from the front step when she saw me loitering. Inside, she was worried about the further news she had to impart. 'He took your little boy. I hope that's okay.'

'Oh . . . yes,' I murmured, accepting the coffee from Linda's hand, and her arm around my shoulder.

'It sounded rough. He's a pig.'

'No, he's been good to me, better than I've been to him.'

'You're blaming yourself, like women always do.'

'I'm not to blame, either,' I said with a sigh. But I knew the cause was north of the border, an explanation Linda would never understand.

Another flatmate, Annemarie, joined us. Feminine support. The pair of them became hotly indignant on my behalf, but their dogmatic prescriptions were utter bullshit. What did they know about men and marriage, what did they know of the letter I carried with me everywhere and how it burned me up?

They saw the heat in my eyes and began fishing for what I wanted to hear. They weren't what I needed and when it all became too much I retreated to the bedroom and lay face to the wall.

The phone rang, making me jump. Not Mike, please. I didn't know what to say to him. But there was no tap at the door. When it rang again, I thought, Oh God, he'll want to patch things up, he'll say he's sorry, that he wants to talk.

Then Linda called through the house, 'Annemarie, it's for you.'

After a late meal, I told myself to phone the hotel. There was a phone box on the corner, away from intrusive ears, but the twilight had gone and I used the darkness as an excuse not to go.

In the morning I left the house without speaking to the others and spent the day wandering the city, sat through a movie, and afterwards rang Diane, reversing the charges.

'You have to give it another go, Sue. Marriage is a precious thing.'

Had I expected anything different?

'Come home to Brisbane, at least. It'll look different up here,' was her final advice. How wrong she was.

I stood outside the phone box thinking of the letter. How could one piece of paper cause a revulsion so powerful I had to move far away from all it represented? Did it even exist? No one else had seen the letter, except John Obermayer, and he was in Melbourne. I thought about calling him. Did I show you a letter, anonymous, handwritten? If I had to ask, was I going crazy?

I needed to show it to someone else, though, to hear myself explain what it meant. Not Linda, and certainly not Annemarie. With the letter retrieved from the house, I found my way to the address of another classmate from the summer school, given freely in the first bloom of friendship. When the bell went unanswered, I waited in the street until the shops were closed and the offices sent their workers home.

'Sue, what are you doing here?'

Not the welcome I was hoping for. 'I'm sorry to turn up on your doorstep like this, Janet. I need a favour.'

Janet hadn't come to the party in Surry Hills. Not her scene. She was older than the others and maybe that was why I liked her.

'Come in. What can I do for you?' she said, once she was over the surprise.

We talked, me through tears, Janet through cigarette smoke, although mostly she listened, and only when I was spent did she offer any response. I passed the letter into her hand – it was real after all – and with it came the story.

'I can't bear to live among people who applaud what happened, who think the jackboot gives protection to their narrow little lives, where thugs like Dolan dare me to go after justice for Terry because he knows he's above the law.'

'Then don't, but there's plenty of it about, here as much as anywhere,' Janet said bluntly.

'It's not the same. I feel a difference on the streets down here.'

Later, I said, 'If I go back there, I'll be saying all right, you win, Mike, let's have more babies, and I'll be a mother in the suburbs and my children will be all I am.'

'Would it be any different if he came down here, like you asked him to? He'd still want children of his own.'

'Maybe I don't want him to change his mind.'

It was late when the talking was done. 'Sleep here,' said Janet.

I was exhausted and slept well into Wednesday morning, waking to find a note that insisted I take my time.

I did, and, alone in the kitchen of Janet's flat, made a decision.

'He came this morning,' said Linda, when I returned to Surry Hills. 'We didn't know how long you'd be so he went off again. Didn't say what time he'd come back.'

I was ready now. I waited, but when the call came many hours later, there was a twist.

'I'm in Grafton,' he said. 'I've got Tom with me. We're going home to Brisbane.'

It was the last thing I'd expected and what it meant was suddenly subsumed beneath more practical issues. 'Is Tom all right? It must be hot in the car. Make sure you give him lots to drink.'

'I'm doing that, and I don't need any lectures from you about how to take care of him. It wasn't good for him in Sydney, either. He's better off at home'

'Bastard. Go home to fucking Brisbane, then,' I said. 'This is the end, you know that, don't you? It's over.'

I hung up in a fury. He'd taken Tom with him to force me back to Brisbane, where he'd persuade me to try again. This wasn't how it was meant to go.

I waited until Friday before ringing and instead got his mother, Helen, who told me, curtly, that Mike was at his new school, meeting the principal. He rang back just after five.

'Are you in a phone box?' I asked.

'No. Mum and Dad have made themselves scarce.'

I looked up to find that Linda and Annemarie had done the same.

A boxing match came to mind: before the rough stuff began, the seconds left the ring. When I told him what I'd decided, would he beg or abuse, would he blackmail, tell me how Tom missed me, and turn the screw from there?

'How's Tom?' I asked.

'The drive took a lot out of him, but he's fine today, running around the backyard right now, chasing the cat.'

I could see it, my son as relentless as a Hollywood Frankenstein and the wily old cat one step ahead.

'He's asked for you,' said Mike.

I stiffened. There was no follow-up, though, and I wondered if it was true. How long would we dance around the ring like this?

Then he caught me without warning. 'Are you coming home to Brisbane?'

Not when, but was I, as though he'd dropped his guard on purpose.

Stuff it then. 'No, Mike, I've made up my mind. I live in Sydney now.'

Nothing came down the line at me, or to me. The silence was agony until I understood he was waiting for my question in return.

'Have you changed your mind, Mike? Will you come down here, like I asked?' No mention of our marriage, of our future together, but that's what I was asking.

'No,' he said, after the briefest hesitation.

He'd made up his mind, just as I had.

Our last phone call had been sulphurous, ending with my angry cry: 'It's over, you know that.' Right now I knew it was true, more certainly than when I'd yelled those words into the phone.

'I think we should separate,' said Mike. 'We already have, really,' he added, with a little laugh that held no malice. 'What you said on Monday was true, our marriage was a mistake. You've said it before, not just in Sydney this week, lots of times, in different words maybe, but the message was the same. I'm sorry I forced you into it.'

'You didn't force me, Mike.'

My throat was tightening with a sentiment I hadn't expected to feel. 'But it *was* a mistake, wasn't it? I'm sorry, too.'

It would have been cruel to tell him that I did feel love, when the sentence must finish with 'but not enough'. A relief swam through my blood stream, loosening muscles.

'Have you got enough money?' he asked.

Oh God, were we going to talk about that now? 'I took out twenty dollars yesterday.'

'You'll need more than that. Use whatever's in our account. I've got enough to last until I get paid, and then I'll set up a separate account for myself. We'll talk about it again then, okay?'

'All right. Yeah, I suppose . . . thank you.'

The money talk was over and I had no idea what to say next.

'How did you go at the new school?'

'Better than I'd hoped. I have good classes – no Seniors, but a Grade Eleven English and another for history. Best of all, no French.'

I laughed. We laughed together! He'd hated teaching French in Bindy.

There were other questions, more talking, as though now that we'd shaken hands in the centre of the ring, we could dance ourselves out with pleasantries. I might have been talking to a friend I caught up with every week or two.

Then the phone was back in its cradle and Linda's head appeared around the door with a 'safe to come out now?' look on her face.

Could a marriage end so easily? Should it?

Linda handed me a glass of iced water and I walked out to the front step in search of a breeze. It was five-thirty, yet even on this shaded side of the house the heat was still a bastard. Legs bared, top uncoupled from my skirt, I longed for the day to cool down, but it would be hours yet before the Sydney sun relented. Maybe Mike was right about daylight saving after all.

On Saturday, I woke to a new life and was immediately suspicious of it. By Sunday, less so. I talked to Linda and she again offered the empty bedroom until its regular occupant returned. Where would I live then? How would I support myself and a three-year-old when the balance in my passbook reached zero? These were simply problems to solve and I wouldn't let myself be weighed down by them.

A bigger worry was the telephone that both beckoned and

repulsed me from its perch beside the sofa. I'd been married to Mike for three years, shared a bed with him, shared a life, and knew to steel myself for when his need grew too strong.

He rang on Monday, Australia Day.

'How's Tom?' I asked immediately.

He launched into a summary, like a conscientious babysitter.

'What have you said to him?'

'Nothing yet.'

'And your parents?'

'You're not their favourite person right now.'

I pictured Helen Riley's stern visage and behind it a kind of glee that the marriage was over.

How long would I stay there in Surry Hills, he asked. More talk of money. There was no begging, no heat. I had a question of my own: 'Why aren't you angry with me?'

'I am. I just don't want to get into a shouting match. I'm angry because I've missed something, I'm sure of it. I can't understand why you're so hot on living down there, in Sydney, when it's all one bloody country.'

I had to tell him.

'Mike, when we got back to Bindy, this time last year, there was . . .'

I knew if I said another word, if I explained about the letter, about Terry and Barry Dolan, I'd be drawn towards him again, or Mike would come to Sydney after all, convinced our marriage could be revived. It took the breath from my lungs when I realised I didn't want that.

'What?' he asked, when I went so suddenly dry.

'Nothing.' I said. 'Nothing that can make any difference now.'

My son was six hundred miles away and with Mike so busy at his new school, while I was pretty much twiddling my thumbs, it was up to me. I booked a ticket on the train, planning to head north on Friday night, sitting up to save money, then come south again on Sunday, in a sleeper. Tom would think it was a great adventure.

On Friday, though, I delayed packing, and knew I was doing it.

The room in Surry Hills seemed so small, and what if there were drugs in the house, not just for parties, either? The girls were fine, but what about their friends? At four o'clock I still hadn't packed for a six-thirty departure. At five, I rang to cancel.

'I can appreciate you're not really in a position to fetch him yet,' said Mike, when I tried to explain. 'I've found a babysitter so Mum doesn't have to look after him and things are working out well. Why don't I keep Tom until you're settled somewhere more appropriate?'

I agreed, too readily and, in a panic, rang Janet's doorbell a second time.

'Brave girl,' she said, over a Friday night glass of wine. It was from a cardboard cask the size of a shoe box, which meant there was plenty to get us both drunk.

Janet began to expand on the whole matter. 'If my mother had her time over, she'd do the same. Never said so, raised four kids and never complained, but it was there in her face all the time. Wife and mother in the suburbs was all there was, back in her day.'

'I'm already a mother. No choice in that now.'

After a refill, I let my thoughts go free-range. 'It'll be hard on my own. I've got no help down here, no sister nearby, can't ask friends to mind a toddler.' And finally, after another glass: 'I'm not a very good mother.'

'I've heard that before. Is your little boy underfed?'

'No.'

'Covered in sores? Is he left to cry when he needs a hug, do you never play games with him, do you smack him, tell him he's a whining little shit? That's a bad mother.'

'It's deeper than that.'

'Is it, or are you expecting too much of yourself?'

'Maybe I don't have the mother gene. I love my son, but I don't want to play the mother game.'

On Sunday, the absent girl returned unannounced and I had to scramble around in embarrassment, cleaning and gathering up my things, which, thankfully, fitted back into my bag. But there was no need.

'I'm moving out,' the girl told Linda. 'Sorry about the short notice, but it looks like you've found someone else already.'

Too good to be true, for me. I could have the room permanently now, or so it seemed until Annemarie spoke up.

'Listen, Sue, about your little boy. When I said it was fine, it was only going to be a week or two, wasn't it? I didn't think it would be, like, forever.'

I phoned the house in Brisbane where my son was safe from drug fiends and had someone to mind him during the day.

'Mike, can you keep Tom a bit longer? Things are a bit fluid here at the moment.'

He was sympathetic. 'Do you need money? I can put part of my wages into the joint account for you. I'll have to do it anyway, child support or whatever it's called.'

I feared the thin edge of dependency. 'No, I'll get work soon, and that'll pay my way here. I'll get by.'

After the call I slipped away to my room, to my bed, to the blank wall in my face. In my face, too, was the truth: I wouldn't be going up to Brisbane to get Tom, not in a week or two, not a month. I cried the first real tears and found there were more inside me than I'd bargained for. I cried for two days, until I heard Linda and Annemarie, bereft and panicky, discussing doctors.

They called Derek, instead, who brought some weed with him and between them they coaxed me out of my room and onto the sofa, where the reefers were lit and my sobs became laughter, or at least the sound of each became indistinguishable, and their sensation, too.

TOM

I visited Sydney many times throughout my university years. During one of those visits, I took myself on a private tour of the city's sights, not the Rocks and Hyde Park Barracks but in pursuit of my *own* history, and so I know that the old pub Dad and I stayed in is still serving beer to retired wharfies in singlets and tattered shorts. Maybe they're waiting for Godot with the same mixture of hope and impotence that Dad must have felt as he waited for Susan just one floor above their heads. When I asked, however, the girl behind the bar seemed surprised that the rooms upstairs had ever been available to the public.

I also stood outside the address where the marriage of Michael and Susan Riley finally collapsed into its hollowed-out centre, but instead of a dilapidated share house for students, a six-pack of apartments stared back at me, ugly in pale 1970s brick.

What was I looking for on my pilgrimage, anyway? A glimpse of Susan hurrying from the house so I could know whether her eyes were wet or dry? Those details were harder to ask for, although it was telling that she could recall the address so readily when I asked her, probably on the same visit to Sydney.

'That was the place you stormed away from, wasn't it?' I said. 'Dad thinks you went to see some lecturer who had it in for him,' I said to her once. 'Some feminist who'd convinced you that all marriage was oppression and a husband from Queensland was sure to be an oaf.'

That surprised her. 'No, I didn't go to see anyone, not that day. I just walked the streets.'

Dad never did discover what drove Susan to turn on him so irrevocably in that house. By the time I made my private pilgrimage I could have told him myself about the letter and John Obermayer and Barry Dolan. If I didn't, it was because I felt it was Susan's story to tell, not mine, but if that was true, why did I walk the streets of Sydney as she had done? What was I looking for?

How *does* a son ask his mother why she gave him up? What answer can she give that doesn't tie itself into knots of self-justification? If I'd left the questions unspoken, would she have told me anyway?

I was in my late teens by the time I started wanting to know – gone from school, gone from childhood, where mothers stand guard against life's harm. She'd missed her chance there. Let's not beat about the bush; Susan missed her chance to raise me the way other mothers raise their children, working up from the ground floor with a child who is entirely dependent at first, then a little less so, and a little less so. She'd got off at the third floor and let me go on rising in the company of others, until I was pretty much at the top.

Love came later. I built a love for my mother in the way Grandma Cosgrove worked on her jigsaw puzzles at the beach each Christmas: a little patch of colour spreading out, over many visits, then jumping ahead in brief spurts that started when she took me to see my father in the nursing home, then slowing for long periods while I continued to live as Mike Riley's son, content and untroubled by the anomaly. Susan would say the vital moment came when she showed me the letter she first read with me in my stroller, outside the Bindamilla post office, but I'm not so sure. That letter explained a lot of things, but not what mattered most to me.

SUSAN
April, 1976

It was months before I saw them again.

'I want to have Tom over the Easter weekend,' I told Mike, during one of our weekly calls. He could hardly refuse, but a bit of compromise seemed only fair when it was such a long way and neither of us had the money to fly. We agreed on Coffs Harbour, where my bus arrived less than an hour before the Holden pulled into the car park of the Pacific Sands Motel.

With Tom latched onto me like a little possum, Mike and I pecked each other on the cheek. Had I really been married to this man for three years? I still was, and it was still his surname I wrote at the top of my assignments and that came printed on the legal documents we'd started to fill in.

He paid for the room and refused the notes I offered as my share, to my considerable relief. Once inside, I wouldn't let Tom out of my grasp. He was over the moon to have so much of my attention, until his boyishness kicked in and my arms infringed his right to charge around like a mad thing. I let him go, chased him, caught him and pretended to eat him up while he squealed and begged for more. I had to take him back with me. This was too much to miss out on.

In the morning I took him to the beach, just the two of us, and the certainty of my decision warmed me more than the sun on my skin.

Afterwards, while Tom took his nap, Mike and I talked, and, although we'd slept in the double bed without embarrassment – and without touching – now that we were seated on the edge of the same bed, the words didn't come easily, as though six hundred miles of phone line allowed for better communication.

We kept to procedural matters. Divorce papers had been lodged, and, since we hadn't been much good at collecting the usual accoutrements of a marriage, there wasn't really anything to divvy up.

'I took Tom round to see Joyce,' he said. 'They were pleasant enough.'

'Half your luck. She's just about melted the phone lines with what she thinks of me. All my fault and she can't believe I haven't got Tom with me in Sydney. I'm a disgrace to motherhood, that sort of thing.'

'Don't listen to her. It's just the circumstances.'

'It hurts all the same when she says I don't love him. I do, Mike, you know that, don't you?'

Who was I trying to convince?

'You're a good mother, Sue. Look at the two of you together this weekend.'

I'd seen the extra bags in the boot of the Holden and knew he'd come prepared.

'Was I, Mike? Getting married saved Tom from being illegitimate, but it didn't save me from being an illegitimate mother. I always felt a fraud, like I was just doing what had to be done. That's why it hurts when Mum gets on her high horse. She's disowned me, won't let Diane talk to me, or the boys. It's another kind of divorce.'

'Excommunication,' he said. 'Catholics don't do things by halves, do they?'

After dinner, with Tom again out for the count, I said, 'Do you want to . . . you know.' I glanced towards the bed. 'I'm still good for a hand job, or whatever.'

'I use my own,' said Mike, with a mocking wink.

'You don't think of me while you're doing it, do you?'

'No, I have a picture of Richard Nixon that works better.'

I laughed, surprising myself.

If he'd simply denied such intimate consolation, I wouldn't have believed him, but to find him so casual – and so callous – offered hope.

I could do without the passionless half-hour in the bed, too. I'd lost all interest in recent months and decided it was because sex meant giving away a part of myself. In the rebuilding of Susan Kinnane, there was nothing left to share with others, not in that most intimate of acts, anyway. The house in Surry Hills was my life now, the place where I'd slowly grown a new skin after the excoriation of January, after conversations with a fading husband and tears over a little boy as slippery as a buttered pig in my dreams.

He wasn't the only presence in my night-times. Terry was there, in a way I'd been able to block out in the years when the wedding band on my finger told of where I'd escaped to. I was glad I'd gone to see him as often as I did while Tom and I were living in the Rileys' granny flat. I would never visit Brisbane again, never set foot across the border, which meant those visits would have to sustain me. But, with what I knew, it was impossible to go back there, and wasn't I persona non grata according to Joyce, anyway?

So the house in Surry Hills was my refuge now, and Linda my friend, if not my confidante, and others came through the door, mostly women, which I preferred. The house was rarely quiet, the many voices vibrant as they argued and declaimed and painted pictures of life as it might be without a thought for that other world of children and husbands. I got rat-faced on cheap wine and wept with laughter in a way I hadn't known since a similar house in Auchenflower.

I'd found a part-time job typing and filing in a doctor's surgery, which paid the rent and for my share of the food. I was no better at studying methodically than I'd been as a teenager, but that didn't seem to matter when I could dash off an assignment in last-minute frenzy and have my tutor write across it, *Sue, you must have been a journalist in a former life?*

Then came Coffs Harbour – reunion, reclamation of what should rightly reside with me. By the Sunday, Tom was over the novelty of my undivided attention and just wanted to get on with having two parents for a change. He played no favourites and engineered an excruciating walk along the water's edge, with himself in the middle, swinging his plump little body into the air while Mummy and Daddy held one hand each.

'Happy families,' said Mike grimly.

It was the closest we came to laughing freely with one another that day.

By then, I was aware of a change in myself. My exuberance had dimmed, I let Mike dress and undress the little figure, which he'd clearly become used to, and I found myself watching Tom only when he called on my attention.

On the last morning, I still hadn't said anything, and knew by then that I wouldn't.

'Mummy loves you, Tom,' I said, hugging him for too long and having to suppress my hurt when he pulled away.

At the bus station, I kissed them both and waved as the Greyhound took me southward again leaving Mike to strap Tom into the Holden and drive him to their home across the border.

The tutor was watching the men, or boys, really, except for the mature-age student who didn't look quite right in jeans.

I was bored because every male in the room was playing possum with this week's topic in case it flushed them out.

'Equal pay for equal work, it's basic justice,' said one of the guys, as though anything else was unimaginable. He couldn't imagine recent history, then, I thought, couldn't imagine the mothers of the many young women around him, or was he simply avoiding an argument, as I suspected.

'How do we arrive at figures like these, then?' prompted the tutor, a woman no older than me, who quoted brick-hard statistics to build the abysmal picture of female earnings compared to male.

As a group, we dutifully ferreted out the culprits in the way Mrs Fenster liked her history class to list the causes of World War I. It was access to jobs, it was gender bias in promotion, jobs for the boys. These boys all showed their disdain for such discrimination, although the older man among them bravely admitted that he would have struggled to work under a 'sheila'. He said the word through his best Paul Hogan grin and got away with it because he'd made fun of himself.

'You can't forget discrimination against mothers with young children, either,' said the serious soul beside me. 'The law still doesn't protect women from being sacked when they start a family.'

This was where the discussion went now, carried by the other girls while I looked on. I was the only mother in the room, although none of them knew this about me. The white line on my ring finger had long since tanned.

'But there's a reason for that,' said the dark-eyed boy who haunted the same corner every week, drawing long stares from girls who would have loved to fold him into their shoulder bags and take him home. 'When a woman starts a family, she's taking on another job, motherhood's a job, a big one. She doesn't have time for work as well.'

'Many women seem to manage it, Ian,' said the tutor.

'Yes, but how well? Both jobs end up suffering. At work, she's tired and has her mind on what's happening with her kids, or maybe she gets called away because her kids are sick and other workers have to cover for her. That's not very fair. Worse than that, she's not there when her kids need her.'

Young Ian had thrown a switch. I saw feminine hair bristle in the static and I sat up at last in anticipation. The tutor sensed it, too, but turned deliberately to the other boys.

'What do you think?'

Some squirmed and avoided the tutor's eye, as though they were back in a Grade Nine science class and afraid to be asked the valency of sodium.

'I think Ian's got a point,' said one. 'Kids need their mothers. You can't really turn that on its head for the sake of academic theory.'

Emboldened, another voice followed: 'The children should always come first.'

I turned to pick out the speaker, Tony D'Astasio. If I knew his name, it was because he was usually more thoughtful and articulate than the rest.

'I'm thinking of the little ones,' Tony went on, 'because those early years are really important, aren't they? It's not the same for fathers, the relationship is different. Kids need their mothers at home with them while they're little, up to school age, anyway. Why have them otherwise?'

Masculine heads rose tentatively, but it seemed clear Tony had summed up their collective opinion.

Why have them? My chair creaked as I shifted, alerting me to my own agitation.

'Do you think women only have babies when they want to?' I asked. 'A lot of them get knocked up by the likes of you and your mates here, for a start, and it's not men who end up with a bulge in their bellies. And when that bulge becomes a baby, what are a woman's choices then? Settle down in the suburbs and raise the little thing while Daddy pays the bills? Is that how it's supposed to be? Because it isn't, you know, for a hell of a lot of women. They get abandoned, they get divorced.'

'I wasn't talking about those women. Married women was what I meant.'

'Oh, so immediately a woman marries she loses her choices, is that right? Where do you get off telling women they have to give themselves over to their children, as though they don't count once the first little tacker pops out between their legs? Women have had enough of that, Tony boy. We're here to do more than raise kids, we've got brains, we've got ability, as good as any man.

'And what's this guff about mothers have to raise their own children? That's a wank of the middle class, a prison called motherhood. Women don't have to stay at home raising our little ones. There are other ways to love them. Who are you to lecture people like me about how to love my son?'

Finally I stopped, and only then found that I was standing over Tony D'Astasio, my hands leaning on the fold-down tray of his chair.

When did I get to my feet? My lips were moist from the passion of argument, my armpits too, the cotton of my t-shirt cold beneath my jumper.

Around me, the other women were merely silent. The men were cowed and poor Tony D'Astasio was petrified.

'I think we might take a break,' said the tutor.

Undergraduate life buoyed me until my first Sydney spring. I had to wait until next year to slough off my marriage entirely, but I'd jumped early by switching my name back to Kinnane: another regeneration. I was seeing more of Janet and sometimes spent two, even three nights a week sleeping on her sofa.

'Here's a two-bedroom place in Paddington,' she said, tapping the Saturday *Herald* while we sipped coffee at her kitchen table. 'Will we go have a look at it?'

Sharing a flat with Janet was a step up and a step closer, although to what, the newly named face in the mirror couldn't tell me. Twenty-five was an odd age to be reborn, but I knew this couldn't be a new childhood, and whatever I'd missed had to be written off.

Janet came in from work one September evening to find I'd swathed the dining table in paper.

'An assignment?' she asked, looking over my shoulder.

It wasn't, or at least it wasn't an assignment to be handed in, assessed and then finished with, letting me move on to the next.

'This is everything I have about the Springbok protest. And it's all useless. Look at this.' I pushed a newspaper clipping far enough to my right for her to get a clear view.

'What's Bjelke-Peterson up to now?' she asked, scanning the headline.

'A student demonstrator's been hit on the head with a police baton.'

Janet took up the clipping, but I couldn't wait for her to work out the significance.

'Happened in broad daylight, in front of a hundred witnesses, there's television footage. Even the police commissioner wants an investigation, but Joh's killed it in cabinet. What chance do I have of getting an inquiry for Terry? Just proves that Dolan was right, the way he taunted me on the phone.'

'Where's the press in all this?'

'Gutless, or just too cosy with a government that can't lose. All the good journos leave, like John Obermayer. What's the point when the man in the street *thinks* like Joh?'

'Not all of them, surely. Where's the outrage?'

'On file at police headquarters, that's where. John Obermayer's still got contacts in Brisbane. Says the Special Branch has a file on everyone. Look at this.' I handed up a letter I'd received a week earlier.

'Who's . . . Trevor?' she asked, reading the name at the bottom of the page.

'A lecturer at UQ. He's queer and can't afford to speak up in case they open a file on him, too. Have a look at what he says there.'

Janet took a moment to read, then looked up. 'The police are tapping the phones of the Opposition? How can they get away with it?'

'No one to stop them. It'll get worse when Whitrod goes.'

'Who's he?'

'The police commissioner. The ordinary coppers go over his head now, straight to Joh.' I stabbed in disgust at the article about the bashed student. 'They'll be kissing his hand after this.'

'His arse, more like. What are you going to do?' Janet asked.

'I don't know. I'm tired, I'm not getting anywhere. If all this didn't boil my blood –' I swept my arms wide over the table – 'I'd dump it in the bin.'

'If you did, maybe you wouldn't feel so angry.'

Oh God, I thought. Was that really an option?

NINE

TOM

Every child knows the story of how his parents met, it's just not usual to be alive when it happened. Or, at least, it was unusual until the modern world forced the word *parent* to evolve like one of Darwin's species. A pedant would argue you can't exist before your real parents meet long enough to exchange bodily fluids. In fact, that was the trick Peter Carey played in *Oscar and Lucinda*, where the narrator's forebears meet long enough for that function alone, with the father killed off only hours later. Nice one, Pete. And nice one, Dad, since he gave me a copy for Christmas when he decided I should be reading literature instead of James Bond. To be fair, he didn't realise the significance I would find in Oscar's fate and, in any case, it remains one of my favourite novels.

I could play tricks with parentage, too, because my own mum and dad contributed not a single strand of DNA to my genes. When people said that I was growing more and more like my father, the smile we offered in return was a joke we happily kept to ourselves.

I was a few months short of my fifth birthday when Mike Riley met Lyn Cosgrove at Kenmore State High. That meeting was on the first day of school in 1977. Then, like the start of World War II, nothing much happened for a couple of months except that the Decree Absolute came through, dissolving the marriage of Michael and Susan Riley.

On Holy Thursday, the Kenmore staff went for a drink after school, which turned into many drinks and the pair who stayed longest suddenly found more joy in the company of another human being than they'd known for a long time.

After Easter, Lyn invited Dad to *A Midsummer Night's Dream*, which some of her friends were putting on at La Boite. It was a romp and he had never enjoyed Shakespeare so much. For their first real date, he took her to La Grange, a restaurant boasting not just haute cuisine but genuine French waiters, where he ordered his meal in the vernacular. Apparently, Mum fell out of her chair laughing at the pained face of *le garçon* (her story), or else she simply chortled with enough mirth to embarrass the poor klutz (Dad's version).

In the meantime, I was in charge of the shopping.

This was quite a responsibility for a five-year-old and I took to it like a ship's captain, standing braced at the front of the trolley like Lieutenant Cook on the poop deck. All I needed was a telescope.

The job was assigned to me because I'd taught myself to read, after first working out the link between black marks on a page and then with help from *Sesame Street* and *Play School*. Once I started school, it was time to put this fabulous skill to work, so Dad allowed me out of the supermarket trolley to find a bag of flour or two cans of crushed tomatoes, or (big challenge) a packet of Arnott's Arrowroot.

What I remember about those days, when it was just Dad and me, was the whistling. My adventures as grocery hunter sometimes took me three or four aisles away, and Dad might have moved on by the time I had the prize in hand. The solution was whistling – not from a five-year-old's lips, but from Dad's. He tootled along like a canary, an unconscious thing that I hadn't noticed until then, or maybe he simply hadn't felt like whistling in the years when I first began to watch him, copy him, bind myself to him. But, certainly, in the days leading up to the wedding and afterwards, when Lyn joined us in the house they'd bought in Ashgrove, he was a six-foot songbird.

SUSAN
Anzac weekend, 1978

'You should have let me take a cab,' I said to Janet.

The rain hadn't let up all afternoon and since it was the Friday before a long weekend, the traffic was a soggy tangle from Redfern to Mascot.

'You'd have been lucky to get one. Might have missed your flight,' she replied, without taking her eyes from the road.

I glanced at my watch, then out through the sweep of the windscreen wipers and finally at Janet in the driver's seat.

'It's not raining in Brisbane, according to Mike. I rang him with my flight number this afternoon.'

'Joh probably arranged a dry day for the diggers. He's got a direct line to God, hasn't he?'

'Up there, they think he *is* God. So does *he*. Would make a great interview – a lot more interesting than 'attitudes to Anzac Day'.

That had been the topic of my final piece for the *Advocate*. I got the feeling it was punishment for leaving just when I was getting good at the job.

'Did you interview anyone, or just recycle copy from the year before?' said Janet, and we grinned cynically, like a pair of seasoned journalists.

'You're taking Tom another present, I see.'

I looked down at the package in my lap. 'He'll think it's his birthday all over again, but it didn't seem right to go up there without something to give him. Lego this time. My brothers loved it.'

'Mine too.'

Shoptalk and birthdays were easy territory, except that mention of Tom seemed to teleport him into the back seat of Janet's car, where he was proudly telling anyone who'd listen that his dad was getting married.

The news hadn't surprised me; I'd been expecting as much since Christmas when Mike told me, nervously, 'I've met someone.'

Forewarning didn't stop my stomach from twisting as the airport emerged from the gloom because in the northern sunshine waited a woman I had yet to meet, much my own age and soon to be a wife. How soon she became a mother was up to me.

On the flight, I tried to imagine her, this rival in motherhood who had suddenly appeared, starting with an image from the *Vogue* on my knee, until the poise and flawless couture made me laugh out loud. At the second attempt, I went for an earth mother with the easy knack of nurturing and the body of a fertility goddess.

I stopped making such pictures as soon as the engines changed pitch on the approach into Brisbane. I was north of the border again, where I'd sworn I'd never go. Through the window, I watched the street lamps of the southern suburbs scoot by until the lights climbed vertically to form the office towers with the black snake of the river coiled round them.

I turned away. Terry was down there, but so was Dolan these days. He'd been transferred to the big smoke as a detective sergeant, according to John Obermayer's sources. If I craned my neck, I could take in Parliament House and remind myself of the latest outrage: street marches needed a permit from the police now, except that Bjelke-Petersen appeared on the news taunting protestors, 'Don't bother applying. You won't get one.'

And the people cheered. Anyone who badmouthed Joh these days was badmouthing Queensland. The whole state was a joke.

At the arrival gate, Tom came running into my arms before I was ready, knocking me back a pace. Mike joined us, smiling, and after a few moments I became aware of a third figure hovering close. God, she'd come to the airport with them. Not a model, not an earth mother, pretty without the burden of beauty, Lyn was well dressed in labels I could name, she wore great shoes, but the pants looked like a comfortable pair from last season. It was the kind of choice I would have made. She stared at me, a tentative smile glued in place to cover her nerves.

Me too, I wanted to say. I'm a jelly. It was hard enough for the new wife to meet the old wife at the best of times, but we had a complication, one attached to my chest as though he would never let go.

A kiss seemed too intimate. 'Hello, I'm Sue,' I said, freeing one hand and feeling Lyn's in mine. Maybe this wasn't going to be so bad after all.

They drove me to Diane's, who'd found the backbone to defy Joyce's ban. Tom stayed with me overnight, played, fought and slept with his cousins until, on Sunday, Mike and Lyn returned, and the four of us went to Lone Pine so Tom could see the koalas.

'Am I the ogre you expected?' I asked Lyn, while Mike took Tom to the toilet.

'I'm relieved there's only one head. Actually, Mike hasn't told me much about you at all. That only made it harder when I knew you were coming.'

The affection between Mike and Lyn was obvious in the way they were aware of each other constantly, in little touches, deliberate and welcome. Mike had done the same with me until I told him it felt claustrophobic and, of course, he eventually stopped entirely. In unscripted moments, I glimpsed my son with Lyn and couldn't miss how comfortable he was with her. The wedding was not until August but the mothering had already begun.

On Anzac Day, Mike came for me on his own and in silence we drove through mostly empty streets, past granite soldiers staring down at tributes of flowers, now abandoned, while the old diggers got drunk. In Coopers Plains, Mrs Stoddard had the front door open before we were out of the car.

I'd been here many times, yet I held back. Terry had come on a lot since I'd been so repulsed by the sight of him in hospital. Those days were gone. It was the uncertainty of emotion that kept me beside the car. What did I feel? Sympathy, because he was the one who'd been robbed of so much, anger at the way it had happened, or was it fury at myself that I'd given up on Dolan?

When Mike realised I wasn't close behind him, he turned, his face a gentle question. Oddly, I wanted him to hold me a moment. I had lovers these days, whoever took my fancy, in fact, but none of them embraced me with the affection that Mike had once shown me – I made sure of that – but at that moment I needed the warmth of someone I could trust.

I was out of luck, though. 'We don't have to stay long,' he said, low enough so that his words wouldn't reach Mrs Stoddard. Then he took purposeful strides towards the front door, and what could I do but follow?

Terry sat in the same overstuffed chair, his hands clutched possessively on the armrests. 'This is the lady I told you was coming, Terry,' said Mrs. Stoddard. 'This is Susan.'

It had been so long. Of course he'd forgotten me, of course his mother needed to prepare him. In the same tone she said to me, 'We've been practising your name,' and sure enough Terry pronounced it clearly and smiled at his own success.

'Good boy,' said Mrs Stoddard.

I took a step closer. There were no scars, like Frankenstein's monster any more, perhaps because his hair had been combed carefully over his forehead to hide them. The hair, once fabulously untamed and falling to his shoulders, was cut like an old man's, with a dead-straight part on the left-hand side and every strand neatly suppressed and shining across the dome of his skull.

I bent forward to kiss him, but he stiffened and pushed back in the chair.

'He doesn't like people coming too close,' warned Mrs Stoddard.

'Susan,' Terry said again.

'It was awful,' I confessed to Diane on the drive to the airport. 'When I think of what he might have been. No one will know his name, no one will remember what he once was. An oversized child now, nothing more. Depends on his mother for everything. I felt terrible afterwards, leaving her to her loneliness. Then I had to front up to Tom. I'm starting to see parts of Terry in him now. He was all Kinnane when he was younger, but I guess the male side is starting to show through.'

'What does Tom make of it all?' she asked.

'Nothing yet. Mike doesn't think it's right to take him along just yet. Might upset him.'

Diane weighed up what she thought of this, but made no comment. Her tone remained serious, though, when she asked, 'What's the verdict on Mike's fiancée?'

'I like her, more than I expected to. They're made for each other and I suppose I'm happy about that, happy for Mike.'

'I was thinking more about . . .' But Diane lost her nerve and began to redden.

'It's all right. I know what you mean. I've made up my mind. The visit to Terry settled it somehow. Tom's staying here, with Mike and Lyn. I told them this afternoon.'

'But Sue, he's yours! You're his mother. It's the wrong choice.'

'Don't, Diane, please. It's done now. It was done a long time ago.'

'I don't understand you, Susan.'

'You don't need to. But I do need you to leave it alone.'

'Mum will go through the roof,' she said. 'She thought Mike getting married again would shake you up, make you see what you were missing out on.'

'Does Mum think of what Tom will be missing out on if I take him back to Sydney with me? I can't be a mother like you, Diane. It's not *in* me. Tom's happy here and I can't make him any happier. I'm starting a new job next week, the *National Times*, for God's sake. Do you know how many people I beat to get it? And they'll want their pound of flesh, too. I'll have to chase stories all hours of the night. I know you can't understand it, but this is the life I wanted, back at uni, before the Tower Mill.'

At the airport, we ignored the parking signs and sat in the car.

'I'm sorry I ranted at you, Di. Say you forgive me?'

'For the rant, yes. As for the other, I'm not so sure. Can I have Tom over to play with my kids? He's still part of the family.'

'That's up to Mike, and his new mother, too, I suppose.'

It was nothing more than a statement of fact but Diane's face showed her astonishment all over again. 'I don't get you, Sue, really I don't.'

I reached for the doorhandle but Diane put her hand on my elbow. 'Can I tell you something?'

I lowered my hand, sat back in the seat.

'I've gone on the pill. Four kids is enough and Jim still likes his Saturday nights.'

At last. Thirty years of Joyce telling you what to do is enough for anyone, I wanted to say. 'I'm proud of you,' I said instead, leaning across to kiss my sister, but her announcement called for more than a peck on the cheek. I hugged her as I'd seldom done before, and when she did the same I discovered the affection I'd craved all weekend.

'I've got a son and a sister who love me,' I said, tearing up. 'Too bad you both belong here and I don't.'

In Sydney, I took a cab from the airport, only to find the flat empty and cold. I sat in the dark for a while, telling myself it was the right decision and it was, too, but I still ached now that it was done.

Something else had floated up through this weekend, and only in the cold and the darkness did I admit it. Jealousy wasn't part of my nature, but that night I envied the man I was once married to, envied the easy intimacy he'd found; I could have done with a little of the joy that rayed out of Mike Riley like the Queensland sun.

TOM

I remember the first time I did it, and why. I was closer to seven than six by then, and memories from that age are unequivocally one's own; they remain deeply rooted to become the bricks of who you build yourself to be.

The day was special. I was taking my costume to school so Mrs Milavic could be sure it was right for the end-of-year concert, but that's not why the day was a marker in my life. I'd been thinking about the matter for some time, and especially in the car that morning, with Dad at the wheel and beside him this laughing, lively woman who'd come into my life. I'd been told to call her Lyn from our first meeting and I was a good boy so I did what I was told; but, all the same, my dad's name was Mike and I didn't call him Mike. I wanted to be like my friends.

When Lyn walked me into school, holding the hanger high, I took her other hand and, once my costume had been safely delivered to Mrs Milavic, said out loud for my classmates to hear: 'Goodbye, Mum.'

SUSAN
1979

The shop assistant was fitting a Bankcard form into the little machine when the pager began to buzz inside my handbag. I didn't need to check the tiny display to know it would be Brian.

'I'll wrap them myself,' I told the girl, and hurried through the ritual of signature, carbon copy and receipt. I'd chosen a racing car and a poster showing the relative sizes of dinosaurs. 'He's obsessed with them,' I'd explained to the assistant earlier.

'Mine, too. They all are at that age.' She'd replied with a knowing smile that was meant to link us as mothers. I wondered what she'd have thought had she known the car and the poster were going in the post.

With Tom's presents loose in a bag, I was quickly onto the concourse and checking the signs overhead. Public phone this way.

I was put through to my editor immediately: 'Susan! Thanks for calling so quickly. I've just seen the copy you showed to Morty. Sensational. This could blow the lid off the volcano. You're sure of your sources?'

'Of course.'

'How much crosschecking have you done?'

'I'm not a doe-eyed novice, Brian. The minister's been feeding details to Ridgeport for over a year, and I've got a sniff on another two donors.'

'Do you need help? This could turn into—'

'No, I'm on top of it and the last thing I want is some cowboy charging in to scare the horses.'

He paused, putting me on alert. 'I was thinking of bringing in Eddie Topfer on this one.'

'No you fucking won't!' I shouted into the phone, drawing the eyes of passers-by. 'It's *my* story, Brian. *I've* done all the legwork to get it this far, and I'm going to see it through on my own. Eddie'll want his by-line above mine, anyway.'

Brian laughed because it was true and left me to it. It was late, and I had notes to type up, which I did best at home. The days were shortening and my new flat was dark by the time I reached home. Janet now had a job with the *Age*, in Melbourne, which was just as well, since I'd have been a lousy flatmate. I grabbed meals on the run, and, once the review of each day's chicken scratch was done, I slept.

Tom's presents sat in their bag on the end of the table while I typed. I'd need wrapping paper; something with rocket ships or zoo animals. Did they make dinosaur wrapping paper? It had been a Christmas photo Mike had sent that prompted my comment to the shop assistant. I carried the photo in my handbag because it was such a lovely shot of Tom, sitting near the tree with a plastic triceratops in one hand and a tyrannosaurus in the other. He was smiling with his whole face, the way Mike used to do, and probably still did. Interesting nature–nurture experiment going on there. The slim feminine legs in the background were surely Lyn's.

Last year, I gave Tom his birthday present in person, but there was no way I could get up there this time. Must have it in the post tomorrow, I told myself, to be sure it was there for him to open on the thirty-first.

TOM

My mum, who happily signed her name Lyndall Cosgrove for the last time at Wanganui Gardens in 1978, is actually older than Dad by more than a year. I suspect that her age had something to do with Gabrielle's arrival only eighteen months after the wedding, or perhaps having one child in the house already reduced the incentive for delay. I was the perfect age to be fascinated by her bulging belly, which I insisted on listening to with my ear pressed up against the taut skin and claimed, once, to hear the baby speak to me. Gabby turned up one night, late in '79, while I was fast asleep at Aunty Jane's. Emma joined us two and a half years later, in time for my tenth birthday.

Somewhere in there, Dad had his first poems accepted by a 'small magazine' and, encouraged by this, submitted the best of a decade's work to University of Queensland Press. I was too young to have the least idea what it meant when shown the first precious copy of *The Unquiet Landscape of Silence*.

In those days, though, it was Susan who was hitting sixes in print. Years later, I ferreted about among the microfiche in the university library to find her articles, and excoriating stuff it was, too, written with just the right balance of worthy opprobrium and 'gotcha' journalism. A minister fell on his sword and there were other triumphs.

I was still a kid, though, when Mum was the scourge of dodgy politicians and even the unions she'd first worked for at the *Advocate*. Despite her idolisation of Whitlam, she was fearless in pursuing left as often as right and, to underscore her bipartisanship, is rumoured to have bedded men on both sides of the aisle, as the Americans would put it. That's not something a son particularly wants to verify.

To me, she was simply my Sydney mother, who sent fabulous presents for Christmas and birthdays and came for visits occasionally, during which I owned her completely. Heady stuff for any kid. She never stayed long, which didn't matter, because I had my Brisbane mum to listen to my woes, tuck me into bed and lend me the warmth of a soft feminine body whenever I needed its comfort. I loved them both as only a child can love, because there was no reason to do otherwise. What a life!

I knew I had two fathers, as well, one remote and one close at hand, just like my mothers, but unlike the mostly absent mum, the father named Terry never came to visit, never phoned and, more importantly, in the view of a seven-, eight-, nine-year-old, sent no presents, and it was this very practical issue that prompted my first serious questions.

'Terry is very sick,' was Mike's answer. 'Too sick to send you anything.'

That sufficed for a few days, until I returned with the reasonable observation that sick people eventually got better, so why couldn't he get with the program?

'What's made him sick is something you never get better from.'

Since Dad wasn't very forthcoming on the matter of my first father, and Mum didn't seem to know much at all, I cunningly took a different route and asked Susan the next time she came to Brisbane.

'Terry lives in a land where no one can reach him,' she told me. 'But you don't need to worry, Tom. He's happy where he is.'

Oh? And how could she know that, if no one could reach him?

Parents hate having their cleverness skewered by irrefutable logic, especially when the whistleblower only recently gave up believing in Santa Claus. I don't recall her response, except that it was vague and unsatisfying.

Although she didn't know it at the time, that visit was to be the last before a lengthy absence of Susan from my life, because, of course, other lives were on the move while I climbed the ladder of single-digit birthdays, hers as much as anyone's. One of the big broadsheets got tired of seeing the best stories in the *National Times* and went head-hunting. At little past thirty years of age, Susan Kinnane was writing front-page articles for a national daily and, after two years of this, when the paper's Washington correspondent resigned unexpectedly, Susan got the nod as his replacement.

My Brisbane mother spent these years crafting two exquisite sisters for me out of her own body, while, on the other side of the mattress, Dad opened the *Courier-Mail* one Saturday morning and saw that a private girls' school was looking for an English teacher. Family folk-lore records that at interview the head of department asked if he was Michael Riley, the poet, since he hadn't had the chutzpah to put this in his CV. He was offered the job there and then, even though a sadly expectant candidate still waited outside for her chance to impress.

God knows, there's no money in poetry, but that wasn't the only time Dad would be rewarded for all his lonely toil. His reputation grew modestly through the 1990s until, in 2003, East Anglia University invited him to Norwich as poet-in-residence for its creative writing summer school. That was why, when the news came about Terry, he was in England and in need of a last-minute flight to Brisbane, like me.

An airline seat might not be the best place for intimate discussion, but there were times on that journey when the hubbub of people moving about and the clatter of trolleys along the aisle offered a chance. Amid the many contemplations that overtook me on that flight, a question rose that I hadn't asked Dad before.

'Did Mum ever meet Terry?'

'Lyn? Only once. It was enough for her to know how sad it all was.'

'She wanted you to take me along as well, didn't she? You had a row about it.'

His answer was to stare at me, clearly caught out. 'I didn't realise you'd . . .'

'I heard you in your bedroom. They were the first cross words I ever heard between you.'

I could count the others on the fingers of one hand and still hold a coffee cup to my lips.

He nodded. 'They *were* our first cross words. It wasn't just the Terry business, more subtle than that. Couples don't normally argue over just one issue. Lyn was every bit your mother as I was your father and she expected the same amount of say. I was the one. I expected exclusive sway over the big things. Wasn't fair. And she was right about Terry, too, only I couldn't see it.'

'How did you work it out?'

'We compromised. I sat you down and I told you, instead of showing you. It was a mistake.'

'Yeah, I still remember it: "Your father had an accident a long time ago. His brain doesn't work properly and he has to be cared for like a child." Was he in the nursing home by then?'

'Yes, Mrs Stoddard died not long after Lyn and I got married. I'm sorry, Tom. I should have taken you to see him. It would have saved you a lot of upset.'

More than he knew. The exchange with Dad on that flight home had been prompted by a memory from my teens, shoved back into focus by Terry's death. I can't say that it was more painful than others I battled over the years, but it stands out because I faced it alone.

On the western slope of Red Hill in Brisbane, where Windsor and Musgrave roads meet at a sharp angle, there's a block of land of no use to home builders. Instead, a Moreton Bay fig had spread its largesse over the busy roads and a small post office that in the 1980s became a cafe.

I passed the spot every day on the way home from school. How old was I on the day I broke my journey for a closer look? Fourteen, maybe. I had no money for a drink, so I tried to hide behind the edge of the building at first. All a bit comical, if it hadn't seemed so serious to me at the time.

On the tip of the corner, beyond the boundary of the cafe's leasehold, I suppose, there was an old council bench. On that day, it was occupied by a single figure, as it was every afternoon, because no one else was likely to sit beside him. Busy with my friends and the delicious presence of girls on the bus, I hadn't given the man a second thought, but that quickly changed once Dad told me about my other father. After that, I became increasingly obsessed with what I saw, until one day I worked up the courage to leave the safety of the bus.

Once I could spy on him from close range, the detail appalled me even more. He was grubby and unkempt, his bare feet traced with black and jagged lines where dirt had become embedded in the cracks of his heels.

What I'd seen from the bus – more than the three days' growth on a bony chin and long greasy locks – was the performance. The man was never still. With the bench as his stage, he carried on a routine for anyone who cared to watch, folding his legs, right over left then left over right. He would twine his arms like snakes in his lap, and when they were locked together he'd rest his chin on the topmost hand. Then suddenly he would unfold, like a flower with its face to the sun, shedding petals of pain and loneliness and confusion.

In my hiding place, I was shaking. A fear had hold of me, no matter how much I told myself it couldn't be him. This man was too old. But the poor bugger might be twenty years younger than he looked.

Could I walk up to the man, ask his age? Why not his name?

But I knew he wouldn't be able to answer. His mind was gone and, with it, probably all memory, all recognition.

'Do you want a table?'

The waiter had sussed me out. My answer was to back away, stumbling over a chair, my bag colliding with a vacant table as I lurched onto the footpath. The man looked up at me, I could smell him, or was it my own fear? The traffic lights changed, leaving me free to cross, to go back to the bus stop where I could resume my journey home. But I stood there, staring, and on the edge of desperate tears. This wasn't my father, but was Terry any different?

TEN

SUSAN
1987

The carriage swayed and rocked to the irregular rhythm of the Tube.
I could have taken a cab to Heathrow and charged it to the paper, but
I liked the Underground and the chance it gave me to see the English
in all their boiled-beef and poorly dressed glory. Two hours from now
I would be in Paris, where the locals wore their clothes with panache,
even something as ubiquitous as a scarf. I wore the new heels I'd
bought in Kensington High Street especially for the occasion.

By Acton Park, though, the train was no longer underground;
grey rain spat against the window and I had to admit I was tired of
London, just as I'd grown tired of Washington.

I looked down at the research notes on my knee and re-read the
telex sent from Sydney overnight. Société d'Europa was rumoured to
be using proxies to take a position in the ANZ, and the editor wanted
me to draw Berringer out on this point to gauge his reaction.

At the bottom of the telex, I read again the teasing addendum:
*You're an ex-Queenslander, aren't you, Sue? You'll be interested to know
they've opened a royal commission into police corruption. Joh must have been
asleep at the cabinet table. Cheers, Joel.*

I shot a disdainful breath down my nose, just as I had the first time
I read it, and smiled privately at the reply I'd fired off: *I'll buy shares in
a whitewash factory. Never get rich on what you pay me.*

The autumn sun was out in Paris. Was it the dazzling light that
turned every Peugeot, Citroën and Renault into a Formula One
racer? My cab driver seemed especially afflicted.

'*Votre nom est Alain Prost, c'est bien cela?*'

'*Oui*, Alain Prost.' He laughed and, as though this boast needed proving, changed lanes for no reason that I could see.

'*Doucement, s'il vous plaît. J'ai tout mon temps.*'

I spoke in my best French, but it wasn't a language he understood, it seemed, and as a result I presented myself at Société d'Europa's offices ahead of time and was shown into a sumptuous antechamber to wait.

The decor of Australia's corporate offices exuded all the warmth of a witch's smile, in my opinion. Not this room. The high ceiling lent grandeur, the doors were double-height and inlaid with understated patterns of rosewood and mahogany, and wasn't that a Louis Quinze sideboard looking me over with Parisian insouciance from across the room? If Société d'Europa brought this sort of style with them, then Labor's decision to open up the financial sector would have secondary benefits.

At precisely eleven, the elegant doors opened and Robert Berringer came out to greet me.

'Ms Kinnane, I hope I have not kept you waiting,' he said, in a tone that instantly outshone the room. The accent was heavy but he'd pronounced 'Ms' perfectly, as though he'd been prepped by the PA who hovered behind his shoulder; a man, not some mademoiselle in a pencil skirt as so many were.

Berringer was barely three inches taller than me, but he carried himself like a larger man. Fine suit, Alain Delon haircut. Why did flecks of grey and crow's-feet bracketing the eyes make a man more attractive, while women became slaves to lotions and dyes? I knew from my notes that Berringer was forty-six years old and divorced for nearly a decade, having produced a pigeon pair of children who now lived with their mother.

'I'm honoured you've come all the way from Australia to interview me.'

Ah, he was trying the naivety-as-charm approach.

'I'm a Londoner these days,' I said, to deflect him, then wondered about the accuracy of my words. 'Not such an epic commute, after all.'

But he knew that.

While we negotiated the pleasantries he was sizing me up from head to toe and clearly approved of my new shoes. Italian men tended to rape you with their eyes, while the French merely noted how well the package was wrapped, withholding judgment about whether to undress you until they'd at least offered a coffee.

'Would you like *un café*, Ms Kinnane?'

The lapse into his own language was deliberate. Could I be charmed as a woman, could my questions be blunted by feminine distractions, would this gauche Australian-come-Englishwoman go starry-eyed at finding herself in the centre of civilisation?

We were seated by this time in exquisite chairs to the side of his desk. Time to set things straight for Monsieur Berringer.

'I'd like to begin by asking about some recent stock market trans-actions. Is Société d'Europa planning to take over one of Australia's big banks? The ANZ, for example?'

Surprise has a way of sneaking out between the cracks, especially when the charming smile is manufactured.

'What transactions are you referring to, Ms Kinnane?'

'Oh, please call me Susan.'

'In that case, you must call me Robert.' He pronounced his name in the French manner, lingering on the long final syllable. But I had beaten him to this offer of informality and tipped him off balance again. I went in hard with the share trading.

He claimed ignorance: 'Wouldn't that upset your Mr Keating?'

'Perhaps that's what your bank is trying to find out. Test the govern-ment's resolve. How open is this new policy and how much are they going to protect iconic brand names in the banking industry?'

'I can assure you, Susan, that Société d'Europa is setting up in Australia for the long haul.'

He quoted the official line, pretty much as I'd read it in the com-pany prospectus, but he was choosing his words carefully, in an English that belied the laboured accent and, as he spoke, he watched me cau-tiously. There was respect in those eyes. The charm of faux seduction had given way to the *pas de deux* of interview, which, for me, carried a certain charm of its own.

I backed my foot off the pedal. 'How will you like living in Australia?'

'I was in Sydney for a few days last month, to sign the lease for our offices. The bank has arranged an apartment for me overlooking . . . is it Rose Bay? Magnificent. It will be like living on the Riviera without the faded aristocrats and American widows in search of one last husband. I am looking forward to it.'

The last part was surely meant to make me feel proud of my home town, but his caricature of the Riviera coaxed a genuine smile onto my lips. We continued to dance around the bank's intentions, drawing laughter from one another on several occasions until he suddenly dispensed with the prospectus and spoke with real passion about the opportunities in a market energised by reform.

'You're a banker, yet your heart hasn't been removed, and your blood hasn't been replaced with iced water.' I said, wondering how he would react.

If he was insincere, this would sour the interview, I'd calculated, but instead my comment earned his freest smile so far.

'The dotted lines are drawn on my chest, ready for the surgeon,' he said, grabbing the lapel of his suit as though he wanted to show me, 'but so far I have avoided the knife. Tell me, Susan, are you always so hard on a man?'

'It's my job.'

'Oh! I'm sure I detected personal relish in what you said.'

Relish! His English was too good. Had I managed to strip back more from Robert Berringer than he realised?

A clock sounded eleven-thirty from somewhere behind me and, almost instantly, the PA appeared to announce the next appointment. Berringer waved him off with a hand splayed wide to indicate another five minutes. When the PA returned, we rose and shook hands.

'I have enjoyed our talk very much,' he said. 'So much, in fact, I would be delighted if it could continue this evening, over dinner. I'm sure we'll find something other than finance to discuss. Chest surgery, perhaps. Blood transfusions.'

I was booked on a six-thirty flight, and had only the outfit I stood in.

'Yes, I'd like to, very much,' I said, and laughed out loud at the madness of it all when, later, I stared through windows in Rue de Grenelle and dared imagine the price tags.

We ate at *Le Cochon à L'Oreille* near Les Halles, starting with *kirs royaux* and progressing on to a bottle of burgundy over *foie gras* and *entrecôte de boeuf*. Since I wore the same skirt and jacket, he had surely guessed at my impulsive change of plan, but despite this I didn't feel I was being talked into bed. The more we sparred across the table, the more his throaty English dissipated, until I had to challenge him about it.

'The accent is something I put on to entertain the tourists. Actually, I spent a year at Cambridge as a postgraduate and then two more in the US for Crédit Agricole.'

When it was my turn, I told him I'd been married, and, breaking a rule, I told him I had a son who lived with his father. Before I quite knew how, it was out there on the table between us that I'd seen little of Tom for five years, and none at all for the last three.

He raised his eyebrows. 'He will have changed a lot. I'm about to experience something similar with my own, but they are teenagers, of course. Their characters are largely formed.'

I hadn't made that connection between us until then.

In London the next day, I submitted my copy about Société d'Europa's plans and a profile of its first Australian CEO. In reply came a note from Joel.

We pay you plenty, especially when you file late. By the way, whitewash factories going broke in Queensland. The royal commission is drawing blood. Fun for young and old.

Before I left the office for my flat in Islington, I read all that the wires had to say about what was being called the Fitzgerald Inquiry. There was blood in the water, right enough – brothels and bookmakers had been paying off senior policemen and the commissioner had been stood down.

I remembered his name – Lewis – the fawning puppet Bjelke-Petersen had installed. Who else would fall, I wondered, while I waited on the crowded platform beneath Charing Cross.

Above ground again and approaching my flat in the autumn cool, I could see an enormous bouquet of irises propped against my front door.

Thank you for a delightful evening. Robert, read the card.

I hadn't given him my address, yet these flowers had come to my home, not the office where they would have been an embarrassment. Had he known as much? Sensitive or not, bankers were resourceful people, or their PAs were, and I loved irises. I was tempted to phone and tell him so.

It was a Friday night. I poured a glass of red and watched the late news, which, as ever, had nothing to report from Australia.

Fun for young and old, Joel's message had predicted. Despite the wine, I didn't sleep well and spent the weekend in an unfamiliar quandary until Monday, when I rang Joel in Sydney.

'I'm thinking about coming back to Oz.'

'Susan, my axe-wielding angel. We'll have you home by Christmas.'

TOM

Mike Riley was a teacher who wrote poetry and he didn't kid himself that those roles could be transposed. He was never going to win literary prizes or have his name spoken by prime ministers and this was why the residency in 2003 was such a thing for him – a tick of recognition, and from East Anglia, a university renowned for its creative writing program, too. What did it matter that it was for a summer school in Norwich, not a semester? When he rang to tell me, his excitement couldn't quite smother the pride; this time it was the dad who was desperate to show off the ribbons he'd won on sports day.

He was never going to fly off to England without Mum, either. They used their long service leave to make a decent go of it and didn't they have a ball. Gabby, Emma and I had all beaten Mum and Dad to Europe, which made them determined to see everything, taste it, swim in it, to make their own what had always seemed so far away. Once Dad started in Norwich, Mum was to head back to Brisbane, and with that day looming they spent the last week with me in London.

Hilary was gone by then. They were too polite to say anything and too open-faced to hide their disappointment. We thought she was the one, their silent glances told me, even though they had never met her. With explanations left unspoken, I did my best as tour guide and snatched a day off work to show them around, as I'd done when Susan came the year before. That was the day we went to the National Portrait Gallery. It sticks in my mind because of a single moment that occurred there, before a portrait of Germaine Greer, of all people.

You'd think a bit of company in a flat that I now had to myself would enliven me, but, in truth, they made me more aware of Hilary's absence. After the first gush of catching up, I felt myself going dry and started in with questions about home, and people I hadn't seen in years – or cared about for longer.

On the second night, Dad shot a breath down his nose and smiled like a happy devil. 'A famous old name popped up in the papers just before we left, in fact. Do you remember the police commissioner exposed by Fitzgerald?'

'Lewis?' I said instantly.

'That's him,' said Dad. 'Wants his superannuation back, apparently. Says it shouldn't have been forfeited just because he went to gaol.'

'You're joking. Has he run out of the money he took in paper bags?'

'You're getting your villains mixed up, Tom. Joh was the one who liked paper bags for his cash. And Joh's on the make, too, now that I mention him. Thinks he should be compensated for lost business opportunities because nobody'd touch him after Fitzgerald. He's made an application to the government.'

If Mum hadn't been there I would have let fly with more than 'Bloody hell! Shows how much he cares about the damage he caused. I tell you, I'm going to piss on that man's grave!'

'That's a bit over the top, Tom,' said Mum. 'What are you so hot about Joh for? He'd gone before you even left school.'

Dad saw it the same way. He leaned forward on the sofa and said more seriously, 'It was our generation that copped all of Joh's crap.'

No, Dad, I wanted to say, that crap was mine, even more than it was yours. But I didn't say it, just as I'd kept quiet a dozen times before when the urge had taken me. It was Susan's story. She'd kept the Bindy letter from him and I wondered what good it would do to tell him now.

SUSAN
March, 1988

They were the hottest seats in town. Even a year into the Inquiry, there was often a queue outside the court, the Brisbane boys told me, and it doubled in length whenever another big fish was about to go belly up. The police pond was already ripe with putrid carcasses.

I wasn't actually covering the Fitzgerald Inquiry for my paper. I had wangled my way to Brisbane a few times on blatantly false pretences, but when the name I'd been waiting for came up, I simply took leave. I couldn't miss his moment on the hook.

I was at the court in George Street in plenty of time and with a borrowed press pass to be sure of a seat, for today the gavel would fall on his head at last. There would be no damage for the surgeons to mend, not like there was for Terry Stoddard, but the bastard's life would never be the same.

I could barely sit still while the hearing room filled. Council assisting appeared, consulted with associates and rifled notes at a lectern facing the commissioner's bench. I didn't see the commissioner take his seat, nor take in the murmur of those around me.

'The commission calls Detective Senior Sergeant Barry Dolan.'

And suddenly he was there. I had stared at his photograph many times, more than one shot, in fact, because the higher you climbed in the police force the more often the media wanted your face. I knew what his voice would sound like, after the phone call years earlier, but this was the first time I'd sighted his flesh, finding it pink, not newsprint grey after all, and with the bulk of it buttoned into an ill-fitting suit. Even so, he couldn't hide his humiliation. I breathed it in as he passed in the aisle.

The years hadn't been kind. What had once been a formidable frame now sagged beneath too many shouts with his mates, or was it too much time at the trough? His jowls were wider than the sweating forehead and even accounting for a sleepless night, he seemed withered. He was forty-five years old, I knew, young to have risen to the rank he would soon lose, thanks to the services rendered and favours proffered in return, which now hung about him like a shroud.

'They're going to bury you,' I said, under my breath.

'Detective Senior Sergeant, is it correct that you have made certain admissions to investigators representing this Inquiry?'

A long pause followed, yet even the most stubborn must yield eventually.

The answer extracted itself like a stubborn tooth. 'Yes.'

'And what was the nature of those admissions?'

I remembered Tom in his highchair, many years ago, with his little mouth clamped shut against the spoonful I was determined to get down his gullet. I wanted to shout at Dolan, Open wide, you fucker. There are no thirty-six-inch batons in this courtroom, no darkness to hide you, no frightened mates to keep their traps shut. Open wide, swallow the purgative, and let *me* be cleansed.

'Senior Sergeant?' prompted Council.

'That I have received payments.'

Come on, Barry, you could do better than that – which Council Assisting reminded him, until it came out at last.

'Illegal payments, yes.'

'Corrupt payments?'

'Yes.' It didn't seem so hard now.

'How much did you receive in corrupt payments?'

'I'm not sure.'

'How much was each payment, in rough terms?'

'Five hundred dollars.'

'And approximately how often did you receive such payments?'

I once interviewed a torturer in Egypt, who trained Alsatian dogs to attack naked men in their cells. The injuries, shown to me in photographs, had turned my stomach, but the moment of purest horror came when I realised he enjoyed inflicting such pain. On that day, before Commissioner Fitzgerald, I understood my Egyptian torturer. The savage bite of Council's questions couldn't elicit enough agony, as far as I was concerned. I wanted the shame to linger in his florid face, so that I could savour it like no one else. Hadn't I come halfway round the world to see it?

Dolan's admissions continued, while the crowded courtroom listened in silence. It was a familiar litany, which I'd read many times in the transcripts stretching back to before I left London. Corruption was so banal, so unimaginative; grubby notes palmed to look the other way when passing the door to a brothel or a backroom casino that half of Brisbane knew was there. No wonder Lewis and his mates dubbed it 'The Joke'.

But this was all Dolan had to answer for. There were no questions about a young man running through Wickham Park on a cold winter's night, no questions about undue force or a conspiracy with an unnamed constable to make what happened look like an accident. Dolan didn't know that a woman in the court wanted to put those questions to him, a woman he'd dismissed as a joke as well, more than ten years ago. He'd got away with that one, and for all I knew he'd forgotten it ever happened.

Today he was being held to account for something, at least.

I began to cry, too loudly to go unnoticed. The commissioner himself glared at me from the bench because I was interrupting vital testimony. Did I seem like a relative, a sister? Oh God, he thought I was the bastard's wife!

I blundered free of the courtroom, and, in the seclusion of the ladies' room, sobbed as loudly as I damned well needed to, for the seventeen years I'd waited and wasted and hated myself because of what I couldn't do, and which today was being carried out by others who didn't even know what Dolan had destroyed.

*

Later that day, I met Tom. Our meeting had been arranged before I was quite sure when Dolan would appear at the Inquiry, and I knew I couldn't simply fail to turn up when I'd been so cruel to him on my last visit.

For some reason, he stopped at the old windmill and was looking away from the Tower Mill Hotel, where we'd agreed to meet. Then, as I tried to join him, he started towards me, throwing his school bag over his shoulder as he walked.

Oh God, Terry once carried an old-fashioned briefcase like that. I saw Terry in his face, too. The nose, the line of his jaw. I'd picked these out years ago, before I left for overseas, but today, after the hearing, the similarities became a fist closing tightly around my heart.

I asked him what he knew about 1971.

He stared blankly at me. I prompted him with the Springboks and the State of Emergency.

He shook his head.

'Come with me,' I demanded, leading him to the place beside the path where Terry had lain for hours while the pressure inside his skull crushed all trace of the man he'd been. 'This is where your father was found. Your *real* father,' I told him, even though the emphasis sounded cruel in my throat.

'This is where it happened?' he asked, that same face darkening in fear.

No, I wanted to say. The worst of it happened somewhere else in the park. Impossible to know where. I couldn't explain, though. Instead I said, 'You've seen what it did to him.'

Another long stare, then, 'No. I've never seen him.'

'Mike hasn't taken you? Not even when your grandmother died?'

'Terry's mother?' he said, stunned. 'I didn't know I had another grandmother.'

'I don't believe this. Come on,' I said. 'It's time you met your father.'

There was a taxi rank downhill from the Tower Mill, for patients visiting the specialists along Wickham Terrace. Tom followed me – I was moving too quickly and we didn't speak until I had him in the cab.

'You mean we can visit him? But I thought . . . I had this idea he was a long way off, that I couldn't see him.'

'No, Tom, he lived with his mother out in Coopers Plains until she died. That's the grandmother you never knew you had. Bloody Mike. I'm going to have a piece of him over this.'

'I asked, but Dad said it wasn't possible. That's why I thought . . .'

He stopped there and said no more during the twenty-minute journey.

His silence only made me more angry, and once the cabbie was paid the same fury made me march him to the reception desk as though I was delivering a miscreant to the principal's office.

'Mr Stoddard's in his room watching television,' the nurse told us, and since I knew the way I was off again without a glance over my shoulder. Only when I arrived at Terry's door did I find that Tom wasn't behind me. He was half a corridor away and motionless.

Despite the half-dark, I could see every line of uncertainty in his face, every fear, every tremor.

'Tom?'

He turned and started away, making me run to catch him before he'd turned the corner. 'Tom.'

'I can't,' he said.

Susan, you're a bigger fool than Mike Riley I told myself. The boy is petrified and he has every right to be; he's about to meet his father for the first time.

'Oh Tom, I didn't understand what a moment this would be for you.'

He fell against the wall, his head limp on his chest and weeping despite manly efforts to silence himself.

I pressed my forehead against his. 'It's all right.'

'What if I can't stand it?'

'You'll be all right. I know you will.' I shifted closer and slipped my arms around him, the first time I'd truly held him like that since he was a toddler.

'But what's he like?' At this lament, I saw deeper into my son than I'd ever been privileged to see before. This was what it was like, being mother to a child you could no longer lift into your arms.

A nurse approached along the corridor, unseen by Tom, who kept his head down. She stopped a few metres off and enquired with her face alone whether she could help.

I shook my head just enough to answer and she continued on her way. Then, as tenderly as I could manage, I spoke into his ear.

'He's like an oversized little boy, Tom, if that makes any sense. He'll be watching cartoons because the colour and the movement make him laugh. He's not a monster and he's certainly not dribbling and pathetic. Come and see for yourself and then you don't need to be afraid.'

I felt his body relax in my embrace and loosened it a little so he could stand up straight, wiping quickly at a tear in the hope I wouldn't notice. I pretended not to, then took his hand and led him to the door.

TOM

Imagination can be as deadly as it is playful and the more apprehensive you are about something, the more sharply it sways towards the deadly.

I had imagined my father in many guises, most often as a homeless man who roamed the streets of Red Hill. To find him in clean clothes and smiling, vacantly perhaps, but well cared for and content within the limited world left to him, brought a relief I owed entirely to Susan. Something changed that day, even if it didn't end.

Terry Stoddard was nothing like any of the pictures I had drawn inside my head, frightening or otherwise. He was pudgy around the middle and losing his hair, with similarities between his face and mine that could be noticed if we stood side by side, but not enough for strangers to pick us out as father and son.

The only heartache I felt in that room came when Susan told him my name and, smiling up at me, he repeated it, immediately and accurately. Because of this, I thought for an instant there might be a real intelligence behind his eyes and a recognition of who I was.

'No, Tom, there's nothing there,' Susan assured me, when I said as much. 'Don't torture yourself and don't waste any time hoping, like I did.'

Mostly what I remember, along with the relief, was the sense that we made a family, just the three of us in that room, my real father in a chair in the corner, the mother who had carried me inside her body standing by the door and between them, their son. Three different surnames, maybe, but one family all the same.

I said so, adding, 'This is the first time we've been together,' and when Susan heard that she surprised me with heavy, painful tears.

I went to her. She had played mother for me in the corridor outside Terry's room and now it was my turn to play the son. I wasn't playing, though, because I'd moved spontaneously, and what was to say she hadn't spontaneously found the right words to coax me inside?

'I've got some things to settle with Mike,' she said, and it took me a few moments to catch up. In fact, we were in the cab before I was fully aware of the change in her. No more tears. She was angry now, and eager to dump that anger over the target area.

Dad's Camry was parked in the driveway when the cab pulled up in Ashgrove.

'Is that Mike's?' she asked.

I could only nod.

'Keep the meter running,' she told the cabbie. 'I'll be five minutes.'

Dad had seen us pull up and was waiting with the front door open and a condescending smile on his face that disappeared when Susan came straight to the point.

'We've just come from the nursing home.'

He stood aside to let her into the lounge room and waited for me to pass as well, his eyes searching my face to see how the visit had affected me, but he was looking for something else, too, I was sure of it. He knew he'd been caught out and he was already trying to guess what this would do to things between us.

In the lounge room, Susan set to work. 'I can't believe you've kept Tom from seeing Terry all these years. He had the right, you know. I had no idea it was like this.'

Another man might have launched into her that she'd been absent from my life for five years and barely present for five before that. Dad wasn't like that.

He looked over his shoulder towards Mum, who was watching from the doorway into the kitchen. Her face was hard to read – full of sympathy for a loved one about to cop a hiding, but holding back a little in an I-told-you-so kind of way. Emma came to watch, too, attaching her six-year-old self to Mum's legs, and at this interruption Lyn picked up my sister and went off calling for Gabby as well. I saw the three of them soon after through the window, the girls bouncing happily on the trampoline at the bottom of the garden. Dad was on his own.

'I didn't think Tom was ready to see Terry. I thought it would upset him.'

'Bullshit! How long were you going to wait? Until he's thirty?'

'When he left school. I was . . .' But Dad couldn't seem to convince even himself.

Susan ripped into him again and this time Dad reacted. Back and forth they went about what was appropriate for me and how I would feel about Terry and when was the right time and what a boy of ten, or twelve or fourteen could handle.

'Stop it, the pair of you!' I called. 'This is me you're talking about. I'm right here. Why don't you ask me what would have been best?'

I'd silenced them as I'd intended to, but I'd turned the focus on me when I hadn't quite worked out what *would* have been best. It meant, too, that whatever I said, I'd end up taking the side of one against the other. It had never been an issue before, there had always been Dad on the sideline during the game, Dad in the audience applauding when I was handed the prize, Dad at the dinner table charting a path through my conundrums. Susan was the sender of presents, the voice on the phone, and so far away no clash was possible. I was well and truly pincered now. No way back, only forward.

'Dad, it wasn't right,' I said. 'I've wanted to meet my real father for years, I asked you about him and you lied to me. It wasn't fair.'

Would I have said that if Susan hadn't been there and on my side? I doubt it. I'd been angry at Dad about a lot of things, mostly what I was allowed to do, to say, or to have as my own, but there had been other times, as well, when something more deeply rooted was at stake. Not that I could remember what those things were at the time; it was the anger unable to find expression that became indelible, and this was the first occasion, at just short of sixteen, I allowed myself to simply go with it.

And I did. I didn't quite work myself into a rage because I hadn't inherited that particular gene from my mother, but I didn't lay it all out for him as passionlessly as a debating argument, either.

'You don't know how much I used to think about what he was like, what a wreck he would be, and then when I finally meet him, he's perfectly all right, just simple, like a big kid, nothing to be scared of. You shouldn't have done this to me. You should have let me see him all along.'

There was more, all of it heartfelt and most of it forgotten now, since it was more the emotion that I was discovering within myself that has stayed, that and the regret in Dad's face as I let out the hurt that I was only then discovering ran deeper inside me than I'd ever imagined.

Afterwards, I went with Susan out to car, very much aware that I had sided with her against everything that had loved me and kept me safe for as long as had memories. Susan was pleased with herself, pleased that she'd righted a wrong. Was she pleased with herself, too, because we'd come closer together that afternoon?

I guess she was, yet her departure left me thinking back to Terry's room, where I'd wanted to step close, I'd wanted us to meld together in a bucket of tears, and once we grew tired of that we would have laughed at ourselves for being such cry babies and she would have told me stories about the man who bound us together.

As she waved to me from the taxi, I felt vaguely cheated, but what could I do except head back inside to Mum and Dad, who were not my parents, and the sisters who were not my sisters.

SUSAN
March, 1988

After the Inquiry was done with Barry Dolan, I lingered an extra day to make sure Tom was all right. He seemed so, and even though he was a little stand-offish when I went round to say goodbye, he hugged me with real affection when it was time to go. I returned that affection in spades, surprised by the need in me.

On the way to the airport, I dropped in on Terry. It was getting easier, now. He was watching TV in his room, which seemed the sum total of his days, despite assurances that patients were taken on regular outings.

Did he recognise me after my recent visits? Again, I had only the nurses' word that he did know faces if he saw them often enough. He smiled in the way the uncertain do, as a form of defence, but the noise and colour of the screen soon drew his eyes away. I sat beside him, wishing suddenly that I could take his hand, for my comfort, not his. But no, touching made him anxious; the nurses were adamant about that.

'What did you think of Tom?' I asked him.

Did it matter if he made any sense of the question?

'I had it out with Mike afterwards, over never bringing Tom to see you. I'm still furious about that . . .'

A male nurse stuck his shaggy head through the open doorway. 'I heard talking,' he said, clearly surprised. 'Sorry, seemed unusual, that's all.' And immediately he was gone.

'You don't talk, do you, Terry? There's nothing going on in there that would let you know your own son. Would you get on together if you suddenly snapped out of the netherworld? Or would you be like me? I didn't like what I saw in him, at first. An awkward boy in his oversized body and watching bloody football over my shoulder while I scratched around for things to say. He was so complacent, so stitched up, a copy of Mike Riley instead of . . . what? You and me? I don't want him to be a copy of anyone.

'I'm glad I brought him here to see you, though. I didn't realise how vulnerable he was, how easily he could break. He seemed so grown up when I came back from London. And then he sided with me against Mike. Maybe there's more of you in him than he shows. That'd be good, wouldn't it, Terry?

'He's going to be a good-looking man, too, like you were, and he's no fool. Top of the heap at school, according to Mike. Wish he wasn't at Terrace, all that testosterone and born-to-rule bullshit.'

I was mouthing off as though I didn't have a say in any of it, and I didn't, really. No point in pushing for a change when he'd be finished next year.

'Too late. Too late for a lot of things,' I said. 'We'd have raised him differently . . .'

Had I spoken too loudly, or was there something in my tone of voice that made Terry turn my way? It was enough to make the fantasy fall in on itself and with his vacant face waiting for enlightenment I told him the truth: 'We talked about an abortion, didn't we? Pretty much decided. No getting away from that. Then the Tower Mill.'

Terry continued to stare, waiting for more, as though he was happy to listen.

'Was I wrong to leave him with Mike? If there's one question I wish you'd answer for me, that's it. He was your son, too, Terry. I'm sorry, more sorry now that I see what kind of man he's going to be, but I had to do it the way I did, if I was going to stay the person you knew.'

If I went on like this I would make myself cry. Ridiculous. It was seventeen years ago.

Could you love a son the way you loved his father? And then I was crying and couldn't stop, even in the cab on the way to the airport.

ELEVEN

TOM

When do you stop talking to your parents? Boys are supposed to become grunters in their early teens, according to the cliché, so what made me the exception, because I kept gabbing to Mum, Dad and the teachers at Terrace, right through to my mid-teens. For me, the silence came later, and focused mainly on Dad. Even then, it was only about certain things, as though I'd built a private room at the end of the hall and went there alone to be with Terry and Susan. I doubt anyone else noticed, except Mum, who could be a winged Cerberus at times, guarding the nest she'd built for her two blond-haired daughters and the gangly youth I had become by my final year at school. I'd started calling myself the cuckoo's child by then, recognising the out-sized comparison I made with Gabby and Em as a telltale sign that the stealthy bird had paid a visit.

Then, suddenly, I wasn't a schoolboy any more, and without quite knowing why, I settled on journalism at UQ.

No, that's not true. The reason was all too obvious and Dad knew it. He would have accepted my choice better if Susan hadn't started flying me down to Sydney to spend time with her and then, of course, there was the holiday in Europe at the end of first year. He and Mum couldn't possibly indulge me like that, with two girls to put through All Hallows' and mortgage interest rates touching seventeen per cent.

How many eighteen-year-olds know about interest rates, though? When Susan dangled an airline ticket in front of my nose and promised Christmas in Paris, I snatched at the chance. Of course I did.

SUSAN
1990

Travelling with a teenager was an education, or perhaps a revisitation, if there is such a word. Since the day I'd started at the *Advocate*, through three years at the *National Times* and my career with the dailies, I'd been up with the sun. It was easy to forget that, before then, I could sleep until noon and think nothing of it.

On Christmas Eve, when Tom finally emerged in search of a late breakfast, I told him what lay ahead for the day.

'Robert's taking his kids out to Chantilly, to visit their grandparents. Rapid fire French all day, I'm afraid. Best if we don't go.'

'Just you and me, then,' he said, and the pleasure with which he spoke grew midwinter blooms in my belly. I'd already played the tour guide for his wide-eyed early days in Paris, when there were so many icons to tick off, and found myself dredging up obscure details about the city.

Robert was impressed. 'How in the blue blazes did you know that?'

He loved inserting what he thought were Australianisms into our banter, especially when Tom was around.

My greatest triumph had been the extraordinary public toilet beneath La Madeleine, which offered the delectable pretence that we'd descended not a flight of stairs but an entire century. From its pissoires, Tom could wave to me if he hadn't been a touch embarrassed.

'What will we do instead?' he asked over his coffee.

'There's a market street Robert says we should visit out near the red light district. And don't get any ideas, you'll be on a tight leash.'

A bitter December breeze channelled along Boulevard de Clichy as we climbed up from the Metro at Pigalle. 'Holy fuck,' he complained.

'Wimp!'

'Where's my mother's care and sympathy?'

'You're twice my size. About time you took care of me,' I teased.

The gawkiness of his teens was washing out of him, revealing a lean young man, broad-shouldered and handsome – I saw the girls eyeing him off, and thirty-something matrons, too – and was I the only one who saw it, or was there a tangibility about his potential?

As Robert had warned, the footpaths along the boulevard were seedy with sex shops and peepshows. After a couple of blocks, I guided him with a hand under his elbow into the shelter of Rue Lepic; and shelter it was, too, from both the wind and the bawdy neon. Stalls spilled amber light and their riotous jumble of wares into our path, first a chaotic butcher's shop crammed with sausage and hung with gutted pigs and unplucked turkeys that needed only a twinkle in their eyes to fly again. A barrow of flowers straddled the gutter.

'Where do they grow flowers at this time of year?' Tom asked.

'Fly them in from North Africa,' I said, the faux expert once more.

He wanted to buy me a bouquet of tulips but I forestalled him because they'd have been awkward to carry round for the rest of the day, then regretted my practicality when he looked so crestfallen.

He was fascinated by the snails, but baulked in horror at tasting one and, at a basket of oysters, had to be tutored in the pronunciation of *huîtres*.

'Not *wheat*, darling.'

I was touching his arm again, hugging him to myself. 'Make an *aitch* sound and turn it into a double u.'

'Still, your French is better than your father's.' I laughed, aware too late that I was forgetting who his real father was.

But Tom knew who I meant and threw back his head in acknowledgment. 'I know, he used to test my vocab. Didn't sound anything like Mademoiselle Lernier.'

'Mademoiselle?'

'A dish, much too pretty to be a teacher at Terrace, but not as pretty as you,' he said.

'Worm.'

He put his long arm around me and kept it there until the next corner when we had to jump our separate ways or be parted more violently by a motorbike. I hoped his arm would return, but it didn't. Robert often looped an arm around me as we walked, my husband in all but name and, while I welcomed it, this intimacy with Tom was something different.

Paris was a lovers' cliché, and, as I climbed Montmartre with my son, I smiled at the absurdity of falling in love.

It was a steep climb to the top, and we were in no hurry: Tom, because each street was a wonderland; and me, for delays of my own that I was too happy to examine. When the ground flattened out, so did Tom's interest, as the city of Parisians ceded the streets to charcoal artists and racks of *I Love Paris* t-shirts.

We broke through to the steps of Sacré-Coeur with the city spread out before us, crowned by a pale, unblemished blue, and here I was suddenly beset by memory.

'What is it?' Tom asked, when I began to cry softly, soundlessly.

I hadn't seen them coming, hadn't imagined that words said for a laugh amid sex-tangled sheets could reach across two decades and round the planet to snatch the breath from my lungs.

'Your father brought me here,' I said.

'Dad! But you two never . . .'

'Terry,' I corrected him, more sharply than I'd intended. 'He took me on a tour, fed me at Maxim's, kissed me in a garret with the Eiffel Tower right outside our window.'

He still didn't understand, and how could he, when it wasn't true.

If I'd tried to explain, there, in the middle of Paris, only my anger and guilt would have escaped into the chill. I knew what had been done to Terry and yet I'd given up chasing the bastards who were responsible. My punishment seemed clear enough, here, in the middle of Paris. This wonderful day with my son, who was Terry's son, too, was to be taken from me.

In the silence, Tom moved closer to put his arm around me, as I'd invited him to do all morning.

'No, it's all right,' I said, putting my hand against his chest to stop him pressing closer. 'I'll be all right in a minute.' And to recover myself I walked away until the worst of it passed.

By then, of course, the fun had gone skipping away from us, and although I tried to fetch it back he seemed oddly reluctant.

In the weeks after Paris, I thought of Tom almost every day, not in passing, but in the long silence before sleep and over coffee in the bustle of the newsroom. I was mother to an almost-man. He needed to know things that a child could not.

That was why, early in the new year, I found myself among strangers who, like me, followed a line painted on the stark concrete until we were inside a room surprisingly alive with children. They had come to see their fathers, of course, attended by weary mothers who didn't share the joy of reunion with quite the same enthusiasm, if I was any judge.

Soon after, a different door opened and men filed in, watched languidly by the uniforms stationed around the room. One man stopped in front of my small table.

'You Kinnane?' he asked, and when I nodded he slipped into the seat opposite.

'You know I'm a journalist, right? I made that plain when I asked to see—'

'I know who you are. I've read your stuff in the papers.'

He was aggressive, an attitude that had surely served him well on the force. No doubt it was a handy shell in gaol, as well. He was slimmer than I remembered from the courtroom and his face no longer the florid crimson of his trial. A year on this prison farm had browned it along with the lean and powerful arms he set in place on the table like twin sphinxes. I tried to forget for a moment what those arms had done.

'Then you know that nothing sympathetic is likely to come out of this interview,' I said.

He dismissed this with a grim chuckle and said again, 'I know who you are. We spoke on the phone once, a long time ago. Your name was Riley, then. Kinnane's your maiden name.'

'If you know that, why did you agree to see me?'

He shrugged and asked, less forcefully this time, 'Are you here as Riley or Kinnane?'

'My name wasn't Riley for very long and, as you say, it was a while ago. The time I want to talk to you about is before I got married. So the answer, I suppose, is Kinnane.'

'Seventy-one, the Tower Mill,' he guessed. 'That is going back a long way.'

'It sticks in your mind when the man you love suddenly becomes a vegetable,' I said, matching his belligerence.

Dolan leaned back, taking his arms from the table while he observed me dispassionately for long seconds, no doubt making connections. He seemed to have a good memory, another valuable skill in a detective. More than likely he'd been good at his job, the one he was paid for by the Queensland Treasury.

'How are you getting on here?' I asked, backing off to let him think. 'It's almost a year since they transferred you from Wacol.'

'It's better. I was segregated from other prisoners for a long time when they first put me away. Saved me from being bashed, but it didn't save me from finding a turd in my shepherd's pie, petty stuff like that.'

'At least you didn't get your head kicked in.'

He made that connection quickly enough.

'Is that why you've come, to gloat, to be sure I'm festering to your satisfaction?'

I had often thought of Dolan behind bars in the aftermath of his trial, not in a pool of his own blood, but among other felons, the fox made to sit among the chickens because he'd made himself one of them. But that wasn't why I'd come and I told him so.

'Then why?'

'Because I have a son. Terry Stoddard's son. I was already pregnant on that night at the Tower Mill. He's at university now, growing into a fine young man. At the moment, he doesn't know that Terry's injury wasn't an accident. He's old enough to know the truth and when I tell him, he might reasonably ask why I haven't done more to see justice done for his father.'

Still tilted away from me, his arms now folded, Dolan asked, 'Have you come to ask my permission or for a confession? You're wired up, is that it, hoping to trap me into saying something?'

'You watch too much television. Besides, you seem to have put yourself away for a long stretch without any help from me.'

It was catty of me and I knew it. Worse, I'd surrendered the moral high ground in exchange for a cheap shot. He had every right to say fuck off, lady, and go back through the steel door. But Dolan surprised me again by smiling faintly and resting his arms back on the table.

'Touché,' he said. 'But what you're saying about '71, there's no evidence. There was never anything you could do.'

I reached into my handbag. Across the room a guard stirred and watched me with interest until he saw I'd simply taken out a sheet of paper. Carefully, for the letter was fragile from numberless re-readings, I opened out the folds and slipped it across the table.

Dolan read it all the way through.

'Still won't get you anywhere. It's unsigned and the man who wrote it is dead.'

Was this a bluff?

'Road accident,' said Dolan, when he saw me weighing up the claim. 'Hit a tree out past Emerald somewhere. He was drunk, not an unusual state for him, apparently. Not that you'll read that in the official report.'

It was the truth, I could be sure of it, and it didn't matter anyway. I hadn't come to trap Dolan or threaten him and he seemed to accept that now. It changed the tone of his voice.

'I was shit scared, you know, by what I'd done. A rage of the moment thing. We were so fired up.' He stopped and looked me in the face. 'That probably sounds like an excuse. It's not. I don't know what difference it makes to you, but it's the one thing I'd change if

I had my time over, even more than . . .' He let his hand wander in a vague reference to his surroundings. You get a lot a time to yourself in a place like this. Not physically, but maybe you can guess what I mean.'

'You didn't show a lot of regret when you telephoned me out of the blue.'

'No, mustn't have sounded that way. When I called you, I didn't know why you'd been asking about me. Once I did, well, it was pointless to pursue me. Different time, back then, different climate. You were never going to get anywhere. When was that, '75?'

I nodded, once again stunned by the accuracy of his recall. 'The same time Whitlam was sacked.'

'Was it?' he said. 'That makes sense. Joh'd helped to get rid of him by putting that clown into the Senate. He was on top of the heap. We knew the score by then. Nothing could touch us.'

He leaned forward and spoke with a sincerity that couldn't be feigned: 'You know, the stuff that happened, the bribes, the raid on those pathetic hippies up north, we did it because we could. That was the main reason. Government wasn't going to stand in the way as long as we kept up our side of the bargain. In fact, the bribes we took seemed like payment for services rendered. There was nothing to stop us. That was the real corruption, not the money, it was knowing there was no check on what you could get up to, except the next guy up the line who was pocketing more than you were.'

He stopped suddenly and held my eyes. His own were as hard as ever, I saw, which was why his remorse seemed authentic.

'When you've told your son, will you want to bring him here? I won't see him, you know. This is not a zoo. I'm not here to be gawped at.'

'No,' I said. 'I'll show him this letter and tell him your name. The rest is up to him.'

TOM

Dad wasn't the only one who held things back from me until I was 'ready', although in the case of the dog-eared letter Susan finally showed me after Paris, it would be more correct to say, until *she* was ready. The trip to France had changed things for her, I think. My birthday was the excuse for the gift of an airline ticket to Sydney.

Did she fly me down for the sole purpose of showing me the letter? She didn't produce it like 'Exhibit A' while I was still fresh from the airport. Thinking about it later, I recognised how she steered conversation and invited questions more openly than during my earlier visits.

I had things on my mind, too, questions I wanted to ask, but until then had lacked, not so much the courage but a pathway into my mother's complexity. I knew all I needed to know about Terry Stoddard by then, but far too little about Susan Kinnane and the decisions she had made fifteen years earlier. Yet I still couldn't bring myself to ask, straight out, why she had let Mike Riley raise me as his own. Instead it seemed better to broach the matter in the way she always seemed to do: I asked why she hated Queensland so much.

'I don't,' she responded, in honest surprise.

'You did once. Dad told me. You were adamant about it. You weren't going back there, you were never going to set foot in Queensland ever again. He says it like he's quoting you.'

'From a long time ago, Tom. I go there now to see you, to see Terry. You can love a place, but dislike the people who live there, and it's only some of them, anyway. There was a time, in the '70s and

239

'80s, when there seemed to be too many who got my goat. I couldn't stand the politics. Had to get out.'

Had she skilfully nudged me towards that question and I simply hadn't noticed? Whether that was true or not, I had created the perfect opening for her, and she took it up seamlessly.

'You're nineteen tomorrow, aren't you, Tom?' Without waiting for me to respond, she said, 'I was nineteen when I met Terry. There's something you need to see. It will answer the question you just asked better than any explanation I can give.'

She rose and went along the hall to the bedroom she shared with Robert, who was off with clients that night. She didn't immediately emerge, and I've since sketched a scene in my mind where she stands considering what she holds in her hand. Until that moment, only a friend she had once lived with and a journalist named Obermayer had ever seen the letter, and neither could have experienced the personal connection that it held for Susan. Only I could share that.

When I looked up to watch her approach along the hall, she was carrying the kind of plastic sheaf that clips into a ring binder. Seating herself beside me, she placed the sheaf on the table, more in front of me than her, where I quickly saw it contained a handwritten letter, a rather grubby, much-folded letter.

Without a word, she waited while I read it.

Dear Mrs Riley,

I seen your face in Queensland Country I reconnise you from a picture in the Brisbane paper a few years ago and your name is the same except your last name is different. I kept the page from that paper so thats how I know you are the same one. I am sending this to you because of the man who got hurt during the trouble over that football team. The paper said you were his girlfriend even if you must have married some teacher in Bindamilla since then. I was the one who went back afterwards and called the ambulance because it wasn't right the way we just left him there like that. I didn't want to but the one who hit him was senior to me and I had to do what he said. He made me help him to carry him to the path. He knew he

240

had hit him to hard and might get put up on a charge for it when the Inspector found out. If we left him next to the path, it would look like he hit his head on the railing and that would be an accident. I did not want to leave him there like that. He looked bad to me, even though there was no light to see him by. He did not move the whole time. When I came out into the street afterwards, there was blood on my uniform. I told ███████ him we should get an ambulance but he said no. Let other people find him so it doesn't come back to us. After that we were ordered back into ranks. I could not do anything then and he was watching me. When we got back to the barracks, it was after midnight. He went to have a drink with some others and I went out through the gate and found a taxi.

Your boyfriend was still there. No one found him after we left. That is why it was me who called the ambulance. I feel very bad about this because the paper said he got brain damage. I did not hit him but I seen it happen. He hit him to hard and he should face up to it.

You should know what happened because the paper said you were his girlfriend. Then I saw you in Queensland Country. I feel sorry about what happened. I cannot tell you his name because we don't rat on anyone no matter what they did. But you should know what happened.

The letter lay inside its plastic sleeve for good reason. The original folds were almost worn through and the edges fraying.

'You carried this with you?' I said.

'In my handbag. Yes, for a long time. After a while I knew it by heart, pretty much, but I still opened it, held it in my hands.'

There were other creases, a drunken spider's web that meant the letter didn't quite sit flat, even in its cocoon of plastic.

'You crumpled it up.'

'More than once. That mark, there —' she pointed to a smudge that had darkened like a liver spot — 'is from when I threw it into the kitchen rubbish.'

I pictured her doing it, and just as clearly saw the frantic retrieval.

'Who sent it?'

'I spent years trying to find out. That was the reason I left Bind-amilla, only it was impossible to get even a list of the policemen who were brought in from the country for the State of Emergency. They blocked me at every turn and I was a novice, anyway. I tried again once I had a few journo tricks up my sleeve, but Joh was at the height of his reign by then and the police were his private army, contemptuous of the media. It was hopeless.'

She leaned forward, bringing her face down close as gawpers do over a museum exhibit. 'Sometimes I don't know who I hate more – the bastard who swung the baton or the coward who sent me this.'

'Coward?' I said. 'It would have taken—'

'Oh, bullshit, Tom. He was drunk, wanted to ease his conscience. See these smears? They were already on the letter when it arrived. I'd say he wrote it one night, when he was pissed and feeling guilty because he'd seen my picture in *Queensland Country*. Once he was sober, he couldn't bring himself to post it, I'll bet. God knows how many times he flip-flopped until he was off his face again and finally shoved it in a letter box.'

'He called the ambulance.'

'Four hours too late! If he'd called for help straightaway, he might have made a difference, but instead he covered his mate's arse. Terry was bleeding inside his skull all that time. It was the build-up of pressure inside his brain that did the damage.'

The full meaning of the letter came then, by stealth. 'He was bashed,' I said.

'With a thirty-six-inch baton.' Susan held her hands apart to show me the length. 'Swung by an average man, the tip can reach a speed of more than a hundred miles an hour. Do you want to know how many pounds per square inch that equals? I worked it out once. Your father's been as good as dead since that night, Tom, clubbed to death by a Queensland copper who's never had to answer for it.'

'What did Dad say about this?' I said, touching the plastic lightly with my fingertips, then lifting them instantly as though it had given me a jolt.

She sat back, making me turn and look at her while she kept me waiting. Her face had hardened. She was disappointed – no, more than that, she was annoyed with my question.

'Nothing. He's never seen it.'

'Why not?' I looked down at the juvenile scrawl with its spelling mistakes and clumsy grammar. 'He calls you Mrs Riley, mentions Bindamilla. It must have come while Dad was still out there.'

'Before then. It was sent to me care of Bindy post office.'

'And you didn't show Dad?'

'It wasn't addressed to him.'

I took her answer at face value, that night. Only later did I want something less evasive. I looked back at the letter.

'There are no names, just what happened,' I said. I was beginning to see what a torment it must have been, to offer evidence of a crime and at the same time deny any chance of catching the culprit. 'There are no names . . . It would have been better—'

'You're wrong,' said Susan calmly.

I checked the bottom of the letter. Definitely nothing. 'The envelope?'

She shook her head, eyes for the letter only. Slowly, reverently, she took it from the plastic sleeve and with the blunt end of a pen touched the letter where a word had been blocked out.

I read the context and saw that *him* had replaced a name.'

'He started writing the man's name, then saw what he'd done and scribbled it out. Looks like he did, too, doesn't it?' said Susan, raising the letter up to the overhead light.

I stared at the letter closely. 'Barry,' I whispered. 'Jesus, you got a name. Could be a surname, though.'

'I thought of that, too,' she said, 'but it's not. I couldn't identify the letter writer, but with help from a reporter at the *Courier-Mail*, I got the surname for our friend Barry.'

She stopped speaking to concentrate on her hands, returning the letter to its plastic sleeve with the care of a conservator. This only heightened my anticipation, although she hadn't intended it that way.

'Well?' I urged.

'Dolan. Barry Dolan. He was one of the brown shirts brought in from regional stations to make up the numbers at the Tower Hill that night.'

'But you had his name. You must have gone after him.'

'I wanted to. I tried, but without the evidence of the letter writer, it was pointless. Dolan had got wind of what I was up to by then, as well. Warned me off. Best I could do was keep tabs on him. I was still doing that when I went to Washington.'

'Where is he now? Are you still keeping tabs on him?'

Susan couldn't resist a teasing smirk. 'Don't you recognise the name, Tom? Detective Senior Sergeant Barry Dolan. He did quite well for himself, you see, rose in the ranks.'

I could only shake my head, making her laugh out loud with a freedom that seemed almost manic in the circumstances. Didn't she hate this guy for what he'd done to my father, for what he'd done to us?

The letter was suddenly a snake ready to strike and I stood up, knocking over my chair and making Susan reel sideways in surprise. It was a moment or two longer before she realised what was happening.

'You're shaking,' she said, hugging me.

My chest was heaving. A panic attack, I recognised later, but at the time I'd never had my body play tricks on me this way. I held on to her for dear life, a full head taller and strong enough to crush the air out through her ribcage if I wasn't careful.

'Darling, I'm sorry. I didn't think it would hit you this way. I thought you were ready. I'm so sorry.'

'No, no, you did the right thing.'

And as quickly as it had gone into spasm, my body relented, leaving me weak and in need of her support just to remain on my feet.

Afterwards, while I longed for sleep in the spare room, my thoughts overshadowed the letter. I must have hugged my mother as a child, when I was afraid or, like tonight, simply cattle-prodded by emotions that defied analysis, hugged her with my three-year-old strength and felt her arms around me, comforted and with never a thought that it would ever be different. She must have said soothing things to me and called me *darling* with a mother's tenderness.

I wished so much I could remember it.

I didn't know who Barry Dolan was until Mum laid it all out for me after Paris. He was in gaol by then, and, because receiving corrupt payments gets you five years at most, he was released not long after and went off to live under a rock somewhere.

Perhaps he'd found salvation, but, for all the Christian charity endlessly impressed upon me at Terrace, I didn't give a fuck if he saved his soul or not. The man smashed my father's head open with a thirty-six-inch baton and left him in the darkness, dead in all but the details.

Later, my lawyer's training told me Dolan would never be tried for murder. Where was the body, the defence would demand. Terrance John Stoddard was still breathing, still ate three meals a day and still squeezed out a healthy shit every morning with the satisfaction of one whose bowel movements were an important marker in his daily routine.

Fucking Queensland.

At least Dolan was made to face a guilt of some sort; he was made to experience that moment in the dock when the people cried, 'Look at what you did, you bastard. The evidence is out there for us all to see. You *did* take the money, you *did* betray the public trust.'

Joh Bjelke-Petersen never suffered such a moment. Susan hoped that he would. So did I, once I knew the story. Without Joh, there would have been no Barry Dolan.

That was why, at the end of 1991, Susan and I sat side by side in a courtroom as the verdict was announced in his perjury trial. We weren't the only observers hoping for vindication that day – not because the former premier might have lied in his evidence to the Fitzgerald Inquiry, but for crimes that would never come to court.

In the most personal sense, we were seeking revenge for a baton charge on a cold night in 1971, when I was no more than a few cells inside my mother, a night when my father came face to face with an angry copper. It could have been any one of them, of course. They'd all had their hatred of rabble-rousing long-hairs primed for an act of brutality, and the man responsible now stood in the dock, not for inciting violence but to answer for something, at least. What my mother and I were seeking was that essential moment when he was forced to admit he'd done wrong.

But when the moment came – it was snatched away. Oh, Christ, what a night that was, outside the court in George Street after the verdict, with my mother howling in rage and my own limbs so robbed of life I could barely keep her upright.

A hung jury. The accused had walked free, spluttering self-righteous claims of innocence through a smugness that couldn't hide how stunned he was to get away with it.

How utterly denied we felt, how unfinished. Within days of the non-verdict the papers carried news of a dodgy juror from the Friends of Joh campaign, who'd held out against the rest. What a knife in the heart that was. The entire state had been given a chance to redeem itself in one cathartic act, and they'd squibbed it.

Susan was inconsolable for days. She'd thought she'd witness another fall, like Barry Dolan's.

'You asked me why I get so angry with everything up here,' she said, once she'd calmed down enough to speak. 'Do you see, now? There are still faithful souls who'd follow him all the way to hell. Anything but admit they were wrong.'

I thought she meant the knee-jerk conservatism that bubbled through into how people voted, but when I said so, she snapped at me.

'God no. I don't give a damn what party they vote for. National, Labor, that's all tribal. It's not even the childish pretence that up here they're better than the poofters and posers down south. There's as much envy in that as there is suspicion.'

'What is it, then?' I demanded. I wasn't a teenager any more and I wanted to peel away my mother's evasions.

In response, she skewered me with a long silence that might have ended with her storming away in typical Susan fashion and more days of silence between us until I came crawling back, a son needing his mother on her terms alone.

Well, bugger that. I was ready to be done with her if she fobbed me off again.

'Tell me, then. There had to be more than that letter to drive you away.'

When she began to answer, with barely a moment's hesitation, I knew the earlier silence hadn't been maternal discipline. She'd been marshalling her response.

'Because when it mattered,' she said, speaking slowly, as though I wasn't to miss a word. 'When it mattered, too many could only sneer at their own right to dissent – that's what I'm talking about, Tom. They decided they didn't need it. They trusted one man, instead, a man as ignorant of history as they were.'

'You're talking about Joh.'

'Or anyone cagey enough to sweep up all the local prejudices and serve them back as some kind of victory for the common man. It takes a stubborn kind of naivety to choose that, Tom. There were two mobs in Queensland back then, one you could see at demos and the other mob that bayed for their blood and cheered old Joh on when he gave it to them. They had no idea what battles had been fought to free them from men like him.

'Can you imagine how I felt watching it happen around me?' she demanded. 'By the time I left, Joh *was* Queensland. Criticise him and you were a traitor to the entire state, and even if there was no law that said it was a crime, there was the court of public opinion. Thank God for the lawyers who brought it all crashing down.'

I saw, then, that in the tension of that courtroom, more than a single defendant had stood accused. In my mother's eyes, millions of others had stood in the dock with Joh, and if a guilty verdict had been returned, all those faces would have been made to look at what they'd flirted with – not Joh, who'd become a parody of himself by then, but the slow dismantling of their own political heritage.

*

When the verdict or, more precisely, the non-verdict was delivered in the Bjelke-Petersen trial, I was in the middle of uni exams. Later, when the results were posted, I'd managed only modest scores in comparison to earlier semesters and it would be easy to join the dots of cause and effect.

But such straight lines would have been an illusion. Through much of that year I'd fought a growing disgruntlement, and for the first time in my life became slapdash with assignments. The truth slipped out one night, unbidden. 'I'm bored,' I told the girl I was seeing at the time.

'Then change what you're doing,' she replied, as though it was the easiest thing in the world.

Rather to my surprise, it was. I filled in the forms, salvaged what credit I could from my journalism courses and started 1992 as a law student.

Why Law? A straight line would lead to Dad, who'd always said I had the right kind of mind for a lawyer – and it wasn't necessarily a compliment. He certainly pushed the suggestion once I'd confessed my disillusion, but, again, his advice wasn't the deciding factor. Susan was the one. Something she'd said played over and over in my mind: thank God for the lawyers who brought it all crashing down.

Did she realise what she was admitting? Ask Dad, or anyone who lived through the Fitzgerald days, and he'll tell you it was a band of crusading journos who brought down Joh and Lewis and the rest of his cronies. The truth isn't quite so romantic. My mother's profession might have wrestled the beast to the ground, but it was the law that drove a sword through its heart.

I'd been absenting myself from the Riley household more and more through those early years at UQ. My many trips to Sydney began to feel like a journey between two countries, despite Queensland being welcomed back into the fold through the early '90s after the Joh decades of wilful separateness. For me, the differentiation lingered, and always in favour of the south. It was personal, and far from reasonable in any objective sense, but each time I crossed the border I felt a change in the current.

I willingly confess how silly this was, when the shake-up that flowed from the Fitzgerald Inquiry meant Queensland's political processes were downright pristine compared to New South Wales'. That wasn't the point, though. Political personalities came and went, they were honest or otherwise; what filled me with quiet disdain were the stories my mother told, over and over, of the tacit consent given by an entire state to a regime that was steadily, deliberately chipping away at the rights of its own people.

'It's still there, Tom,' she'd insist. 'It might be lying dormant for the time being, but the seed is still in the soil.'

Oh, how my mother loved the dramatic. She'd interviewed John Sinclair, the man who saved Fraser Island from sand mining. A public servant in his day job, Sinclair had been hounded out of the state, and Susan saw herself in the same light, following the grand tradition of writers and artists who found Queensland too stultifying to remain.

Not that I was content to sit at her feet drinking in every word. How many times did Robert leave us bickering on the balcony, resigned to his own exclusion, and with a wink at me that said I'd found the way to my mother's heart – argue politics.

Lurking in the shadows behind us both was Terry Stoddard. The three of us were a family in a way I could never feel within the loving quartet that welcomed me back to Brisbane whenever I returned. The verdict in Joh's trial had robbed my father's ghost of closure, so Susan and I were perpetual wanderers as well, and if she continued to rail against her bête noire, out of all proportion to his crimes, this was why. I knew it was over the top, but let myself be swept up in it all the same, for no other reason than it bound us together as mother and son. At least I thought it did.

During the inquiries I'd made about changing courses, I'd looked at universities interstate. In the end, UQ took me in without demur, but the idea lingered. Why wait until holidays, if there was a way to see Susan every day?

When I told her about it, she was chuffed and before I knew it she was sussing out flats near the University of New South Wales. 'I'll pay the rent until you find some flatmates,' she assured me.

Her response was both natural and generous, yet as soon as she started on about a flat in Paddington my interest waned. I lied and said Dad wouldn't let me move, only to be found out when Susan rang him, demanding he change his mind. How could I come right out and say it, that I wanted to live with her in Rose Bay, for a month or two, anyway, until I found my feet? There was a spare bedroom, after all.

But she hadn't even considered the idea.

TWELVE

TOM

'Come and look at this, Tom,' said one of the paralegals one morning, when I'd been working at Coghills for more than a year.

By the time I looked up, she was already gone from my doorway and I had to follow her to a conference room where the television screen was filled by a talking head.

'That woman from Ipswich, it's her maiden speech,' came the explanation.

'The fish shop lady?' I said, only to be shushed by one of the partners standing with arms folded and a scowl I hadn't seen since I'd stuffed up some research in my first year.

From the speaker came a nasal, faintly indignant voice: 'Present governments are encouraging separatism in Australia by providing opportunities, land, moneys and facilities available only to Aboriginals. Along with millions of Australians, I am fed up to the back teeth with the inequalities that are being promoted by the government . . .'

Was this woman actually peddling such twaddle in Federal Parliament? I listened, caught between dismay and laughter.

'Today, I am talking about the privileges that Aboriginals enjoy over other Australians . . .'

'Like low life expectancy, no government services, harassment from the police,' I began to enumerate, until the partner glared at me a second time.

I watched the face on screen, trying to decide whether it was the ignorance or the audacity that appalled me more. I should have gone back to my desk, but her distortion and bigotry held a macabre attraction. I simply couldn't believe what I was hearing, and if the partner beside me could stay to hear it all, so would I.

At my desk afterwards, I felt sorry for the poor woman for the inevitable jibes about her red hair and her irritating voice, but mostly for the vilification she would suffer for stirring up prejudices that we'd outgrown. Reaction to the speech was sure to be savage.

SUSAN
1996

'Downward envy, they're calling it in the office,' I said from in front of the TV, where the news prattled away with the sound turned low. I'd kicked off my shoes to recline with my feet on the coffee table, and the first glass of red in my hand.

Only Robert's top half was visible above the island bench where he was cooking dinner. My culinary skills were on a par with my French – adequate, but lacking nuance. The kitchen was his own little Paris, he'd told me, and I let him 'go home' whenever the mood took him.

The news moved on, extinguishing the face of Pauline Hanson, who had prompted my remark.

'We have the same with Le Pen,' said Robert. 'He has a surprising amount of support.'

'This galoot of a woman will do the same, you watch. I had Tom on the phone the other day saying no one will take any notice of her. He lives in a bubble, that boy. Got to get him out of that lawyers' sweatshop, shake him up. If he's not careful, he'll work twelve hours a day for thirty years and wonder where his life went.'

'Only twelve? I slept on the floor behind my desk some nights,' said Robert.

I threw a cushion at him, but without enough conviction for it to reach the bench.

'He'd have been a lousy journalist. He can't see what a story Hanson is. I've heard *Sixty Minutes* is sniffing around.'

'Perhaps she'll expose herself.'

Sudden nakedness filled my mind. Sometimes Robert's way of phrasing things begged a belly laugh, but he corrected my French howlers only gently, and I'd learned to return the favour.

'Make a fool of herself, you mean. The producer could make sure of that with a bit of judicious editing, but why kill the story? She's a hundred per cent news fodder, this one. Talk-back loves her.'

Hanson would become a lightning rod for every nutter from Cape York to Perth, she'd legitimise anyone who felt threatened by 'the other'. Despite my cynicism a familiar anger stirred in me. Look where the woman came from. Should anyone be surprised?

TOM

For a man with eight grandparents, the death of one shouldn't have affected me the way it did, but, in '97, when Len Kinnane drew cancer's short straw, I found myself unaccountably overwhelmed. I went up to the hospital to see him after the surgery and listened to him talk of how he would fight this like he'd fought the Japanese.

'Good on ya, Grandad,' I muttered, with the rest.

Weeks later, when the chemo did little but make him frail and miserable, I was warned of the inevitable. Finally, the hospital sent him home with a drip in his arm so he could die in his own house, another vow he'd made and one he'd soon kept. He and Grandma Joyce had raised their kids there and, after her too-early death, he'd stayed on, even though every stick of furniture, the prints on the walls, even the doilies must have reminded him of her.

Aunty Diane moved into the bedroom she'd once shared with my mother and called in the rest of the family to make their farewells. I picked Susan up from the airport and together we drove straight to Holland Park to find Grandad propped up on pillows and still lucid, despite the morphine.

Why was I so affected? I barely knew the old guy, I told myself, and in that simple truth lay the answer to my question. Len was the last of my real grandparents, the ones whose blood ran in my veins. Soon, there would be only Susan and Terry left in that direct line and this left me lonely in a way I couldn't explain.

Such sentiments didn't stop me becoming annoyed with Len, though, when he took my hand and said, 'I wish I'd known you better when you were a young nipper. There you were, just across the river all those years.'

He didn't need to cross the river to see me – didn't have to go anywhere – not when, every winter Saturday, he'd come to watch my cousin play football for the school. Gary's B team were always the curtain-raiser for my As, so it would have been simple to stay behind, and he surely saw Mike Riley among the faces waiting for my game to start. Yes, he knew, but he never said a word to Dad, never stayed to tell me I'd played well. That would have been something, at least.

I said as much to Susan when we retired to the lounge room to await the tea Diane had promised.

'That was my mother's doing,' said Susan, and suddenly Grandma Joyce was so fully in the room there was barely air to breathe.

I was grateful for the convenient 'out' she'd offered, because I didn't want to be so hard on Grandad, not with the end so close and a need in me that still had no name.

Susan seemed to take my football story as a cue for her own. 'Ritchie and I gave Mum hell in this house, you know,' she began, with a smile. 'No wonder I remember her screeching at us so often. The things we got up to.' Then, as I suspected it would, her smile took on some subtle adjustments. 'He was worse than me, the little devil, but he had a cheeky way of sucking up to Mum when she lost patience. I never learned how to do it.'

Her smile became a wince and then a frown, just as her childhood mischief had become an urge to be gone that itched like sunburn and bled whenever she scratched it. We were sitting on the same sofa where Joyce, with Len beside her, had tried to lay out their daughter's future, as though Susan had no say in it at all, except Susan hadn't talked about her future on the many occasions she told me the story. How had she phrased it? 'They planned my motherhood, down to the last nappy and who might deign to marry me.'

Her bitterness was justified, no doubt, but I'd listened to her stories many times and wanted something else from my mother at this moment – family, forgiveness, softer sentiments more suited to a house where a man lay dying. Susan said something, but I didn't pick up what it was. I think she was trying to get the conversation going again because my edginess had rendered me silent.

'Are you all right?' she asked.

I responded with a shrug.

'There's nothing we can do for Grandad,' she said quietly. 'He's resigned to it and the pain's under control. We don't need to stay if—'

'I'm fine.'

'No you're not. I can tell from the way you're sitting there, jumpy as a cat. Nothing to be ashamed of—'

'It's not about Grandad,' I said, too sharply.

She tried another tack, which left me equally dumb, then, as she did so often, Susan filled the void with the issues of the day. 'It's this Hanson thing, isn't it?'

We'd talked about it on the phone in recent weeks. The maiden speech had turned Hanson into a convenient *piñata* for the chattering classes, but the stuffing she spewed out was making her a hero, for Christ's sake. My mother had seen it coming, but not me.

Since she'd put the matter out there, I took hold of it. 'Some girls at Dad's school have been having a go at the Aboriginal boarders, saying they get everything for free, stuff white people have to work for.'

Susan shook her head. 'Half-truths are harder to argue against than outright lies, especially in politics. Those girls are only quoting Hanson from the television, of course.'

With spectacularly bad timing, Aunty Diane came in with the tea tray and her own opinion. 'Some of the things she says aren't so far from the truth, you know.'

Susan and I glanced at each other, but we loved Diane too much to embarrass her. What we hadn't said came out later, while we drove to the nursing home through the lassitude of a Sunday afternoon in Brisbane.

'Don't be too hard on your aunt. She's good at heart,' Susan concluded, after we'd each let off a bit of steam. It seemed enough for her, yet left me more hollowed out than ever and my mood didn't improve when we found Terry in bed with a drip in his arm.

'Chest infection,' said the nurse in charge of Terry's wing. 'The doctor doesn't want it to turn into anything worse. His head injury makes him more prone,' and she went on to explain why in terms that neither of us understood.

My poor father. He lay in bed as ghostly white as Len Kinnane, but with no idea of what was happening to him. That seemed to make his condition worse, despite the nurse's assurances that he wasn't in any danger. They had secured his right arm to the bed frame to stop him pulling out the drip from his left, and, defeated by this, he remained unnaturally still through our entire visit.

Grandad would be dead by week's end, and, with Terry making an almost identical scene, it struck me again that my personal history was slipping away. It was too late to know Grandad, but with Terry there had never been a chance, not since the day I was born.

'I wish I'd known him,' I muttered.

On the other side of the bed, Susan stirred. My words might not have formed a question, but that's what they were, yet another variation of 'What was he like?' It was as though I couldn't get enough of the stories she told, willingly and sometimes through tears. I'd first heard them back in the Fitzgerald days, but I kept asking, because none of her answers quite satisfied.

On that day, the Hanson thing gave her an easy hook.

'He'd have taken her on, head to head if he could. He'd have dismantled the scaremongering and jealousy with hard evidence instead of prejudice. He was learning so quickly, you know, Tom, back in '71. He could see the street protests would take a cause only so far. Only real power could bring change. He might have been premier, one day.'

It wasn't the first time she'd made that prediction. It was something to be proud of and I certainly felt proud when she spoke of what he might have been. It formed part of the familiar theme I picked up in all her stories – we had all been deprived of Terry's political potential. Since she offered nothing more personal that day, as on every other, it was all I could latch on to. And, as always, I felt angry, without quite knowing what I was angry about or who I was angry with.

When Susan suggested we leave, I was on the move almost before the words were out of her mouth. At the car, when I couldn't fit the key into the door the first time, I wanted to punch through the glass. It was a rage I recognised, half against the world, half against myself.

'Tom?' said my mother tentatively. She'd come round the car and was suddenly at my side.

'I felt so ashamed sitting there beside him,' I told her. 'Terry's in there because he stood up against the same rubbish Hanson is peddling all over again, twenty years later. I thought we'd all moved on. Now this. Nothing's changed at all, especially not here.'

'There are too many like your aunty Diane, I'm afraid. The mindset is rooted way down deep. There's talk that she'll form her own party. It's all about the leader, you see, and we know where that leads,' she said, nodding towards the nursing home.

'I've had a enough of this place,' I heard myself say. 'Even the stuff I'm doing at work . . . I don't know, it's so trivial when you look around at . . .' I couldn't finish, because the thought simply wouldn't form.

'Then leave – go overseas. I still have contacts in London. Maybe one of them can swing something for you. Do you want me to make a few calls?'

'Yes, today, right now,' I begged.

Suddenly, she was laughing. 'Tom, it's four in the morning over there. Can you wait a few hours?'

It did seem funny, once she put it that way. 'Yes, a few hours,' I said, pulling her hard against me for comfort.

Did I really leave Queensland because of Pauline Hanson? My mother put it in those terms a couple of times, halfway between a private joke and something more serious. At the time I felt it was simply time to go. Many of my friends had already taken a working holiday in England. There was nothing special in what I was doing.

Susan's contacts didn't prove much use, as it turned out, but I had money enough to be patient and London held things for me

261

that I hadn't anticipated. While job hunting, I'd sometimes sit by the Thames and stare across at Westminster, feeling that I'd come home, at last. This was odd, because, when asked where home was by some nameless drinking companions in a nearby pub, I answered 'Brisbane' without hesitation. I even turned spruiker when they stared blankly at my reply.

'A thousand kays north of Sydney, in sunny Queensland. Great place.'

Yet I didn't carry around with me any strong images of the home state I'd been so quick to own. Let poets like Dad memorialise its landscape; my training was the law and that was how I experienced places. To me, Queensland was a political entity and since its laws and parliament had grown out of the buildings I could see across the river, yes, I found a homely contentment in London. It became stronger when I began at the Crown Prosecutor and found, in the work I was doing, a second homecoming.

How much did Hilary have to do with that happiness? I'd been working at the Crown Prosecutor for two years when, on a bus to London University for a postgrad course I was doing, I noticed the same girl three weeks in a row. On the third night I said hello and after we'd laughed at our matching accents, discovered a Brisbane connection, as well. If she'd been part of the Catholic mafia we might have met at school dances, and the fact that she wasn't only made her more attractive to me.

And Hilary *was* very attractive. Hair like Susan's, about the same height, and pale-skinned, which she put down to the English weather. By the Christmas of '99 we were living together in a cosy flat in Kennington, ten minutes' walk from The Oval, where the Australians occasionally came to play cricket.

They weren't the only Australians to make a beeline for Kennington, either. My sisters, Gabby and Emma, camped on our floor for a week in 2001 as part of their grand tour, and a year later Susan turned up.

'Thought I'd pop over to check out my old stamping ground, and to visit my son, of course,' she said, but it was obvious she'd come to run the ruler over this young woman I talked so much about in my emails.

SUSAN
2002

Was there ever a more fraught role to play than the partner of the father of the bride – and in a foreign country, too, amid a language that could deliver the stiletto's thrust with such charm? No doubt, the Parisians had a title for what I was, a variation of *La Bitch*, most likely. Torment would be lingering, as well, because we'd arrived well ahead of the wedding so Robert could be part of the excitement, and he adored Sabine, in any case.

Fortunately, the solution proved both acceptable and very welcome.

'Je vais rendre visite à mon fils, à Londres pendant quelques jours,' I announced after one night's penance among the aunts. *'C'est possible qu'il y ait un mariage bientôt,'* I couldn't help adding.

Tom was waiting for me at Kennington tube station. My God, look at him, I wanted to shout at everyone within earshot. He was no taller, but the self-assurance made him seem so, a man to pick out among others – or was that a mother's bias? I embraced the feeling and welcomed his long arms around me, hugged him, clung to him as much as our coats would allow. It was early April, but the sun was gone for the day and there was a bite in the air.

The business of the moment was Hilary, however, and I pulled away quickly to smile at the young woman who watched us with an anxious smile. Despite the darkness, she stood out in a red coat and beret, so much more lively than my mania for black.

She offered kisses and the right words: 'So good to meet you, nothing like I expected.' She was almost trembling as she delivered her lines.

I had my own stock phrases ready, as well, and delivered them on cue at the dinner table after Hilary had pulled out all stops with a culinary welcome.

'Fabulous,' I declared. 'How did you do the peppers?' They'd been stuffed with mushrooms and some herb I couldn't identify.

'Aren't they great?' gushed Hilary. 'And so easy. The secret is to cook them slowly.'

I nodded politely at this advice and wondered whether a comment about the fish would be overdoing things. Hilary, however, wasn't finished with the entree.

'You won't find the recipe in any cookbook, either. It's a traditional peasant dish from Slovakia. A woman at work wrote it all down for me,' she said, and before I could stop her, she'd run to the kitchen to fetch it. 'I'll write you out a copy, if you like.'

The name of the mystery herb would have been enough.

I glanced towards Tom, who had seen my embarrassment, but he treated the whole thing as an excuse to chuckle at both of us. If Hilary had seen this exchange, she might have pulled back a bit, but no, she continued to monopolise the chatter, and the wine bottle, until ten o'clock, then dumbfounded me further by saying, 'Oh, you two must have so much to catch up on,' and promptly waved her way off to bed.

In the morning, she looked pale. Hung-over, I decided, until an alternative shook me. Oh Christ, she's not pregnant, is she?

'Did you pick up the drycleaning?' Tom called while he was getting dressed.

'Damn, I forgot again,' came the sheepish reply.

Tom made a further comment, which I couldn't make out, but the tone hinted at exasperation.

I was being unfair, I decided. Shouldn't have been listening in to their domestic back and forth like this. I withdrew to my room, closing the door after me until a knock called me to breakfast. Hilary was half dressed for work and half for a return to bed, a decision Tom was having no luck helping her to resolve. Eventually, she opted for work and went off towards the tube station, utterly cured by a bowl of cereal, it seemed.

Was she enough for Tom? I didn't want him to sell himself short.

Oh, shut up, Susan, and enjoy the reunion. Tom had taken the day off.

'Hilary is worried she made a fool of herself last night,' he confided over a mid-morning coffee. 'It's only nerves. Your reputation alone is enough to intimidate, Mother Susan,' he teased. 'Heavyweight journalist, confidante of kingmakers. She tried too hard to impress you. Things will be better tonight.'

And, at first, they were. 'We thought we'd take you out for dinner,' Tom announced. 'An Indian place. Used to be John Major's favourite restaurant when he was prime minister.'

'Is that recommendation or condemnation?' I asked, with a roll of my eyes.

'Depends on your politics,' said Hilary. 'Doesn't seem to be bipartisan, because we've never seen Tony Blair in the booth next door. At least you won't have to share your *vindaloo* with the secret service.' She was smiling confidently as she said this, which I put down to a pep talk from Tom.

The Kennington Tandoori wasn't far. 'You two know the menu. Order for me,' I commanded. This was going to be fun. 'Where's that waiter? What'll you have to drink?'

I downed the first beer as though I was back in Bindamilla and teased Tom that he couldn't keep pace with me, which he trumped by finishing his in a single gulp and ordering two more.

Hilary sipped at a Diet Coke. Shit, she might be pregnant after all; I hadn't had the gall to ask Tom during our day together. For a moment I was chilled by visions of airheaded granddaughters.

The food came, and over *aloo paratha* and prawn *balti* Hilary's twenty-nine years slowly yielded to my journalist's probing. She was a Brisbane girl, Dad with one of the banks, Mum a pharmacist, two sisters, no brothers; she wished they'd come for a visit, just as I was here now.

'You miss them?'

'Of course.'

'Why don't you go see *them* instead?'

This provoked a glance towards Tom, I noticed, but we were soon on to other things. Questioner became the questionee and I quite enjoyed the interrogation. No, I wasn't giving up writing, just moving to a more leisurely focus. My first feature, a sad piece about Alzheimer's, had appeared in the weekend supplement only last week.

Later, as we waited for coffee, Tom asked, 'How long did you actually live in London?'

I sat back to count the time, since he sounded serious and a vague figure wouldn't do. 'Let's see. Left in . . . '83. Two years in Washington, which puts me in London about this time in '85. I went back to watch Fitzgerald light the bonfire under Joh and that was . . . Must have been here close to three years.'

'You didn't have any problems with your passport? Work permits, that sort of thing?' he asked, once again with more seriousness than the question warranted.

'It's not an issue for a foreign correspondent,' I explained.

He accepted this with a wince around his eyes and asked no more, but the topic, and his disappointment at my reply, were out there now.

'Why? Are the immigration people hassling you?'

'No,' Hilary answered for him.

I was more aware, this time, of the look between them and the sharpness of her reply. Tom plunged ahead, however.

'No hassles yet, but only as long as I stay with the Crown Prosecutor. They've convinced Immigration that I'm doing work no local can do, which isn't quite true but it's the way the system works.'

'Then why the question about passports?'

'Because I'm hoping to stay longer, maybe move to the bar. Hilary has an English grandfather so she can stay as long as—'

'So do you,' I said, enjoying the way I'd silenced him so abruptly.

Tom looked flummoxed. 'Grandad Kinnane? He was born in the backblocks of Queensland, wasn't he? Are you telling me all that hardship in the good old Aussie bush was bullshit?'

'Everyone has two grandfathers,' I said, making him work it out for himself.

'You mean Dad's father is English? I never noticed any accent.'

'If you mean Rob Riley, then of course you didn't. I'm talking about your *real* grandfather.'

Even as the words were leaving my mouth, I scrambled to retrieve them. My eyes flew to Hilary, then quickly lost their panic when there was no sign of confusion.

'Don't worry. Hilary knows the story,' said Tom. But he was eager for the rest of *my* story. 'You mean Terry's father, the Stoddards?'

'They were from Yorkshire, one of the hard mining towns. You never knew your grandmother, thanks to bloody Mike, so you never heard her accent. In fact, you've got more than English grandparents. Terry was born here, before they emigrated.'

'Are you serious? I never thought about it, just assumed . . . Jesus, I can get more than extended residence, I can have a British passport.'

I was thrilled to be the one to give him the news, and, swept along with his enthusiasm, I added, 'All you have to do is get your birth certificate changed. Shouldn't be hard for a lawyer. I'll sign a statement. Whatever you need.'

Hilary remained quiet, although there was more going on behind her solemn face than even a journalist's antennae could pick out. The coffee came and was merely sipped at while our bill was prepared, then it was out into the April night. The rain seemed all the colder by the sudden contrast with the warmth of the restaurant, and we hadn't thought to bring an umbrella. Heads down, we hurried into the squall.

'I don't know what you want to live here for, Tom,' said Hilary, while we waited to cross a busy road. 'You've got to be born to this kind of weather. Never get used to it. I'd go home tomorrow if it was up to me.'

I'd felt the same when caught on rain-swept corners twenty years ago, but it was Hilary's final words that lingered in my ears. There was something I'd missed about the passport business.

TOM

On that long flight from Heathrow in 2003, I carried two passports, one with the diplomatic blue of Australia, the other, British red. That red passport had caused me no end of trouble in the eighteen months beforehand, not through all the red tape, but in the arguments it stirred in Kennington. I don't think Dad was half as hurt by the whole thing as Hilary.

I shouldn't forget Mum among the wounded, either. She phoned me at six one morning to explain exactly what she thought of the statutory declaration I'd asked Dad to sign, while Hilary stood close by in her dressing gown, arms folded and face as cold as the dawn outside. God knows, I deserved her frowns, but I wanted that passport and I didn't see how it could threaten our relationship. There was no doubting what we felt for one another. We were comfortable together; our friends actually used that word about us, to our faces, no less. When your social circle were all between twenty-five and thirty-five, that was the way your life went; people partnered up, tied the knot, got on with it. There had been times Hilary and I hadn't bothered to explain that we *weren't* married, when the assumption was so naturally made.

As far as she was concerned that passport was the enemy, and she started in with guerilla tactics against it. On one of our regular visits to the Kennington Tandoori, she pointed out, with heavy sarcasm, 'They have Indian restaurants in Australia, you know. Good ones. It's not all *rogan josh* and chicken *tikka masala.*'

Only the week before, she'd read aloud from the *Guardian* about

Australian chefs matching it with the world's best, and the pick of the crop was some new place off Adelaide Street.

'See that, Tom?' she insisted, shoving the paper under my nose. 'In Brisbane!'

Another time, while we were walking and a chill breeze chased her hands inside her pockets, she'd told me, 'I want to have kids one day, Tom, and I don't want to walk them to school in the dark and the freezing rain. England's been fun, but it's not for the long term, not for Australians like you and me.'

'I'm only half Australian,' I'd said stupidly.

'Bullshit! You didn't even know where your father was born until Susan told you. Besides, it's Queensland you've got the problem with.'

She walked on beside me for half a block, shoring up her courage. 'It's time you got over it, Tommy,' she said, a catchphrase I was rapidly coming the loathe. 'This whole business with your father, it's a tragedy, an injustice, it burns a hole right through you, I know, but you can't hold an entire people to account. That's what's at the bottom of all this, isn't it? You can't go home because you feel let down by the whole bloody state.'

'No, that's not it. I don't give a damn about Queensland.'

This only seemed to exasperate her: 'Then why do you go on about the place so much?' she said, pulling her hands free and thrusting them wide.

Did I? When I later caught Queensland on my lips a few times, I had to concede she was right.

And then, with no more warning than it takes to quit a job and book an airline ticket, Hilary went home to Brisbane. That was late in May, 2003, less than three months before I was to make the same journey, with Dad at my elbow the whole way.

THIRTEEN

SUSAN
August, 2003

'Mike, it's Sue,' I said, gently, into the phone. 'I hope I didn't wake you.'

'It's fine. You know me, up with the sun,' he replied. 'Even with daylight saving it's light before five over here right now.'

'Daylight saving,' I repeated, without quite meaning to. Did it still carry the same resonance for him that it did for me?

'I have some sad news,' I said.

'Oh?'

'Terry died this afternoon.'

'Died!'

'The nursing home phoned me an hour ago. A chest infection turned into pneumonia and they didn't catch it in time.'

'The old man's friend,' said Mike.

'He wasn't old. Same age as us.'

'True, true. I'm sorry, Sue. How are you feeling?'

'A little numb. Isn't that what they say? It's not like when Joyce died, or Dad. We knew it was coming for them, and we'd said our goodbyes. Poor Terry, there was nothing to say, was there?'

He made no reply to this, as though he'd retired to his own corner of memory, just as I had.

'Do you want me to ring Tom?' he asked.

'I've already done it. Maybe you could go down to London, if you're free. He should have someone with him, someone who knew Terry, I mean. He wants to come back for the funeral.'

'So do I.'

'No, Mike. There's no need to come all that way. I tried to talk him out of it.'

'Of course he wants to be there, to see things out after all these years. Me too. I finish here tomorrow, anyway. We'll come home together.'

I was suddenly jealous of his place at Tom's side, enough to say as much when Robert came in from work.

'You're not still competing with Mike, are you?'

'Competing? What do you mean?'

'For Tom,' he said bluntly.

'No, of course not.'

Over dinner, though, I didn't have much to say and before long Robert was glancing tentatively at me, in that way that he has, and which I love him for.

'We were a family once, you know – Mike, Tom and me. If things had been different, we might still be.'

He took my hand in a faux gesture that had me smiling even before he'd said a word. 'I would be a poorer soul if fate had turned that way.'

The sentiment was put on, and his voice was a parody of Maurice Chevalier, but it masked a truth I was glad to keep safe.

Whatever the unlived possibilities, the three of us would stand together at Terry's funeral, a family of sorts again. I was glad of that, too. How would we arrange ourselves? Would it be me in the middle, the men on either side, or would Tom take the centre? It didn't matter. What mattered more was that something lift from all three of us once it was done.

To that end, I flew to Brisbane the next morning. By then, Terry had been taken to the funeral home, where I was allowed to see him at rest. With nothing left of the man I'd once loved, my eyes stayed dry, something the attendant was too polite to notice. Would I cry at the service, when Terry was present in the bones of our son's face, in his bearing, and even the timbre of his voice?

'I wish I'd known him,' Tom had said, yet again, when I'd called him with the news; but you didn't have to know someone to be so like him that it stung the soul of those who could see it, hear it, remember.

After the chill of the mortuary, I was shown into a sombre office where the director was both solicitous and business-like while we settled questions about the coffin, how he was to be dressed, the service.

'That's everything, Ms Kinnane,' he said, after what seemed far too short a time.

'You mean that's it?'

He shrugged apologetically. 'It doesn't take long when there's no religious service involved. When will you decide on the day?'

'I'll call as soon as I get word from my son.'

'You have my number.' He nodded at the card stapled to the receipt I was clutching. Even a funeral could be paid for with a credit card, it seemed. 'Can I get you a taxi?'

By lunchtime, I was twiddling my thumbs at the Park Royal, while they scrambled to get a room ready for me so early in the day. When my mobile phone trilled, I pounced on it, expecting Tom with news of his flight.

'Susan, this is Hilary. Tom's Hilary.'

'Oh, yes. What a surprise!' And instantly I jumped ahead, thinking Tom must have been in the air already and she was ringing from London with the flight number. But Hilary wasn't delivering a message from Tom, and she wasn't on the other side of the globe, either.

'I'm back in Brisbane these days,' she said, without embellishment, and only a journalist's discipline kept me from blurting, Oh!

'I'm sorry to hear about Tom's father. I'll be at the funeral, of course. But, Susan, I'm ringing because . . .' I heard a breath being expelled. 'Look, could we meet? I'd like to talk to you before Tom gets here.'

She'd caught me on the hop and before I could ask why, we'd agreed to meet after she finished work. When there was still no room ready for me at the hotel, I said to the girl at reception, 'Don't rush. I'll go visit my sister,' and spent the afternoon speculating with Diane about lovers' tiffs and, not for the first time, pregnancy.

*

'Hello, again,' Hilary called through a forced smile, when she found me waiting in the lobby soon after five.

I nodded towards the bar. 'Will we sit in there?'

'I'd prefer we walked in the gardens, if that's okay.'

She meant the Botanical Gardens across the road, and already she was backing away towards the door onto Alice Street, which at this hour on a Friday was lousy with traffic. While we waited at the lights I contemplated going back for a jacket, but the little green figure called us forward before I could make up my mind. Hurrying into step beside Hilary I thought of another winter's night I'd ventured out without enough care for my clothes.

Hilary, on the other hand, was wearing the red coat I'd first seen at Kennington tube station, an observation I kept to myself. This really was a night for staying shtum, I decided, when, fifty metres beyond the gates, we passed the bench where Mike Riley had asked me to marry him.

'How long have you been back in Brisbane?' I asked.

'Two months now. My visa ran out in June.' Then, after a strategic pause, she added, 'That's not the reason I came home, though.'

She stared into my face as she spoke, a harder gaze than I thought her capable of, and one that dared me to suggest my own reasons for her return. In case I settled on the wrong one, she spelled it out: 'I came back here to force Tom's hand.' With this said, she snapped her eyes forward and surged on beside me in crisp, determined strides.

Was this the same girl I'd met in London? To Hilary, I said, with matching frankness, 'You're worried I've told Tom not to marry you? Is that it?'

This brought her to a halt and the naked surprise tangled in her features showed she hadn't even considered it.

'I don't believe you'd do something like that.' Then a grim smile crept across her lips. 'I did make a mess of those days in London, didn't I? I couldn't really blame you if you *did* say something to him.' The smile was gone, though, when she answered my question more directly. 'No, I'm not looking for a second chance to earn your respect, if that's what you're thinking.'

'So why *are* we here, and why so keen to see me without Tom?'

Hilary had been uncomfortable since her opening hello and now the preliminaries were done with, I half-expected her to make a run for it. She certainly stared with longing towards the gate into Edward Street.

'We may as well sit down,' she said, backtracking to a bench behind us.

When I joined her, leaving a healthy space that seemed required, she fixed her eyes at some point just beyond my shoulder. 'It's because Tom can't come home. It's not that he likes London so much, or the work he's doing there. He's got this thing about coming back.'

She paused to see what I made of this and found my face blank, no doubt, because this was the first I'd heard of it. Her shoulders wilted a little at finding me so mystified, but she'd made a start now and seemed determined to get the rest of it out.

'I thought it was because of what happened to his father, the bashing, the way people got so taken in by old Joh. Seems crazy, I know, when he doesn't even remember that time himself.'

'It's not so crazy, not when you know the whole story,' I said. 'Maybe you need to understand what an important thing it is in his life.'

'You think I should cave in, then,' she snapped, almost before I'd finished. 'Go back to London. If I love him so much, I should want to be with him wherever.' And she flung her hands about at random to mock me. 'No, Susan, I don't buy that. Tom talks about Brisbane with too much fondness for it to be so simple. I thought for a while that it was pride, donkey-stubborn pride that wouldn't let him come back here. I mean, Brisbane's not the most exciting town, in the scheme of things. But that's not it. At heart, he knows he's part of the place. It's like some wires have been coupled up all wrong inside him. It makes him talk about Queensland with contempt, yet the next minute he's missing everything about it.'

Where was she getting this from? I'd never sensed any crossed wires.

'You don't get what I'm talking about, do you?' she said, more a sigh of regret than an accusation. 'We could talk all night and you still won't get it. It's you, Susan. Tom can't come home because of *you*.'

Well, nothing if not blunt. Where had the girl from London disappeared to? I surprised myself by feeling little anger, but angry or not, it was time to return fire. 'You mean I've set him against this place with my stories about the Tower Mill? Tom thinks he'll betray his parents if he lives here. Is that it? Well, Hilary, to borrow your own words, I don't buy it. So much has changed and Tom knows it. The way Hanson imploded so quickly was proof of that. He's said as much over the years. No, the politics here is—'

I'd been going to say 'more mature', but my final words never made it into the night air.

'There it is, you see. *Politics*,' she interjected. 'In a way, I agree with you. Tom's past all that. He's heard so much about the politics of it all it's a wonder there's room in his head for anything else. But that was never what he wanted from you, Susan. He wanted to know what was in here,' and she struck her chest so hard I heard the echo in her lungs. 'He's been trying to get that from you for so long.'

'Tom hasn't said this to you, has he? Not in so many words?' I demanded.

'No, not the way I'm saying it, but I know him. There's a part of him he won't let me into, won't even let me touch.'

Hilary was fighting the first tears, and to hide them she avoided my eyes. Not a great one for arguing: she expected others to appreciate her sincerity, even if she couldn't make them agree. She wasn't about to cede the field, though, I discovered.

'Forget the politics, Susan. Tom can't come home because you won't let him.'

This left me utterly bewildered. I could only shake my head, close to laughter at how absurd she was becoming. 'What makes you think I won't let him?'

Perhaps she was aware of her own silliness, too, because she went quiet while her eyes searched my face in the fading light. What did she expect to find? Whatever she'd hoped for didn't appear, it seemed, and with her own eyes closed in what looked like defeat, she said, 'It's true, Susan. It took me a long time to see it, but I'm certain of it now. That's why I asked to see you, alone. Tom's stranded over there, like some stateless refugee and not even I can make him come home.'

I was right about her defeat, then. 'I take it he hasn't succumbed to your brinkmanship.'

It was a savage thing to say, as I'd meant it to be, and I expected real fury in return.

'Blackmail,' she said. 'You may as well call it by the proper name. Makes me look desperate, doesn't it? I hate doing it this way, and you're right, it hasn't worked. It shows what an influence you are in his life, though. You must see that.'

'Oh, for God's sake. Tom's thirty-one years old. I can't tell him where to live.'

'You don't have to, when everything you've done has pushed him further and further away from you.'

The claim was so patently wrong I could only ask in wonder, 'When have I *ever* pushed Tom away? Even when Mike and I split, it wasn't like that. There was no pushing away.'

'In Paris, there was,' she said instantly. 'You were crying in front of some cathedral. He wanted to comfort you, and instead you pushed him off like some groper in the street and walked away.'

'He shouldn't have taken it that way,' I murmured, letting my thoughts become words. Before I could steady myself, they had prompted more from Hilary.

'He wanted to live with you in Sydney, too, but you wouldn't let him. He thought he'd have a chance to get back some of the years he'd missed, but you weren't going to let him get that close.'

Live with me! Did she mean back in . . . when was it? But Tom had changed his mind about coming. Before I could say so, she came out with something even more outrageous.

'Then you sent him off to England.'

This was too much! 'I didn't *send* him. He wanted to go. He asked for my help, for Christ's sake! He's got things mixed up – both of you have. Everything round the wrong way.'

'Looks the right way round to me,' Hilary said calmly. 'It's what it looks like to Tom that matters, anyway. Then you came up with that passport idea. Why didn't you just say you didn't want him to come back at all?' There was a willingness to hurt in her voice now, an anger in search of retribution, not for herself, but for Tom. 'So many times you've drawn him in close, then shut him out,' she blundered on. 'Why do you do it? Do you hate him because of what he reminds you of?'

'Of course not,' I snapped, angry enough to walk away. But behind the girl's desperation lay a need for my son that I recognised. I had been in love with his father once, just as strongly. 'Tom's my son and I've always loved him, no matter what you might think.'

Looking up at me once more in the last of the day's light she said, 'What I think is there's a hollowness in Tom that he won't let me fill. He's always on about how lucky he is, that he's got two mothers, but that's a bullshit story to hide his fear. Inside the hollowness he's afraid he has no mother at all.'

'Where do you get off saying such a thing. Lyn's not even here to defend herself. She's been a fucking marvel and Tom loves her to bits.'

'She's not his real mother. Whatever he says, there's only one that counts.'

'So we're back to me, then. I'm a blank in his life. Yet a moment ago you were saying what an influence I was. Pardon me if I see a contradiction there, Hilary. Tom knows how much I love him.'

'Then why does he grieve, every day, like it was his mother who died at the Tower Mill. It's you he longs for, Susan. He's waited thirty years for you to be his mother. Tom and I could be happy, if only you'd learn how.'

After Hilary walked off towards Edward Street, I must have found my way to the main gates and crossed to the hotel, although I have no memory of doing so. A restless night followed in the company of her words and, when I closed my eyes, her face. Since there had been so little light in the park, my half-conscious mind borrowed memories from London to give her flesh and colour. That the images didn't match up was alarming, somehow.

I'd hoped for a Saturday lie-in but gave up by seven-thirty and went in search of breakfast, only to start like a nervous pony when a girl at the cereal bar looked like Hilary. I was back in my room when the text arrived from Lyn Riley.

Boys on their way via Singapore and Sydney. Arrive Brisbane noon Sunday.

Monday for the funeral, then. I called to confirm as much, then, in a reprise of yesterday, found myself with nothing more to arrange – and the clock beside my bed insisting it was only 9.17 a.m. What was I going to do for twenty-hour hours? I could feel Hilary inside my head, waiting for a quiet moment.

Qantas offered escape and by twelve I was on the ground in Sydney, half-convinced that an evening with Robert justified the airfare.

He knew, though, once I'd told him about Hilary in the Botanical Gardens; and, with none of his teasing humour, he flushed me out. 'You're going to meet Tom off the plane, aren't you, before that young woman can get to him?'

Later, he came to me as I stared out at the harbour with my arms doubled across my body – protecting myself from a punch in the belly, he said.

My uterus was down there, too, I might have replied.

'I can't get it out of my head that she might be right,' I told him.

The day wasn't done with me yet. During dinner came a call I should have anticipated, perhaps.

'Ms Kinnane, this is Barry Dolan,' said a voice that somehow fused both confidence and hesitation.

'You've heard the news then?'

'Yes and I was sorry to hear it. You know that I mean that, don't you?'

I did. Since his release we had spoken a number of times, and not just on the phone. 'I'd like to be at the funeral,' he said. 'Would you mind?'

'No, I wouldn't, but I'm not the only one who has to be okay with it.'

'The boy.'

'Tom's hardly a boy any more. But yes, I'll have to speak to him before I can give you an answer. He's on his way back from London right now.'

Robert had guessed who the caller was. 'You'll have a lot to discuss with Tom tomorrow, then.'

It was no less than what I was thinking. I checked my watch and tried to make numbers work in my head. 'What time is it in Singapore?'

'He'll be exhausted,' said Robert, but despite the protest he found the dialling code for me.

'Susan! Good timing. I've just switched on,' said Tom when he answered.

'How long are you stuck in Singapore?'

'Hours yet. Wouldn't be so bad if we were flying straight to Brisbane.'

'Lyn said you were coming through Sydney. I'm back there now, myself. What's your flight number? I'll try and get on the same plane.'

With the numbers safely scribbled on a scrap of paper, I said, 'Listen, Tom, about the funeral . . .'

'What do you need me to do?' he asked.

'Nothing. That's all taken care of. No, it's something else. I've had word from Barry Dolan.'

From the distant tropics came a long silence.

'He wants to be there,' I said finally.

'Tell him to bugger off.'

'No, Tom. Don't dismiss the idea so quickly. I told you how I went to see him in gaol.'

'He thought you were still after him. Laughed at the letter, said the man who wrote it was dead. Dolan's not coming to the funeral.'

I recognised my own anger in his voice and wondered why it wasn't mine any more. Had I passed it over to him, let it become his burden at a time when I'd lost the strength to carry it any further? Oh Tom, I didn't do it on purpose.

'Tom, you need to think about this. Death puts an end to things. This is an opportunity to—'

'I don't want to talk about it,' he snapped, before I could get up any momentum. 'I've said too much already.'

'Tom, will you at least think about it some more?'

'Ring him now. I don't care what time it is in Australia. The answer is *no*.'

It's a mistake, Tom, I wanted to say into the phone when he'd rung off. We needed to finish this thing, all of us. Dolan knew it, I knew it, and before we reached Brisbane my son had to see it, too.

FOURTEEN

TOM

I sat for long seconds, staring at the phone in my hand, because I didn't want to see what lay in Dad's face. He was right there with me, amid the little nest we'd made for ourselves in the airport's Burger King. But who was I kidding? He'd heard every word and he was clearly intrigued, I saw, once I dared look across the table.

'That sounded like fun. Hope you don't always speak to your mother like that,' he said in a tone he hadn't used since I was fifteen.

The sardonic air was to give me a moment to collect myself, I suspected, but it was a signal, too, that he expected an explanation.

'I'm sorry you had to hear that. I should have gone out of earshot.'

'I'd have heard you from the far end of the terminal, Tom.'

No smile from me, if that's what he was after. When I still had nothing to say, he dropped the pretence. 'Who's Dolan and who's this dead man who wrote a letter? I don't remember any letter.'

'No, you wouldn't.'

Already I could sense what I was going to do. If I'd been touchy with Susan on the phone it was because I'd carried something under my skin for years, and these days the slightest bump was enough to rouse it. It didn't help that Hilary had left me alone in Kennington, where the extra space made me bounce off the walls like a pinball until I was ready to trash the furniture.

It was more than that, though, and a different anger rose in me, not at Susan but at the face I saw reflected in the massive pane of glass beside us. For ten years I'd told myself the story was hers to tell, ten years in which I'd left uni, left home, put a dozen men in gaol.

'Not here. There are too many others,' I said, nodding at the tables close by.

Dad reached for the little daypack he used for carry-on luggage and as soon as he was ready I led him off into the wastes of Changi airport. The irony of this march was that the best place I could find was the most public – in the long, long halls leading to departure lounges thirty-four, thirty-five, thirty-six and on into the distance, all of them utterly deserted.

'Dolan was a policeman,' I said, taking Dad's questions in the order he'd asked them. 'He was at the Tower Mill, the same night you were there with Susan. And Terry, of course. The letter was about him, this Dolan character, about what he did once you'd all been chased down into the park.'

At first I tried to recall details of the letter, until I realised the wording didn't matter and the entire page could be summed up in a single sentence. 'Terry didn't fall, he was bashed by Barry Dolan.'

It was done and so quickly I could barely believe this was all it had taken. After ten years – no, twelve, but what did that matter when, for Dad, it was close to thirty?

I'd told the story for him, without a thought for what the telling would do for me, and this made its impact all the greater. I sensed a lightness that I'd known only once before, in the heady days when Hilary first moved into my flat and every breath had been a joy. I began to weep and glanced apologetically towards Dad.

He was too tightly wound within himself to notice.

'I'll kill her. I'll bloody kill her,' he said softly.

My throat was tight and sluggish and even if there had been more to say I would have struggled. Sensing this, Dad lifted his head, revealing no tears, but some of my restless anger had jumped across the narrow gap between us.

'I couldn't feel worse if you told me she'd slept with every man in Bindamilla,' he began. 'What's the word? Cuckold. Shakespeare liked his cuckolds to be unaware. More pathetic that way, because they couldn't make right what they didn't know about.'

'I'm to blame, too. I should have told you back . . .' But I squibbed the rest, flapping my hand in substitution, because no arbitrary number of years could soften it.

'It would have explained a lot of things back in Bindy,' said Dad. 'I can't even begin . . .' And defeated by his own words, he walked off.

'Dad,' I called.

He turned briefly. 'Just need a minute,' he said, and with that he wandered slowly past the empty departure lounges and at the end of the concourse slipped out of sight.

I settled down to wait for him, but after twenty minutes I picked up his little pack and my own satchel, and returned to the Burger King.

An odd memory from my schoolboy reading found life in the scene around me. In the days when sailors navigated by dead reckoning, the best of them could tell when land was near from the currents, the birds overhead and even the detritus on the water's surface. Returning to Australia was a bit like that, I decided. The place counted for little in London, but in Singapore its tidal pull was there to see on the departure boards and especially the newsstands. I bought the *Sydney Morning Herald* and set about reading it from cover to cover.

An hour later, Dad found me there, hunched over pages I'd already taken in with more interest than they deserved. I waited to see whether he had anything more to say about Dolan, or the letter, or Susan. He read as much in my face and said, 'I still don't know what to make of it all, Tom. Until I do, it might be best if you didn't tell your mother that I know.'

'Our little secret,' I said.

'Secret,' he repeated. 'Yes, let's keep it from Susan,' he said, with a grim smile that drew me into his conspiracy.

He dropped into the seat opposite and nodded at my newspaper. 'Seems we had the same idea,' he said, slipping a copy of the *Australian* onto the table. 'Did you see the Rugby score?'

Yes, I'd seen it. Australia had beaten the Springboks in a Tri-Nations match. 'The game was played in Brisbane,' I said.

'Yes, in Brisbane,' he responded wistfully. 'The protests are all forgotten now. They were never about the football, anyway. I don't even know how much they were about apartheid, either, and that's all gone, too.'

'And now Terry Stoddard, as well,' I added bitterly. 'Must have been for something, Dad.'

He thought about this for a moment and seemed on the verge of an answer – then kept it to himself. There was no need. I knew what the Tower Mill had been about.

SUSAN
August, 2003

A bottle of Robert's burgundy helped me sleep, until I woke, dehydrated and headachy, an hour before dawn. My mind was immediately full of what I had to do that day, so, while the kettle boiled in the too-bright kitchen, I used the laptop to check flights into Sydney. There it was – ex-Singapore, due at eight-thirty. Tom was already over Australian soil, then. What was I going to say to him? The winter morning was no colder than any other but I tugged my robe tightly around my body.

Hilary had thrown me in a way I hadn't been unseated for years. It hadn't seemed so hard last night, defending myself over dinner with Robert in the judge's seat and blatantly on my side. This was different.

Hilary had accused me of crimes I'd never thought of, a form of neglect through substitution, if there could be such a thing. Instead of what might have been between a woman and her son, I had inserted politics and grand ideas.

Guilty, a voice shrilled in my head. How many times had we talked about justice, policy, the myopia of governments?

But what was supposed to fill the space between mother and son? I had three hours to find out before Tom emerged at the arrivals hall at Mascot, sleepy and expectant and looking for me in the crowd. Panic gripped me. I didn't know. I simply didn't know.

It was easier to focus on the physical things, packing for the return to Brisbane and the nuts and bolts of getting to the airport. Only I knew that something so profoundly elusive awaited me there. In the cab, I found it better to focus on the other thing I had to do: I was going to convince Tom to accept Dolan at the funeral tomorrow. Was that mothering? It would be something, a least.

'Are you late for your flight?' the cabbie asked.

'No, plenty of time.'

He saw my surprise. 'You keep looking at your watch, that's all.'

'Oh! Actually, I'm meeting a plane first. My son's flying in from Europe.'

'Been away a long time, has he?'

'Too long.'

Further and further away. Those had been Hilary's words in the Botanical Gardens, and, among all she said, this frightened me most. I had pushed Tom away, sent him off to England, as far away from my life as it was possible to be.

There was a punchline to Hilary's story about Tom and me. It was the last thing she'd said before we parted, and it was the last snatch of memory I took from the cab into the arrivals hall: my son's happiness depended on me.

I saw Mike first, tugging his suitcase behind him on its tiny wheels and looking over his shoulder for the figure who was yet to appear. Moments later, there was Tom with a much smaller bag in tow, hinting at a brief visit, an interruption to his life that would be dealt with, then put behind him.

I hurried to greet them, aiming squarely for Tom. 'It's so good to see you,' I cried, and now came the tears I'd avoided in the taxi. 'It was the right thing to come for Terry, and for me, too. It's so sad that he's gone.'

When I showed no signs of letting go, Tom began to laugh. 'Hey, there's someone else here you should say hello to.'

With barely a glance at Mike's face, I embraced him with the cordiality of an ex-wife.

We took a cab to the domestic terminal where I tried, once again, to get a seat on their flight. But it was the same story from last night: the plane was full and I was stuck with a flight thirty minutes earlier.

I had to act quickly then, and, turning to Mike, I said what had to be said. 'I need Tom alone for a little while. I'm sorry, it's something between the two of us.'

He glanced at Tom and even managed a smile, which Tom returned with similar ease. I was too distracted to care. 'I'll wait in the departure lounge,' he said.

I took Tom by the elbow and I led him along the concourse to a lift beside gate thirteen.

'Where are we going?' he asked.

'There are meeting rooms on level two,' I explained. 'I'll tell my paper I was getting background from a visiting legal expert.'

That earned another of Tom's smiles, for me this time.

The receptionist greeted us cheerily and asked, 'Will you need any AV? Tea, coffee?'

When, finally, she closed the door behind her, I sat back in the plush leather. 'I'm sorry about all this, Tom.'

The apology was for the farce I'd subjected him to, but I might have been speaking of Terry's death – or my thirty-one years as his mother. 'I couldn't talk about Barry Dolan in front of Mike.'

He shrugged at this. 'That's what happens when you keep secrets.'

'Yes, Tom, I kept it from Mike,' I said, without rancour, 'but don't you see how that letter gave me my life back?'

'And took away your son.'

'Don't say that. It was never cut and dried, not with you. You said it once yourself, I could stop being Mike's wife, but I couldn't stop being your mother.'

'That bloody letter, what happened at the Tower Mill . . .' Tom said bitterly. 'It's still there, getting in the way, for all of us.'

'Those things have harmed us for thirty years, Terry most of all,' I agreed. 'Now he's dead, is the rest of it going to end tomorrow, as well? Are we going to stop letting these things harm us? Because if the answer's yes, then Barry Dolan must be at the funeral.'

'No,' he said, not harshly, as he had on the phone from Singapore, but with equal determination. 'He killed my father. It's taken thirty years to hold the funeral, but Terry died that night.'

'All of that is true,' I conceded. 'But I told you what he was like, didn't I, when I went to see him in gaol? He'd had time to think about what he got caught up in. I've met him a couple of times since then, too. I didn't tell you because I didn't want you to search him out, but he called me once he was released, and the next time I was in Brisbane, I took him to see Terry.'

'Jesus, Susan, how many secrets do you need? Why always alone? Was I still in Brisbane?'

I answered with a nod. 'It was before you left for England.'

'Then why wasn't I there, too?'

I couldn't say that I didn't know, even if the answer that bubbled out of me was too emotional to have come from any reasonable part of my being. 'Because I'd already brought you far enough into that night beneath the Tower Mill, Tom, and I couldn't bear to lead you any further. I was protecting my son, as mothers are supposed to do. You'd come to mean far more to me than Terry, who'd become a cause I couldn't put right, but you were different, you were part of me. I didn't invite you along that day because Dolan had taken Terry away from me, and I was terrified that meeting him would take you from me, as well.'

He seemed stunned by this. I certainly was. Where had it come from, and how much more could I say without reaching so deep there would be nothing left to salvage?

'He sat with Terry for half an hour, seeing more than my eyes were taking in. I wish you *had* been there to see it, you should have been there,' I said, confessing. 'He regrets what he did, Tom. You'll see as much in his eyes, if you let him come tomorrow. Dolan wants to be at the funeral because he needs an end, too, like you and me, and Mike.'

'I don't know what to think,' said Tom, sounding more vulnerable than angry. 'I mean, does he want absolution, is that it?'

'I don't think it matters. Forget what Dolan's after, Tom, and think of what he means for you and me. There were never going to be any public admissions about what happened, never going to be any punishment for men like Dolan or those who egged them on. That's all you and I have been able to see for years, but now, maybe there's something real for us at last. If he's there, you and I can bury more than a man's body tomorrow.'

Tom stared into my face as I spoke. Now that I seemed spent, he focused on the floor near his feet, to weigh up what I'd said, perhaps, or to avoid a reply. I wasn't sure.

I watched him now, not in anticipation of his answer, more in wonder that this man was my son. How could I have pushed him away?

'Tom, I've done a lot of thinking in the last day or two. All the time you've been in the air, to be honest.'

His head bobbed up at this. 'Me too,' he murmured.

'What I said before, that death can bring other things to an end. It's time I said something else that's been stuck between us for too long.' I leaned forward in my chair, sure, at last, of what I would say.

'Tom, back when you were three years old, I chose myself, instead of you. There were all sorts of reasons and I can justify what I did until I'm blue in the face, but what matters is how that looks to you. Hear me say it: I didn't put you first, and it's stood between us ever since.'

Perhaps he was still taking in what I'd said, but he didn't respond.

'I'm not asking you to forgive me, Tom. The best I can do is admit the truth of it. All these years I've told myself, told anyone who'd listen that I was a poor mother, that I don't have the gene. None of that matters, though, does it? I should have seen how it looked to you, Tom. I'm your mother, and I let you down.'

'Don't say that, Mum,' he said through tears.

I put up my hand to stop him saying more. 'There's one thing I want you to understand. Please, Tom, you have to understand this. When I came back from Europe and you were still a teenager – from the time I took you to see Terry in the nursing home, really – I've tried to be your mother, and if it seems like I've failed all over again, it's because I didn't know how. Please believe that. It wasn't for want of love, or because I was afraid of what you'd take from me. What I didn't know, what I'm still learning, is how to take from you, to take what you want to give. I need it, Tom. I need my son, for the funeral tomorrow and every day until they put me in a box, too. Maybe by then I'll have learned the rest of it.'

A knock came at the door and moments later it opened enough for the receptionist's face to appear. 'They've just called your flight, Ms Kinnane.'

'I can get a later one,' I said to Tom. 'Do you want to stay, talk it out?'

He closed his eyes and in no more than a whisper, said, 'No, I can't. Not now, not yet.'

He walked with me to my departure gate, too full of his own unspoken words to hear any more from me.

'I'll wait for you in Brisbane,' I called, as my boarding pass was scanned, and didn't miss the irony in what I'd said.

Would Tom let Dolan attend the funeral? It was out of my hands now, yet whatever he chose, it wouldn't end there, for he was my son and I would always worry that he might be unhappy, or ill advised, dumped on by others or by his own folly, that he'd be unloved, betrayed, or the culprit in betrayal, that he'd be lonely, overworked, or overly pleased with himself. Such fears would stay with me, not so much that I lay sleepless as I had for the last two nights, but as the background hum to my life.

On board, I found my seat and settled beside a window with a view of the terminal.

What had I done, back in that unlikely room? Something *had* shifted in me. I could use up every minute of this flight to Brisbane trying to name it, or I could simply embrace the peace it brought me.

TOM

After I'd seen Susan off down the air bridge, I joined Dad and we went in search of a coffee.

'Your mother had a look in her eye,' he said. 'I haven't seen her like that since . . . it's not right to say it, maybe. Since Terry was struggling for life in the hospital.'

'First time I've seen her like that, too,' I said. 'She put herself on the line, Dad,' and I might have added 'for me', but was there any need? 'Before, she'd always held back a part of herself. This time was different . . .' I needed to think. The coffee helped, and so did Dad's weary silence.

Later, after our plane had levelled out on the final leg to Brisbane, I reached into the seat pocket for Dad's copy of the *Australian*, or the part of it I'd kept, at least.

Time played dizzying games around me, as it does when you stare too hard at the one thing. I could sense him watching me. He'd seen that I was studying the legal appointments.

'Force of habit,' I said. 'I bet you check out the teaching jobs when you get the chance.'

'Only to find out who's moving on. I'm not planning a change in my life, unlike some,' he added.

'What makes you think *I* am?'

'Oh, the mysterious Hilary to begin with. You haven't come home just for Terry's funeral, have you, Tom?'

His wry smile showed that denial would be thrown out of court. He shifted his weight in the seat, as he so often did in the creaking cane chair on our back deck in Ashgrove, and said, 'I've been reading over kids' shoulders for thirty years, Tom. You're looking at that CMC job, aren't you?'

What could I do but admit it? 'It's the second time they've advertised. That's the usual procedure, two weeks apart, to be sure word gets around.'

'I didn't think you bothered with the *Australian* in London.'

'I don't. Hilary cut out the page and sent it to me.'

He considered this for a few moments. 'The Crime and Misconduct Commission. Sounds like a good fit for you, Tom. You've cut your teeth at the Crown Prosecutor in London, and then there's the Tower Mill. After what you told me in Singapore, it must rankle that the police were never held to account. That's why the CMC was set up, to make sure men like Joh don't get ahead of themselves.'

'I know what the CMC's for,' I said sharply, 'but don't you see what would happen, Dad? I'd be setting myself up as the avenging angel who rides in to smite ordinary mortals who'd given way to their baser instincts. I'd be seduced by my own righteousness, my own self-importance. That's precisely what Joh suffered from.'

He waited until my little tirade had played itself out, then, with his face as hard and serious as I'd ever seen it, he leaned into my ear and said, 'Tom, if you can say that to me, and to the mirror every morning, then maybe you're exactly the type who should apply.'

I didn't feel up to an answer, not after twenty-four hours spent more inside my head than the cabin of a 747. And not after the brief stop in Sydney, either. 'A few things are up in the air,' was all I could manage.

Dad seemed to think on this in the way I'd seen him come up with an elusive line for one of his poems, and it didn't surprise me when he said, 'You know what Auden said about poetry? That it doesn't make things happen. That's why I'll never be more than a scratch on the eyeball of history. But you're different, Tom, and I think you know it. You've spent ten years getting yourself ready for that job, whether you'll admit it to yourself or not. Why all that post-grad work in London, if you weren't? You don't study admin law to put more burglars in gaol.'

I have a fair idea of how my face must have looked when he said this. I'd seen it often enough in court, that delicious moment when the defendant's shoulders slouch in the dock because he knows it's all over, that hard evidence has overwhelmed his barrister's diversions and it's only a matter of time before the guilty verdict is handed down. That was me.

It was what he said next that mattered more, though.

'Tom, if do your best work on the other side of the globe, you won't make things happen where it means the most to you.'

'So you think I should move home to Brisbane?'

'I'm not the only one who thinks so,' he said, with a studied glance towards the legal appointments. 'Finding the right woman's the big one, Tom. Trust me on that. But it seems to me a few other things have been getting in the way.'

'I've been thinking about that all the way from Heathrow.'

'I can't tell you whose son you are, mine or Terry's, or even Susan's. I can't tell you to use your Australian passport or your British one, or maybe make up a special one to say Queenslander. I can't tell you where you belong, Tom, or what you owe to your countrymen once you make up your mind.'

He went back to his novel, leaving me to stare out of the window, aware that it was still New South Wales below the wings. There was no border marked on the ground, but at some instant in the next half-hour we would cross over, a transition that had once meant so much to me. It did again, though in an entirely different way.

On a weekend stay with me during his residency, Dad had visited the National Portrait Gallery to worship his gods, Tennyson, Thomas and Zeus himself, Shakespeare. I'd gone with him.

'All Brits, of course,' I said, for the want of something to say since he'd drifted into such a euphoric state words seemed beyond him.

But my timing was poor because we'd just arrived at the large portrait of a woman with hair like windswept mulga, face on the tilt, her body sitting low on a sofa with knees up and her skirt draped informally between her legs. It was a rare woman who would let herself be depicted in such a pose, and Germaine Greer was certainly that. It's a fabulous portrait, but it was something Dad said while we stood in front of that painting that came to me during those waning moments of our journey.

'Do you remember what you said about old Germaine while we were standing in front of her portrait?' I asked him.

He looked up from his book, a little flummoxed. I prompted him with his own words: 'You said she wasn't one of us any more. That she'd lived over there so long, she was English, and that was why her portrait was in their national gallery, not ours.'

'Did I say that?'

He'd forgotten, but I hadn't.

Not one of us, and with those words he'd made something shift deep in my guts as though a vital core had been ripped out of me. I never wanted to feel that wrench again, and, as our plane crossed the invisible border below, I knew that I wouldn't. Without fanfare, without a word of declaration to Dad beside me, the matter seemed settled and the relief that came over me urged the question – Why had it taken so long to work out? Wasn't I the same man I'd been twenty-four hours ago, when I'd boarded at Heathrow? More than something nameless in my guts had shifted, even if I couldn't explain what, or why.

'It's time you and Mum met Hilary,' I said. 'She'll be at the funeral tomorrow. Not exactly an occasion you'd choose for a first meeting,' I said, with a shrug. 'You'll like her, though.'

I expected a smile at this, but Dad's face was serious again. 'There's someone else who should be there tomorrow, Tom. I imagine your mother had something to say about that, back in Sydney.'

I nodded. Things had been decided in that matter, too, it seemed.

Neither of us spoke again until the engines lowered their pitch and I felt the aircraft slowing, losing height on the approach into Brisbane. When the first officer took to the microphone he seemed pleased with his news.

'. . . landing on time. We'll be coming in over the city, where it's a sunny nineteen degrees.'

Soon the suburbs were below us and then the CBD, so well defined in the winter sunlight I imagined my hand reaching through the window to touch the buildings.

'Looks different,' I said, with my nose to the glass.

'Does it?' Dad shifted in his seat enough to push his face close to mine, and together we watched the high-rise and the twin peaks of the bridge slide under the wing.

'I suppose, to someone who's been away a while,' he said, then sank back into place to hitch his belt a little tighter. 'Certainly a lot different from the city your father knew.'

Which father did he mean? I grew up knowing of two. But Dad was talking about Terry, who had stopped knowing anything before I was born and tomorrow would go into the Queensland soil, leaving me with only one father, the usual quota, and as the plane sank through a solitary wisp of cloud I felt myself join the ranks of the ordinary, at last.

The parks of Bulimba stood out among the houses and the river flashed briefly beneath us, the reflected blue of the sky hiding its khaki water. We glided lower and still lower until the blur of green beside the runway became grass growing out of solid earth and then, finally, came the jolt of journey's end.

Acknowledgments

I would like to thank the women who helped me with *The Tower Mill*: Teresa Carroll, Janet Allison, Mary Nosworthy, Kate Moloney, Moya Hickey, Jane Connolly, Brigid Hickey, Siobhan Zielinski and the publishing team at UQP, Madonna Duffy and Rebecca Roberts.

277

BORROWER CODES
Please write your code here